Books by **Louise Rozett**
from MIRA INK

CONFESSIONS OF AN ANGRY GIRL

Find out more about Louise Rozett at www.miraink.co.uk
and join the conversation on Twitter @MIRAInk or on
Facebook at www.facebook.com/MIRAInk

Confessions of an Almost Girlfriend

xXx

LOUISE ROZETT

Mira Ink is a registered trademark of Harlequin Enterprises Limited, used under licence.

Published in Great Britain 2013
Mira Ink, an imprint of Harlequin (UK) Limited,
Eton House, 18-24 Paradise Road,
Richmond, Surrey, TW9 1SR

© Louise Rozett 2013

ISBN 978 1 848 45229 9

047-0713

Mira Ink's policy is to use papers that are natural, renewable and recyclable products and made from wood grown in sustainable forests. The logging and manufacturing processes conform to the legal environmental regulations of the country of origin.

Printed and bound by
CPI Group (UK) Ltd, Croydon, CR0 4YY

In honour of the fifteenth anniversary of
Matthew Shepard's death

For Matthew Shepard and Tyler Clementi and young people
everywhere who are just trying to be who they are

SUMMER

homophobic *(noun):* scared of homosexuality
(see also: the Swim Thugs, and half of Union High*)*

———————

1

"JUMP, FAGGOT! JUMP!"

And just like that, summer is over.

Symbolically, anyway.

I've been at this party for sixty seconds and already the tyranny of the swim thugs is so suffocating, it's like I never even had summer break to detox from freshman year.

Not that summer can really be considered a break when you spend the whole thing either folding clothes at the Gap or in therapy. With your mother. Talking about how you had every right to go behind her back and build a memorial website for your dad.

Who's dead.

Obviously. Hence, *memorial*.

"Come on, homo! Let's go!"

Mike Darren's backyard is packed with students from every level of Union High's caste system, but it's obvious that this is a swim-team-initiation party. As Mike struts around checking the beer level of the bottomless red plastic cups that were given only to the prettiest freshman girls when they skittered through the tiki-torch gauntlet, Matt Hallis and the rest of the swim thugs are lined up on the edge of the pool like a firing squad. A freshman swimmer dressed in a red polo shirt, rolled-up white jeans and loafers with no socks stands on the diving board, backing away from them, inching closer and closer to the end while looking down at the water every other second. Matt ceremoniously raises his arm in the air and then shows off those leadership qualities that got him elected swim captain even though he's just a sophomore: he fires the first shot, hurling his cup of beer at the freshman.

Thanks to the fact that Matt is an annoyingly talented athlete whose parents paid for him to spend the whole summer in a weight room, it's a perfect throw with a ridiculous amount of force behind it. The beer splatters on the freshman's blond head, the impact nearly knocking him backward as liquid pours down his cheeks, nose and neck, drenching his perfectly pressed shirt. His legs shake a little with the force of the blow and he jostles the diving board. For a second I think he's going to fall—loafers and all—into the kidney-shaped pool with blue floodlights shimmering just beneath the waterline. He throws his arms out to the sides and steadies himself, and I can tell by the relieved expression on his face that he thinks he survived, that the hazing wasn't so bad after all.

He slowly lowers his arms and takes a defiant step toward the firing squad. The relief on his face disappears as Matt's underlings lift their cups in the air to follow their leader's example.

"Jump or die, fag!" yells Matt, his drunken slurring making his speech sound even less intelligent than usual, which is hard to do. The cups nail the freshman like a spray of bullets, and he staggers backward, arms pinwheeling as he tries to cope with the beer in his eyes and mouth. He missteps and falls into the water on his back. The thugs cheer as loafers pop up and float on the pool's surface.

Ironically, "Take it Off" by Ke$ha starts playing.

"What are we *doing* here?" Tracy asks next to me as she watches her ex-boyfriend parade around collecting high fives. It occurs to me that this is exactly the kind of party that Matt spent time at last summer, before freshman year, which is probably what turned him from the nice guy he was in eighth grade to the total jerk he is now.

I look at my best friend. A year ago, all she could talk about was how she couldn't wait to be at parties like this in her cheerleading uniform with her swimmer boyfriend. Now, she's dressed like a normal person—well, a very fashionable normal person—and she can't remember why she wanted to be here in the first place.

I'm so proud of her.

"'We are putting in an appearance at the biggest party of the summer so we can start sophomore year on Tuesday with our heads held high,'" I say, quoting her.

"What a dumb idea," she replies.

The freshman hauls himself out of the pool with no help from anyone. He is shivering a little in his soaked clothes, probably trying to figure out whether he should fight back, leave or grab some beer and pretend everything is cool. There's a radius around him of about 10 feet, as if being the swim thugs' target of choice is a communicable disease. He takes a towel off a wicker stand and tries to dry his shirt.

"He picked the wrong team—in more ways than one," Tracy says. "Not that being gay is a choice," she quickly adds, repeating what our health teacher from last year, Ms. Maso, drilled into us, even though she probably could have gotten fired for stating as fact what some people think is just a belief about homosexuality. As far as we can tell, Ms. Maso's the only teacher at Union High who is actually interested in giving kids useful—aka truthful—information.

Matt stumbles over to kiss Lena, the new captain of the cheerleading team who he had sex with a lot last year while claiming he was a virgin in order to get Tracy—his girlfriend at the time—to sleep with him.

Which, eventually, she did.

I glance at Tracy to see if she cares that Matt and Lena are making out in front of half of Union, but she's not looking at them. She's watching the freshman as he leans over the water with one of those long-handled nets for cleaning the pool. He nabs his shoes and lifts them, dripping, out of the water. "The chlorine is going to totally trash that leather. God, those look like Gucci, don't they?"

I'm about to remind my fashionista friend that I wouldn't know a Gucci loafer from a loaf of bread when suddenly Kristin is standing right in front of us. In her uniform. With her pom-poms.

"Tracy! You can't quit! We can't do it without you!" she shrieks. Or actually, screeches. Kristin, the only freshman to make "The Squad" last year besides Tracy, has a voice straight out of a nightmare. In fact, at Tracy's big Halloween cheer party, she dressed up as some sort of weird demon fairy, with creepy little wings sprouting from her back. It really suited her.

"Now that Regina's off the squad for good…" Kristin trails off, her eyes finding their way to me as if it's my fault that Regina Deladdo made my life a living hell last year and then got kicked off the squad, even though she was supposed to be the new captain.

I wonder if being captain was going to be the pinnacle of Regina Deladdo's high school career. Or maybe her whole life. I try to muster up sympathy for her but I can't. It's hard to feel anything other than deep dislike for someone who spent half the year writing *911 Bitch* on all my desks and lockers after I sort of blew the whistle on a homecoming after-party.

Regina should have written *Boyfriend Stealer* instead, since that's what she was really mad at me for. Not that I stole her boyfriend. All I did was like him. And it sort of seemed, for a minute there, that he liked me, too.

But that was just me, being an idiot. Because Jamie Forta does not like me.

How do I know? Two ways. 1: I haven't seen or spoken to him all summer—not since Regina got him arrested right before he was supposed to pick me up for his junior prom. The last I heard from Jamie Forta was a note, delivered by his best friend Angelo, that said, *Rose. Like I said. I am not right for you. I'm different. Believe me. Be good.*

Whatever that means.

2: Jamie only became my friend because my brother Peter asked him to. Peter was worried about me when he left for college—or actually, maybe it was my mother he was worried about. Anyway, Peter wanted someone to "keep an eye" on me. Which Jamie did.

And then...there was some kissing.

But he's not my boyfriend. I think his note made that pretty clear.

So, what *is* a guy who broke up with somebody else and asked you to the prom? Who spent a whole year looking out for you? Who gave you the best first kiss in the history of kissing?

I can see every second of that kiss like I'm watching a movie. It happened in the parking lot during homecoming. He was at the dance with Regina. I was there with Robert. But still, somehow, Jamie and I ended up sitting in a car together. And then he kissed me. This junior I've had a crush on since the first time I saw him play hockey when I was in seventh grade.

It was surreal.

It was also the only good thing that had happened to me since my dad died right before I started at Union High.

I miss Jamie. I missed him all summer, even though I tried

not to. What's the point in missing someone who tells you flat out that he's not right for you?

"This year?" Kristin is saying to Tracy, looking a little manic, like if she doesn't lock Tracy down, the world as she knows it is going to implode. "We want you to be our choreographer! Wouldn't that be perfect? I mean, look, last year was kind of lame. But we're actually going to *dance* this year, with totally hot moves."

Kristin says this as if choreography is a novel concept for a cheerleading team.

"You don't need me," Tracy says. "It's not like we're a competition team. Even with a choreographer, we'll still just be bouncing around in bad polyester blend."

Kristin scowls, looking seriously offended by the idea that her cheers are just *bouncing around*.

"What's the problem, Trace? Is it that Lena's with Matt? Because they're just hooking up. It's not like she's his 'girlfriend with a capital *G*.'" Kristin uses her pom-poms to make little air quotes as she says this, and I consider grabbing them and throwing them in the pool.

I wonder if I actually made a move to do it because Tracy shoots me a look. Tracy has had a lot of talks with me about my anti-cheerleader stance, reminding me that not all cheerleaders are like Regina, citing herself and a bunch of other nice, smart girls on last year's team as examples. While I see her point, I still haven't managed to let go of the idea that, in general, cheerleaders suck.

I recognize that this viewpoint may be indicative of a character flaw on my part, and I'm okay with that.

In a fake, buttery voice, Kristin says, "Trace, let's go talk in private for a sec, 'kay? Official business," she barks at me as she threads her arm through Tracy's. Tracy looks at me and rolls her eyes as Kristin yanks her toward the patio, her thick blond ponytail swaying with determination. My hand automatically goes to my hair, which is doing what it always does—hanging limply around my shoulders, straight and thin and mousy brown.

I take out the hand-me-down iPhone that Peter gave me before he went back to Tufts, even though I know I have no messages because the only person who has ever called or texted me since I've had it is Tracy. And my mother, of course. But if there's one thing I've learned about these phones, it's that they can make you look busy when you have absolutely nothing to do.

Normally, when I'm trying to look busy, I click on my vocab app and study for the PSAT, which is six weeks away. This year is just a practice run, but I need to totally rock it so I can show my mother that I'll be able to get scholarships and go to college even if she never sees the insurance money my dad's company promised and somehow hasn't managed to deliver yet. But the idea of getting busted studying for the PSATs at a party is kind of horrifying, so I click on "Photos" instead and continue my project—deleting all the pictures Peter left on the phone when he gave it to me.

At first I was annoyed that my mother insisted Peter give me his old iPhone—which looked like it had been drop-kicked multiple times—rather than letting me get a new one with my own money. But when I synced the phone to my laptop for the first time and the computer asked if I wanted to erase everything on it, I realized that Peter's phone contained all sorts of information about his life that he had stopped sharing with me the minute he set foot on a college campus and got a girlfriend.

There are over 800 photos on his phone, and my plan is to look at every single one before I make room for mine. I'm hoping it'll give me an idea of just how bad things are with him. So far, I've learned that he smokes and drinks a lot, and takes pictures of his friends smoking and drinking a lot. No surprises there, I guess.

I get through ten pictures of Peter's friends having a much better time at a party than I currently am. Then I look up, see people talking to other human beings, feel like a dumbass and decide to go find something to drink.

I push past the freshman girls huddled together for safety as the swim thugs circle like sharks, and find my way to a cooler that's filled with all sorts of things we're not allowed to drink yet, and soda. It takes me a full minute to find a Diet Coke buried under all the ice. I can barely feel my hand when I pull it back out.

"Wouldn't you rather have some Red Bull and vodka, Rose?"

It takes me a second to recognize Robert, probably because he looks happier than I have ever seen him look in four years. It could also be because he let his hair grow long and he seems somehow...cooler. Or maybe it's just because he has his arm around one of the prettiest girls I've ever seen, and she's smiling. At him. Like he's a god.

"Holly, this is Rose Zarelli. Rose, meet Holly Taylor. She just moved here from L.A." I postpone studying the beautiful new girl by noticing two more things about Robert: he is calling me Rose instead of Rosie—which he's been calling me since the day we first met in sixth grade—and he is sipping his drink in a way that suggests he's at a cocktail party at a swanky country club, not a kegger in a backyard.

When I can no longer put it off, I turn my attention to Holly. You'd think I'd know better than to shake hands with someone at a high school party, but because I'm a little intimidated by the amount of beauty in front of me, I stick my hand out like a giant dork. Holly graciously does the same, and she doesn't even wince when my hand—frozen and wet from my arctic Diet Coke expedition—touches hers.

Not only is she pretty, she's classy. No wonder Robert has that idiotic grin on his face.

"Hi!" she says. Her teeth are shockingly, blindingly white, and they immediately make me sure that I've got spinach stuck in mine. "I'm new at Union. My dad's teaching drama at Yale."

The reply that immediately comes to mind is: *I'm not new at Union. My dad was blown to pieces in Iraq.* It's accompanied by some horror-movie images that I can't seem to keep out of my head these days.

"Hi," I say too cheerfully, trying to drive away the carnage in my brain. I know that I should offer Holly some interesting piece of information about myself but I'm unsure of what, exactly, that would be.

Definitely not the thing about Dad. Nothing shuts down a conversation faster than telling someone your father was killed by an IED in Iraq.

Holly, it turns out, has totally perfect, long, dark hair that's super thick and looks like it's been flat-ironed by a professional. Her eyes are huge and brown, I can't even tell if she's wearing makeup and she smiles like she does it for a living. She has on lots of silver jewelry that clanks and jingles when she moves, and she's so petite that I actually stop inhaling in order to feel smaller.

"Rose is the…friend I told you about," Robert adds meaningfully, with a slight hesitation before the word *friend*. Holly nods, and I wonder what he told her—*I used to think I was in love with Rose* or *Rose treated me like crap last year* or *Rose is the one with the dead dad*. "Holly and I got cast opposite each other in the drama department's summer show," Robert says. "Leading man and leading lady hook up—total cliché, right?" He smiles down at her and plants a kiss on the tip of her perfect nose.

If Robert weren't standing here with his arm around Holly, there is no way I would ever believe that she was his girlfriend. First of all, Robert has some problems with telling the truth—he likes the things he makes up more than he likes reality. Second of all, Holly Taylor seems out of his league. Like, *way* out of his league. But here they are, all entangled and entwined and so very couple-y.

"Did you see the show, Rose? Robby was the best Joe in the history of *Damn Yankees.*" Holly is literally beaming up at Robert.

"And Holly was the hottest Lola," he says, grinning at her like she's the only girl in the world.

I'm torn between irritation at her calling him "Robby" and embarrassment over all the hours I spent at the beginning of summer daydreaming about getting cast as Lola. Last spring, after my mom took me to see the opera *La Bohème,* I decided that I want to be a singer. Not an opera singer, though I did learn this summer, when no one else was around, that I can sing really loud. Just…a singer. Of some kind. So I considered auditioning for Union High's summer musical. I wanted to sing my heart out onstage as Lola—a vixen in a red dress and heels—and make everyone see me in a totally new way. But now, standing here with the person who actually played Lola, I'm suddenly so mortified that I feel like I have to leave the party immediately. I mean, how dumb could I be? Lola is beautiful and sexy, and the whole point of her character is that she can seduce anyone and get anything. Her big number is literally called, "Whatever Lola Wants, Lola Gets."

I can't even get the guy I like to call me back.

Standing here in front of Holly Taylor in an outfit that my best friend put together for me with things from her closet, I'm painfully aware that I ain't no Lola.

"Holly's dad is a stage, TV and film actor," Robert says, obviously proud of himself for using the word *film* instead of *movie.* "You'd totally recognize him."

Holly looks embarrassed and quickly changes the subject. "Do you act, Rose?"

"Rose is a runner. She plays the French horn, too," Robert answers for me, like I'm a kindergartener who needs positive reinforcement for her cookie choice at snack time.

It pisses me off.

"Actually, I'm not playing French horn this year. I'm trying out for the musical," I tell Holly.

Robert could win an Academy Award for the series of looks that cross his face in the next five seconds. First startled, then stunned, then irritated, then worried and then falsely happy. I feel like I scored a point or something.

I believe that would qualify as petty.

"You're auditioning? That's great!" Holly says. "Maybe we'll all be in it together. It's *Anything Goes*. Do you know it? Maybe you could be Reno Sweeney! Can you tap dance? Reno's the best part. Although Hope is a great part, too. Ooh, but then there's the funny one…what's her name? She has that great number, right, babe?"

It's then, when Holly turns to Robert, that I see Regina. She's with Anthony Parrina, the huge hockey player she's dating just to make Jamie mad. For a second, I'm worried about retaliation. But then I just feel…shame.

After Regina had Jamie arrested, I decided to finally tell Principal Chen that Regina was my graffiti stalker. The principal personally stopped Regina and Anthony at the entrance to the prom. I heard Regina threw a fit in a sequined blue tube dress and four-inch heels, and it actually caused her up-do to fall down. It must have been some fit, considering how much hairspray she uses. She was suspended and banned from cheerleading, and she missed finals and had to go to summer school so that she'd be able to graduate on time this year.

The thought of Regina leaving the prom in disgrace made me smile for a few hours. Then it made me feel pathetic, like I'd just gone running to the principal. Which I had.

When Regina turns toward me, my first instinct is to get a

very important phone call. But it actually doesn't matter what I do because she doesn't notice me. She's staring at the freshman who is now pinned against the house by the garden-hose-wielding swim thugs, who claim that they are helping him by rinsing the chlorine off his clothes.

Anthony bursts out laughing so loud that some of the thugs turn to see who's making all the noise. When their eyes land on Regina, they actually step back, like they're trying to distance themselves from what's happening, terrified of facing the Wrath of Regina. But Regina is standing stock-still, her face frozen.

"Do you want some, Rose?" I hear Holly ask.

Holly hands a joint to Robert as she exhales. The smoke settles in a kind of halo above her head as I decide not to remind Robert that his stepmother once said she'd kick Robert out of the house permanently if he ever came home smelling of pot again.

Robert takes a hit off the joint and then gives it back to Holly, intentionally bypassing me.

"Rose isn't that kind of girl," he says, giving me a condescending wink.

I want to punch him. I'm actually considering it—even though my mom's therapist, Caron, told me I need to start curbing my violent instincts and redirecting them to "a positive place"—when a howl rises up from the crowd.

Matt has grabbed the hose from his teammates and redirected the water so it hits the freshman right in the mouth. He is choking and sputtering, trying to move his face away from the stream so he can get some air, but Matt keeps walking toward him, bringing the hose closer and closer to the freshman's mouth as if he intends to jam it in there.

Suddenly, Regina's frozen face cracks. She's in front of Matt in two steps, shoving him backward as she yanks the hose out of his hand. She tosses it away, spraying the cluster of freshman girls, who shriek and scatter in every direction, their hands flying up to protect their hair. Matt lands on his butt, unsure what just happened.

"Who is *that?*" Holly asks, her big brown eyes already red-rimmed from the pot.

"Rose can tell you all about her, can't you, Rose?" Robert says drily.

Matt grabs the hose off the ground and struggles to stand up, nearly falling into the pool. He loses track of the spray, drenching his own shoes.

"Conrad, are you really gonna let your sister mess with your initiation?" he asks, staring at Regina.

His *sister?* The party punching bag is Regina's *brother?*

Matt looks back at Conrad.

Conrad says nothing.

Matt turns the hose on him.

Regina goes for Matt but Anthony catches her, pinning her arms and spinning her around. He leads her away and she doesn't put up a fight, her face blank, her body slack as he talks into her ear, his dark eyes hard.

I can't believe Regina is walking away while the swim thugs are drowning her brother. If anyone could take them on, it would be her. What's she doing?

Matt and two thuglets grab Conrad and hurl him back into the pool, even though he's still choking. As soon as Conrad hits the water, Matt spits out one final "Faggot!" then loses interest and wanders off. His brainless underlings trail after him.

"What's with all the homophobia?" Holly asks, looking up at Robert for an explanation. "Is it always like this out East?"

"Union's special," Robert answers. "Let's get out of here."

"Um, shouldn't we do something?" she says, turning toward the pool.

"We'll just end up in there with him, and you're too stoned to swim, darling," Robert replies. I nearly gag for multiple reasons, not the least of which is Robert calling his girlfriend *darling* like he's a 1940s movie star. "The guy's a swimmer," he continues. "I'm sure he can find his way to the surface of a pool without our help."

"Okay," Holly says uncertainly.

I follow her gaze to the water and see that Conrad is making zero effort to swim—in fact, less than zero. He's letting himself sink.

"See ya, Rose," Robert says, taking Holly's hand.

I look at the cup Robert's still holding. "Wait, you're not going to drive right now, are you?" I ask.

For a second, I see the old Robert, the one who was always looking for my approval, even after I kept not giving it to him. But the new Robert surfaces quickly. "Holly's driving the vintage Mustang tonight."

I look at Holly, who seems embarrassed again, then at Robert. "So she's too stoned to swim but not to *drive?*"

"It's okay," Holly says. "We can just walk to my house from here." Holly glances one last time at the pool. "So cool to meet you, Rose! See you at school on Tuesday," she adds as Robert pulls her into the crowd that has no interest whatsoever in the fact that Conrad Deladdo is intentionally drowning himself.

Although, to be honest, drowning oneself is not a surprising response to one's first Union High party.

I should do something.

The thing is, after last year, I want to keep a low profile, and I definitely do not want to be the party buzz-kill again.

Plus, he's not *really* drowning—he's just messing around.

Right?

I look at the pool. I can't see him anymore from where I'm standing.

I wait a second for him to come up. I wait another second.

Nothing.

I go to the edge of the pool and look in. Conrad is still drifting down, as if he's being pulled to the bottom by some current I can't see. He looks up at me and it seems like our eyes meet through the water for a second. Then his close.

I drop to my knees and reach into the water to grab him but of course I can't get to him. I lean forward a little more, and the inevitable happens.

From across the pool, Tracy yells my name but it's too late. Someone shoves my shoulder and I fly face-first into the glowing blue water.

My first thought is, I'm destroying the dry-clean-only silk T-shirt Tracy lent me after practically making me sign a contract in blood, promising that nothing would happen to it.

My second thought is, I didn't realize how much the noise of the party was making my brain hurt until I ended up in the pool. It's so peaceful down here—all the music and the yelling get lost beneath the sound of my pulse and the blood in my veins. It's perfect.

I haven't felt this calm in more than a year. For a while after my dad died, I had these weird episodes that my mom said were panic attacks—they felt more like rage attacks to me. They're mostly gone now, but sometimes, out of the blue, I'll be doing something totally normal when suddenly I see these crazy-violent images. I have no control over it.

Here, under the water, I don't feel like that can happen. Maybe I need to spend my life floating around in a pool.

Conrad looks like he feels the same way. But he also looks like he might be turning blue from lack of oxygen.

I swim down to him and reach for his arm. He yanks it away and gives me the finger.

So much for underwater tranquility.

What did I ever do to him?

I grab his arm and pull as hard as I can. Conrad fights me for a second but then lets me win. As we break the surface, a crowd of people at the edge of the pool is watching Tracy calmly shred Matt, who, of course, is the one who pushed me. I know that without having to watch the instant replay.

"…and get her and that freshman out of the pool or I'll throw you in myself."

A big chorus of "Oohs" goes up from the crowd. Matt is too drunk to formulate any kind of retaliation, so he just does as he's told, stumbling to the edge and reaching for Conrad. Conrad is lifting himself out of the pool for the second time in less than an hour when someone shoves Matt aside, sending him sprawling again, and holds out a hand. Conrad looks up and half laughs, half snorts, like he's disgusted.

"Go help your savior-complex girlfriend," he says. "Leave me the hell alone."

I'm trying to figure out who the savoir-complex girlfriend is and why she needs help when I'm lifted straight out of the pool and set down—dripping wet, mascara running, silk T-shirt and white capris probably see-through—on the deck. The warm hands feel familiar on my arms, and I know who it is instantly. But even though I've been waiting an entire summer to see him again, it still takes me a second before I can look up into the beautiful, furious face of Jamie Forta.

dissidence *(noun):* conflict; discord; warfare
(see also: the general state of being in Union)

2

IT'S A STRANGE FEELING TO BE STANDING IN A DRIVEWAY
at a keg party, fully clothed but soaking wet and wrapped in an
oversize towel, talking—or not talking, as the case may be—to
the guy who may or may not like you and who you haven't seen
in months, who is standing next to your worst enemy, who may
or may not be his ex-girlfriend. Throw in the pacing, wet vic-
tim of a Union High hazing and a few onlookers, and you've officially got a three-ring circus.

I'm shivering as I wait for Tracy to get our stuff so she can
drive me home. Jamie Forta is two feet away and he looks totally different. He's tan, his arms are super cut and his hair is
sort of dark gold—he looks like he spent the entire summer at
the beach. He looks…beautiful.

I imagined a bunch of scenarios for when I finally saw Jamie
again, but I didn't think he would ignore me, which is what he's
been doing for the past few minutes. But why would I think
that he'd do anything else, when that's exactly what he did all
summer?

He didn't return my calls after the night he spent in jail, and he wasn't allowed to come back to school to finish the year. After a few weeks, I started to think that I'd imagined him. I could almost convince myself I had, until I thought about the kiss. That kiss was the most real thing ever—there's no way I could have made that up.

Which takes me back to wondering why he didn't call. It's infuriating.

But no matter how hurt or mad or *whatever* I'm feeling, Jamie looks amazing and I can't stop staring at him.

Neither can Regina, which Anthony Parrina has just noticed as he heads up the driveway on his way back to the party from a beer run.

He doesn't look too happy about what he sees.

Anthony puts down the case of beer he was balancing on one massive shoulder and wraps a possessive arm around Regina. "What, no chain gang for you tonight, jailbird?" he says to Jamie. "Oh, right, they only let the juvie kids work road crew during the day. I honked at you once on the highway in your little orange vest, but you didn't wave to me," Anthony says, making a fake sad face.

I can't tell if there's any truth to what Anthony is saying because Jamie's face is a mask. Jamie's dad is a cop—a cop who left his son in jail overnight to teach him a lesson—and I wouldn't be surprised if he arranged for Jamie's community service to involve spending his whole summer in the blazing hot sun fixing the town's potholes.

I look at Regina. She is staring hard at Jamie, as if she's trying to tell him something, but Jamie keeps his eyes on Anthony. I have no idea if Jamie and Regina have talked about what she did to him. But they do live next door to each other, so that probably answers my question.

"What, you got nothin' to say, Forta?" Anthony challenges.

Jamie and Anthony have unfinished business. Jamie used to play hockey for Union with Peter until he got kicked off the team during the big Union vs. West Union game for high-sticking Anthony in the neck. I saw it happen, and I always figured it was some stupid trash-talking thing. But now I'm starting to think it was something bigger.

And Anthony *is* dating Regina, who Jamie grew up with and has…what? Liked? Gone out with?

Been in love with?

Jamie slowly turns to Regina, not taking his eyes off Anthony until the last second. When his gaze meets hers, concern fills his face. How can he possibly look so worried about her after what she did to him? *What* is going on?

"You okay?" Jamie asks Regina in a low voice, as if they're the only two people in the driveway. That weird, blank look comes across Regina's face again as Anthony tightens his grip on her and smiles like he won a prize.

"She's fine," Anthony answers for her. "It's Conrad who don't look so good." He sort of chuckles.

Anthony is a total meathead.

Jamie turns to watch Conrad pace back and forth on the same spot, water still dripping off his rolled-up jeans.

"Conrad," Jamie calls out.

Conrad stops. "Don't *you* fucking talk to me."

"Don't swear at Jamie," Regina warns. It's the first time I've heard her speak all night.

"Oh, that's great, 'Gina, stick up for the guy who treats you like shit. Should I start calling you 'Mom'?"

Conrad is shivering in his wet red shirt, which is bleeding pink streaks on his white jeans. His eyes land on Anthony, and I'm hoping Conrad will just keep his mouth shut, for his own sake. I can't tell whether he has tears or pool water on his face, but the overall effect is the same—with the bleeding shirt and the streaked face, he looks like he's slightly out of his mind.

"Take him home," Jamie says to Regina.

"You know what, Forta?" Anthony interrupts. "You don't get to tell her what to do anymore."

Jamie takes a step toward Anthony. "And you do?"

"Stop acting like you actually give a shit about us, Jamie," Conrad snaps.

"I said watch your mouth," Regina says.

"All right, kids, don't make me send you to your rooms." Anthony suddenly sounds annoyed and bored. "I'll drive you home. Just don't get my interior wet."

"Why would I get in a car with you? You're even more of an asshole than Jamie."

"Conrad, if you don't stop talking shit about Jamie—"

"Why you gotta defend Forta, Regina?" Anthony asks.

I can answer that. Because she loves him.

But of course she's not going to admit that to Anthony.

Regina goes mute again. Anthony grabs her arm hard enough to change the color of her skin, forcing her to turn toward him. For one weird moment, I actually want to pry his hand off her.

"Let go of her," Jamie warns.

"Fuck off, Forta," Anthony says. He takes a step toward Jamie, his chest puffed out, fire in his eyes.

Jamie doesn't budge. It occurs to me that someone who has just finished community service probably can't afford to get into trouble again. I should get between them, like Jamie did for me last year with Regina. But based on the way Anthony just grabbed her, I'd say the presence of a girl between him and the person he wants to punch isn't much of a deterrent. So instead I just blurt out the first thing I can think of.

"Conrad, your shirt is staining your pants."

Everyone turns to look at me as Conrad looks down at his

pants. The red is now more of a general pink wash than individual streaks. "How symbolic," he says.

"Tracy and I can drive you home if you want to get those in the wash before they're ruined."

The wash? I'm talking about washing pants right now? What is wrong with me?

He snorts. "*You* are the reason this all got so fucked up in the first place," he says, waving in disgust at Regina, Jamie and Anthony. "I'd rather walk."

"Wait, wait, wait," Anthony says, looking at Conrad. "What are you talkin' about? Who's the reason everything got so fucked up?"

Conrad gestures to me with his chin. "Her."

Anthony points at me, his eyes practically bugging out of his head. "*This* is Forta's little freshman? The girl who went screamin' to the principal?"

He looks like he can't figure out whether to laugh or punch me. In my head, I'm telling him that I'm actually a sophomore now, which, if you pass your classes, is what happens after you've been a freshman, generally speaking. But in reality, I'm totally embarrassed and freaked out. It never occurred to me that someday I'd be face-to-face with West Union's hell-on-ice star hockey player and would have to answer for getting him thrown out of the prom after he went to all the trouble of taking off his skates and putting on a tuxedo.

I wonder if Jamie will come to my defense if Anthony decides to kill me here and now.

"Matt just passed out," Tracy says as she comes around the corner of the house with our bags. She takes one look at Conrad's now-pink pants and visibly cringes. "Were those Marc Jacobs?" Then she looks up at his face. "Are you okay?"

I don't realize I'm expecting Conrad to smile at Tracy gratefully and thank her for asking until he glares at her like she's an idiot. "Do I *look* like I'm okay?" he asks.

I want to tell him that I know how it feels to be targeted. But I know it's not the same thing. I kissed someone I shouldn't have kissed. Conrad, on the other hand, was just being himself at a team party—a team that he's supposedly a member of.

"Is somebody going to drive you home?" Tracy asks.

"Why does everyone keep asking me that?" he snaps.

"Probably because no one wants to fish you out of the pool again," she says.

"Well, I'm not getting in a car with either one of them," he replies, referring to Jamie and Anthony, who are still standing face-to-face with about an inch of space between them.

It is simultaneously totally hot to see Jamie like this—is that weird?—totally depressing to know that it's not me he's defending and totally awful to think that the school year hasn't even started and already Jamie is in a situation that could land him in serious trouble.

"Fine. *I'll* drive you home," Tracy says. No one moves. Tracy looks around at our cozy little group and then back at Jamie. She raises her eyebrows in surprise and possibly approval of the new-and-improved version—Jamie 2.0, I bet she's going to say later—that she didn't notice by the pool because she was too busy yelling. Without taking her eyes off him, she asks, "You coming with me, Rose, or...?"

Jamie turns away from Anthony and makes eye contact with me for the second time tonight—or rather, for the second time since June. I can't read anything in his expression to give me a single clue about where I stand with him.

What else is new.

"Uh..." I eloquently begin.

Jamie looks at Regina and says, "You call me if you need me." He gives Anthony another long, hard stare, and Anthony bares his teeth in what's supposed to be a grin. Jamie heads down the driveway. Regina watches Jamie go, a flicker of desperation in her eyes as if she wants nothing more than to go with him. Anthony grabs the case of beer at his feet, slings his arm over her shoulders and drags both the beer and Regina back to the party.

Jamie gets in his car, slams the door hard enough to set off the alarm on the SUV he's parked in front of, and takes off down the street.

I watch his taillights get smaller and smaller.

The first time I rode in Jamie's old, green car was when he drove me home on the third day of school last year. He did it only because Peter had asked him to look out for me, but I didn't know that at the time and I thought maybe, just maybe, Jamie Forta might think I was cute or something. It was kind of a terrifying prospect. I babbled like an idiot the whole time.

When I realized Jamie knew where I lived without me having to tell him, my stomach dropped out like I was on a roller coaster. Sitting close to him made me so nervous I couldn't put a sentence together, but I still managed to memorize every detail I could about that ride. The car smelled like rain. The hood had been polished with something shiny and when the sun hit it, the glare was so bright it hurt my eyes. The seats and the floor were clean enough to eat off. It was clear that Jamie loved his car.

Now that I think about it, I bet Jamie cares more about that car than most of the people in his life.

Possibly more than *all* of the people in his life.

But definitely more than me.

"I already said I'm not getting in a car with her."

Conrad, standing next to the red Prius that Tracy's dad got her for her sixteenth birthday in July, points at me. Tracy rolls her eyes and leans into the backseat, clearing away some junk. Tracy wouldn't appreciate my calling her magazines *junk,* but they've been stomped on and sat on, and pages have been torn out and folded over and marked up, so they're junk in my book.

Last year was all about *Teen Vogue* and *Lucky,* but this year Trace is reading *Vogue* and *Elle,* with the occasional *InStyle* thrown in, "because not everyone gets couture."

Thanks to my trusty PSAT app, I surreptitiously learned that *couture* means custom-made, high-fashion clothes. I have to admit that there are some occasional topic-specific gaps in my vocabulary. My dad—Mr. Vocabulary himself—would not have been pleased. But the fact that I have a PSAT app on my phone would have gone a long way toward redeeming me in his eyes, I'm sure.

"Conrad," Tracy says as she extricates herself from the backseat to move her magazines into the trunk, "Rose ended up in the pool for you. So maybe try a little gratitude. Sit," she commands, pointing to the mostly clean backseat and dropping several torn-up *GQ*s in the process. "Love your shoes, by the way. Stuff paper towels in them when you get home so they dry in the right shape. They're Gucci, right? And those pants *are* Marc Jacobs, aren't they?"

Conrad doesn't miss a beat. "Stop talking about my clothes. You're making me self-conscious."

Tracy looks shocked, like she can't conceive of a world in which Conrad wouldn't want to talk about fashion. I think this is actually less about stereotyping and more about Tracy forgetting that not everyone cares as deeply and passionately about fashion as she does. Whatever she's into takes over her entire worldview. She was like that with cheerleading last year. And Matt, unfortunately.

Getting dumped by Matt after she lost her virginity to him was the best thing that ever happened to Tracy. Well, okay, not the *best* thing. Actually, it was terrible. But as soon as she was forced to accept what a loser Matt had become, she realized she was spending too much time worrying about what he—and everyone else—thought of her. She vowed never to do that again, and she hasn't looked back since. Her obsession with fashion isn't just about magazines and being pretty. Tracy wants to be a designer someday, or an editor at a fashion magazine, or a… something. According to her, her education has already started. She reads every fashion magazine she can get her hands on, follows about twenty different blogs, and spends more hours on Lookbook than most gamers spend playing *Call of Duty 17,* or whatever number they're up to.

I envy her. She found her thing and is already figuring out how to do it.

Actually, if I think about it, I'm not *that* far behind her—at least not in terms of knowing what my thing is. I just have to… start doing it.

When I was thinking of auditioning for *Damn Yankees,* I sang in front of the mirror and discovered that I look like a giant freak. When my mom's shrink, Caron, asked why I hadn't auditioned after I'd said I was going to, I just shrugged. Then she declared that I'm depressed.

Brilliant, right? But Ms. Shrinky-Dink had a point. I *was* excited about auditioning. And I was disappointed—in myself—when I chickened out. So I'm going to that *Anything Goes* audition, even if I look like the world's weirdest weirdo when I sing.

"What are you doing with all this shit?" Conrad says, looking down at the issues of *GQ* that Tracy dropped.

"I like fashion," Tracy answers, sounding a little peeved as she grabs the magazines and puts them on top of her pile. She dumps the magazines in her trunk and takes out the blanket from the monstrous roadside emergency kit that her dad bought for the car—there are enough supplies in there to survive simultaneous natural disasters. "Here," she says, handing it to him.

Conrad wraps the blanket around himself and with one more nasty look at me, slides into the backseat. Tracy slams the trunk shut and gets into the driver's seat. I barely have my seat belt on over my wet towel when Conrad starts in.

"So was it guilt that made you pull me off the bottom of the pool?"

Tracy eyes Conrad in her rearview mirror. "If anyone should feel guilty, it's your sister. *She* was the psychotic maniac last year."

"That's not what I heard," he mutters.

"Two sides to every story," I reply.

"All right, let's hear your side. How did someone like *you* manage to steal my sister's boyfriend?"

Conrad's question rings in my ears as I turn off the air-conditioning that came on full blast when Tracy pushed the car's power button. My teeth are chattering because my skin is still wet. I hope my mother isn't waiting up for me when I get home. If I have to explain to her how I ended up fully clothed in a pool at the party, she'll probably call Caron to schedule an emergency midnight session. That's Kathleen for ya.

I've been calling my mom by her first name—Kathleen— in my head. It makes me feel better for some reason. Less "depressed," you might say.

"Hello?" Conrad says, still waiting for an answer.

If I were a different person, I would see this as an *opportunity,* as Caron likes to call complicated situations. An opportunity to tell my side of the story, or something like that.

But really, it just sucks to hear Conrad ask a variation on the very question I spent most of the summer asking myself: What would a hot guy like Jamie Forta ever see in someone like me?

"I think the real question is how did *you* end up in a pool with the swim team trying to drown you?" Tracy asks.

"Oh, please. I saw the YouTube video of your initiation last year, pretending to be Beyoncé in your bra in the freezing cold after homecoming. You don't need me to explain a damn thing to you."

Tracy didn't see that coming. Conrad is giving her a real run for her money, and she's not used to it.

"Dancing in a parking lot and practically being killed by your teammates are kind of different, don't you think?" I ask.

"Being straight in Union and being *me* in Union are kind of different, don't you think?" he mocks in a high, girly voice that sounds nothing like me. Then he sighs, more annoyed than defeated. "Your ex went the extra mile with me because the thought of me looking at him naked in the locker room scares the panties off him. God, what a fucking cliché."

Tracy doesn't respond. Neither do I. Ms. Maso would not be pleased with our inability to be supportive of someone who just came out to us. Even if he did do it in a way that was carefully crafted to make us feel as stupid as possible.

Conrad misinterprets our silence. "I'm *gay*," he says with exasperation.

"We know," Tracy responds with ice in her voice.

"You mean someone in Union actually has gaydar? Shocking," Conrad grumbles. "Although if anyone would have it, it would be the girl with back issues of *GQ* and *Vogue* in the trunk of her Prius. Everything about Union is so typical." Conrad slouches down, jabbing his knees into the back of my seat. "So, Rose— that's your name, right?—are you and Jamie together or is he just doing his usual dark-and-brooding, now-you-see-me-now-you-don't thing where he shows up at your door every once in a while and does something sexy just to make sure you're still dangling on the line, waiting for him?"

Tracy and I are both stunned into silence, for different reasons. I'm sure she's not surprised by my inability to keep up with Conrad, but it's pretty rare for Tracy to be without a good comeback. I'm also marveling at Conrad's ability to go right for the sweet spot and stick a knife in it. It's a gift. Must run in the family.

Suddenly, I'm angry. Sure, it's true that Conrad was just humiliated in front of half of Union High, but that's no reason for him to take it out on me, especially after I just dove, fully clothed, into a pool for him. Well, okay, I was pushed. But the whole reason I was close enough to get pushed was because I was going to dive in.

Snark doesn't come naturally to me, but I just happen to have some deep inside. I take a breath and let it fly. "I have no clue what's going on with Jamie because we haven't talked since your batshit-crazy sister had him arrested for committing the apparently horrific felony of attempting to take *someone like me* to the prom."

Tracy takes her eyes off the road to look at me. She stops just short of giving me a thumbs-up. I feel Conrad's knees in my back again.

"So, Jamie didn't call you once this whole summer? After standing you up for the prom?" He lets out that angry laugh again that sounds like it should come from someone a lot older. "Wow, that is *cold*. Well, he was busy chasing after 'Gina in summer school." Conrad pauses, knowing full well that this is information I didn't have. "Of course, *she* was busy throwing herself at that puck-head Anthony, just to drive Jamie crazy. And it worked. He totally wants her back. 'Oh, what a tangled web we weave.' Is that Shakespeare? I think that's Shakespeare."

"Sir Walter Scott," I correct, trying to sound unfazed although my brain is reeling.

So Jamie was avoiding me all summer *and* hanging out with Regina. That's fantastic. Well, at least now I know why he doesn't want anything to do with me. Apparently, the way to Jamie's heart is to have him arrested. I'll have to remember that.

But what about Anthony Parrina? If Regina just wanted Jamie back and now Jamie wants Regina back, what is Regina still doing with Anthony?

This is all so far over my head it's not even funny.

"Where am I going?" Tracy asks Conrad impatiently.

"Take Hill to Barry and turn left. My house is halfway down the block. Next to the Fortas," Conrad says pointedly.

All three of us fall silent, which is kind of a relief. We leave the fancy part of Union, where all the houses are huge with perfectly edged bright green lawns, and we drive into the next neighborhood, where the houses are smaller—some nice, some not so nice. We pass one with dark metal siding and an American flag hanging over the front door, with a "Support Our Troops" banner tacked up beneath the windows, practically glowing in the dark because of all the floodlights trained on it. If Conrad weren't here, I'd ask Tracy to stop so I could take a picture for Vicky, who likes to post photos of troop-support banners from all over the country on her son's memorial site.

Kathleen hates it when I say it, but Vicky is my friend. Her son, Sergeant Travis Ramos, was one of the people who died with my dad when the convoy they were traveling in blew up. I discovered Travis's memorial site last fall, and it inspired me—eventually—to start designing the one for my dad. One night when I couldn't sleep, I posted a comment on Travis's site, explaining who I was and asking for advice about how to—and whether I should—launch my site. And that's how I met Vicky.

She emailed back right away, full of reasons why a memorial site is a great way to honor someone. It was Vicky who suggested I launch the site on the first anniversary of the explosion, and Vicky who later contacted everyone on her mailing list to let them know that there was finally a site up for Alfonso Zarelli, which is how I ended up getting tons of posts on the anniversary. And how I learned that my dad had decided to stay in Iraq for a year, when he'd promised me that he was coming home after six months.

I kind of got a little obsessed with the posts for a few days, but Vicky and I emailed a lot, and she helped me. She understood what I was going through.

The day after the anniversary, my mother came to my room and flipped out about Vicky, claiming that I didn't need to expend my "emotional resources" on a grown woman who was grieving. I knew right away my mother had been reading my emails, which wasn't hard for her to do—she'd set up my account for me in middle school, and I'd never changed the password. I'd never thought I needed to.

She doubled our therapy sessions that day.

To be honest, I think my mother was jealous that I'd said more to Vicky about missing my dad than I'd said to her. That's probably why I didn't change my password right away after I found out she was reading my email. In a way, I sort of liked that she was jealous.

Sometimes it's just easier to talk to people you don't really know.

When we pull up in front of the Deladdos' place, it takes exactly one second to figure out which house is Jamie's. The house to the left of the Deladdos' is perfectly maintained and lit up like the Fourth of July. I can see a TV on the wall and a dog bouncing up and down on the couch, barking and wriggling furiously as we idle on the street in front of his territory.

The house to the right of the Deladdos' is small and rundown. The lawn is scraggly with bald spots where grass refuses to grow. Brown shutters droop on their hinges and white paint has peeled off the house and landed in half-dead shrubs, creating a dirty-snow effect. The gutters are bursting with dead leaves and branches that look like they're sprouting from the house itself. There are no lights on and no one seems to be home.

This is where Jamie lives with his dad.

Jamie turned eighteen this summer. Technically, he doesn't have to live here anymore. And considering what his father did to him when he got arrested, it's hard to believe that he'd want to. But I'd be willing to bet that Jamie won't leave his dad alone unless he has to.

Jamie can be loyal to a fault.

I wonder what Jamie's mother would say about his father leaving him in jail overnight.

I saw Jamie's father from a distance last Thanksgiving at a restaurant, and he seemed way more interested in the football game that was on than in talking to Jamie. I don't know a lot about him—I know that he's a cop, and that he went a little crazy for a while and Jamie actually had to live with the Delad-doses for a few months, which I try not to think about because it drives me crazy.

But I know even less about Jamie's mother. Only that she didn't live with Jamie and his dad because she was in some kind of institution near Boston. I also know that it was soon after she died that Jamie got kicked off the hockey team.

Which is when he became one of my mom's patients.

Yes, I am the very lucky daughter of an adolescent psychologist who is in therapy herself. No wonder I avoid conversation with her at all costs.

It drives me nuts that my mother knows more about Jamie than I do. Although, at this point, that would be true of anyone who actually had a conversation with Jamie this summer—the cashier at the grocery store, the guys he worked with on the road crew, his probation officer.

Regina.

"What do you want me to do with this blanket?" Conrad asks, unbuckling his seat belt. Before Tracy can answer, the Delad-dos' front door opens. A woman looks out at us, her hand hovering over the screen-door handle as if she's unsure what to do. She shields her eyes against the glare of the light above her front steps in order to see us better.

"Shit," Conrad mutters. He runs his hands through his hair

and looks down at his ruined pants and his red shirt, which now looks vaguely tie-dyed.

"Just leave it there," Tracy answers.

Without another word, Conrad gets out of the car, slams the door too hard and starts up his front walk. As I watch him, he seems to physically transform, like he's trying to become invisible. He ducks his head and looks at the ground, pulling his shirt down as far over his pants as he possibly can and then giving up and jamming his hands into his pockets. The woman holds open the screen door for him and he slides in sideways so as not to touch her or let her touch him. She asks him something and he shakes his head while moving past her as if his life depends on it. She watches him take the stairs two at a time and then, after he has disappeared from her sight, turns back to us. She lifts one hand to shield her eyes again, and then gives us a hesitant wave before slowly closing the door.

expiate *(verb):* to make up for doing something wrong
(see also: Jamie...apologizes?)

———————

3

"MATT IS A TOTAL *SADIST.*"

"Trace," I say, pretending to be shocked. "Did you finally open that vocabulary study guide I gave you, like, a year ago?"

She rolls her eyes at me. "He *is.*"

I'm tempted to remind Tracy that I spent almost all of freshman year telling her that Matt had turned into a sadistic jerk, but we've been getting along so great, the last thing I want to do is say *I told you so.* Even though I kind of do want to say it.

Tracy pulls a pair of super-soft yoga pants and a blue T-shirt that she knows I love out of her dresser and hands them to me. "Here. And don't forget the leave-in conditioner. There is nothing worse for your hair than chlorine. Matt's hair felt like straw all the time."

"Gross," I say as I pull her silk T-shirt over my head. I know it's ruined—it now feels more like Styrofoam than silk. As soon as I get it off, Tracy rushes it into the bathroom to begin a special washing ritual in her sink involving a "delicates" soap—I had no idea there was such a thing—that comes in a black bottle shaped like a corset.

"I'm really sorry about your shirt," I say as I follow her slowly. I hate Tracy's bathroom. I try to avoid using it because the entire thing is full of mirrors—there is literally no escape from looking at yourself, unless you're in the shower. And looking at myself is not one of my favorite things to do. I actually took the mirror off the back of my closet door this summer because I was constantly checking my hair and my face to see if anything good was finally happening.

It never was.

Tracy, on the other hand, has what Caron would call a "healthy sense of self-esteem." She checks herself out constantly to make sure that the outfit she put together works from every angle and that her hair and makeup are achieving maximum effect. When I watch her do this, I don't think, *my best friend is vain,* like I used to. Instead, I think, *What is it like to actually enjoy looking at yourself?* I mean, it's not that I expect to look in the mirror and see Giselle. But there's got to be something in between "I'm so gorgeous" and "I'm so hideous." Right?

There's got to be.

"Don't worry about the shirt," Tracy says as she swishes it around in the water over and over in a figure-eight pattern. Unfortunately, I can tell she just doesn't want me to feel bad. I know it's totally killing her that the shirt got trashed before she even got to wear it once.

"I'll get you a new one if it's ruined, okay?"

"Uh-uh. If it's ruined, Matt is getting me a new one. And he's also getting Conrad some new pants."

"Yeah, good luck with that," I say.

"I should threaten to call his mother. She always liked me. I bet she'd love to know he was trying to drown a freshman for fun." She lifts the shirt out of the sink, gives it a sniff and puts it back to soak some more. "Blackmail might work. And if it doesn't, at least I'll get to tell his parents that he's having sex, and his birth control method is to say to the girl, 'You worry about it.'"

I look at Tracy in the mirror. "I thought you said you guys used a condom."

Tracy sighs. This is a conversation we had over and over last year, when Matt kept trying to convince Tracy that she should be on the Pill, and I kept telling her that she had to make him use a condom. "We did, Rosie. But only because I had them. He was only thinking about himself. So not worth it. Be glad you're still a virgin." She points at a bottle sitting on the edge of the tub, knowing that of course I had already forgotten all about it. "Don't forget to use that leave-in conditioner."

Tracy closes the door behind her, leaving me standing in the room of mirrors in my bra and the loose-fit white capris I borrowed from her—I couldn't get my runner's thighs into her skinny jeans if I covered them in cooking oil. I turn to face the shower curtain and peel the damp clothes off, trying not to catch a glimpse of myself—I don't feel like seeing my naked body in the mirror while wondering if it's weird that I'm still a virgin.

I'm a fifteen-year-old high school sophomore—it shouldn't be weird that I haven't had sex yet. But somehow, when Tracy points out that I'm a virgin—which has happened more than once since she slept with Matt—it feels weird.

Once the water gets hot enough, I stand under it for at least 10 minutes, feeling the heat soak into me. It's the warmest I've felt since Jamie pulled me out of the pool, his hands hot against my skin, his eyes practically on fire with anger.

Is he mad at me? He's the one who stood me up, I keep re-minding myself. So what is he so pissed off about?

Caron says I have to stop feeling like everything is my fault. And she follows that up with a question about whether I feel like Dad's death was my fault. My mother always looks like she's going to vomit when we get to that part.

I turn off the shower and dry myself while I'm still standing behind the curtain. Then I put on the yoga pants and T-shirt and get away from those mirrors as fast as I can.

Tracy is on the floor, meticulously working her way through *Vogue* with a Sharpie in one hand and a pad of Post-its in the other. I sit down next to her and get to work on a back issue of *Elle*, carefully tearing pages out that Tracy has marked by folding the corner down.

I have no idea why she wants some pages and not others, because all the models and outfits look pretty much the same to me. But as Tracy carefully explained when I first started helping with her magazines, each outfit is an individual work of art that needs to be studied. When I looked skeptical, she reminded me of the monologue Meryl Streep has in *The Devil Wears Prada*, where she smacks down Anne Hathaway for laughing at a bunch of magazine editors who are trying to describe the specific shade of blue on a belt. I knew the speech she was talking about—when I first heard it, it made me see fashion as a kind of art, and I'd never thought of fashion that way before.

As I play the role of Tracy's assistant, I take a look around the room. A year ago, I would have been on her orange shag rug and she would have been in the beanbag chair, asking me whether or not she should sleep with Matt. Now, the shag has been replaced by a flat black rug with gray lines that I think are supposed to be flowers, and two clear plastic armchairs sit where the beanbag used to be. And we're doing something meaningful—or at least, meaningful to her.

To be truthful, I don't actually know what we're doing.

Tracy's walls are covered with magazine pages and blog photos, but they're not just taped up as part of a collage, like they would be in most girls' rooms. She has painted one entire wall with special magnetic paint so she can use these tiny magnets to hang up the images, which she moves around daily and covers in different colored Post-its. Sometimes she's written a word or a phrase on the Post-it like "Bubble!" or "Blue sky"; other times, just letters.

If I ask her what she's doing, all she says is I'll find out soon enough.

We're not supposed to be keeping secrets from each other this year, but she looks so happy when I ask about her project that I decide not to remind her about that.

"So, Peter went back to school?" Tracy gets up, disappears into the bathroom, and comes back with the leave-in conditioner I forgot to put in my hair.

I nod.

"Back to what's-her-name? That rich pot freak?"

Tracy—who has had a crush on my brother for most of her life—knows what Peter's girlfriend's name is. She just can't bring herself to say it. I get it. Sometimes I can't bear to say that girl's name, either.

"Yup, back to *Amanda*." I take the bottle from Tracy and squeeze some of the conditioner into my hands. It smells like tomatoes fresh off the vine. "And I'm sure she just couldn't wait to get him high," I add, the words sounding funny—for a whole bunch of reasons—as they come out of my mouth.

It's hard for me to think about Peter getting high. I never thought that my brother would be one of those guys who would get into drugs just because his girlfriend liked them.

Caron says that people's reasons for using drugs are "often very complex." It's the one thing she says that doesn't get an instant nod of agreement from my mother. Mom and Caron know each other really well—they used to be in the same practice together—so I usually feel ganged up on when Caron is talking and Mom is just nodding at everything like a bobblehead. But when Caron talks about Peter's "complexity of motivation for using," Mom gets very quiet and looks at the floor.

I don't think there's anything complex about it. I think he's doing it because Amanda wants him to, and he's desperate to impress her because he's never had such a beautiful girlfriend in his life. He's never really had a girlfriend at all, now that I think about it.

"So how is Peter doing?" Tracy asks after a pause that is meant to make the question seem way more casual than it really is. "Have you talked to him?"

I shake my head.

"Well, you're going to call him, aren't you? To check on him?"

"At some point."

"You're still mad."

I nod.

"Maybe you should be worried, not mad."

"And maybe you should just call him yourself if you want to talk to him so badly," I tease.

"It's not that I want to talk to him," she says too quickly, though we both know she does. "It's just that I'm worried." She fixes me with her most serious stare. "And you should be, too."

About a week before they had to go back to school, Peter and Amanda came to visit. They'd been working in a hotel on Martha's Vineyard for the summer, and the first thing I noticed was that they looked like they hadn't been in the sun the entire time. What's the point of dealing with snotty, demanding hotel guests on Martha's Vineyard if you're not going to go to the beach?

Then I thought maybe they were just being really conscientious about sunscreen. Amanda definitely seemed like the type to want her pale skin to stay as pale as possible.

But that didn't explain the bags under their eyes.

It was the first time my mom and I met Amanda, and I hadn't been looking forward to it. I was still pissed that she'd invited

Peter to go to her house last Thanksgiving, even though she knew it was our first Thanksgiving without Dad. When Peter had called to tell me he wasn't coming home, I'd actually hung up on him.

So Amanda and Peter drove up in her hand-me-down silver Mercedes convertible that her father—who is also a shrink, by the way—gave her when he upgraded, and they looked like they hadn't showered in weeks. When I said something about it to my mom, she said that that's what college students do. Something about rebelling against their parents' enforced hygiene rules once they finally get out of the house.

Amanda is definitely pretty—there's no getting around that, no matter what Tracy says about how she's so super skinny that her head looks too big for her body. She wears baggy clothes that are supposed to make her look like she doesn't have any money, but they're so nice that you know she totally does. She has super-long blond hair and green eyes, and when she smiles she looks like a sleepy cat.

Or a high cat.

For a few days after they got home, I actually believed that they had just been working really, really hard, and Peter was too exhausted to speak. He barely deigned to acknowledge my existence until he said that he was giving me his old iPhone because Amanda had gotten him a new one. That was on the third day of their visit.

Not talking may be normal for some brothers and sisters, but it's not for us. Peter and I were really close. He used to look out for me, and he was even nice to me in public. Maybe that's because we're four years apart—we were never really interested in each other's toys when we were little, or each other's friends when we got older.

I could go to him if I needed advice for practically any situation. And when he came home with Amanda, I was planning to tell him how nervous I was to go back to Union after ruining

Regina's life, and that I needed some real "coping strategies," as opposed to the ones that Caron and Mom were coming up with in therapy that involved telling Regina how her actions hurt me, by filling in the blanks of this sentence: "Regina, when you *blank,* it makes me feel *blank.*"

The first—and only—time I've ever laughed in therapy was when I tried to imagine saying that sentence to Regina.

Anyway, there was no way I was going to ask Peter for advice on anything while he was walking around with such a huge superiority complex. When he gave me his stupid iPhone, he actually patted me on the head and called me "kiddo." And Amanda gave me a weird little sad-face smile and told me I was just unbearably cute. "Pete, what's it like to have a little sister?" she said in front of me, using a voice that most people reserve for talking about puppies, kittens, or babies. "Oh, look at her—how sweet. It must just be so fun!"

Of course, now I know that they were both totally high at the time. The only thing I don't know is what else they were on besides pot.

It's really the last thing I want to talk about.

"So, did Jamie even say hi to you tonight?" Tracy asks.

Actually, it's the second-to-last thing I want to talk about.

I shake my head without looking at her. She leans over to turn up the Feist album she's been playing nonstop since I told her to get it, and she doesn't ask me anything else.

I've been lying on the trundle bed in Tracy's room for more than an hour, trying every trick I know to fall asleep, when I hear it.

At first I don't even recognize the sound.

And then I do. It's my phone, vibrating.

Somebody's calling me.

I look at the clock. It's 1:00 a.m.

I look at Tracy, who falls asleep in all of about three seconds and can sleep through anything. She's passed out.

I feel around to find my phone, which has vibrated itself off the rug and is now practically jumping up and down on the hardwood floor, probably waking up the entire house.

As my hand closes around it, a familiar tightness creeps into my throat. My heart starts to skitter and skip beats, and my breathing gets shallow. Supposedly once a person recognizes the symptoms of a panic attack, she can sort of wrangle them and keep them under control. I haven't mastered that fine art yet, but at least now a part of my brain stays rational as my airway tries to close, and instead of screaming, "Am I dying?" it can ask, "Why now?" which is apparently a much more constructive question.

Caron would say— Oh, forget Caron. I'm tired of hearing her in my head all the time. I feel like she crawled in there and installed a whole bunch of automatic scripted responses to things. I don't need her to tell me why I'm on the verge of a panic attack—I already know why. It's because the only reason anybody ever calls anybody at 1:00 a.m. is if something is wrong. Terribly, hideously wrong.

The phone is now vibrating in my fist and I know with every fiber of my being that this is the call about Peter that I've been expecting. Amanda probably crashed that stupid fancy convertible into a telephone pole and Peter got thrown from the car, smashed headfirst into a tree and is dead or paralyzed. Either that, or he overdosed on whatever stupid drugs she forced on him while they were at a party.

All I know is, if Peter leaves me all by myself with Kathleen, I'll never, ever forgive him.

I try to take a deep breath, fail and then look at the phone.

It doesn't say *Boston Mass General Hospital*.

It doesn't say *Mom*.

It says *Jamie*.

I blink. I'm dreaming.

It can't be. Can it?

"Hello?" I whisper, my voice scratchy and rough from lack of air.

There's a pause, and then, "Hey."

As soon as I hear his voice, I feel Jamie's hands on my arms again. The warmth begins to travel up into my neck, across my face, under my hair. It drives away the tightness in my throat and my lungs, and everything seems to open up again, to take in the feeling that is now suffusing my entire body. "Hey," I manage to say.

"You okay, after what Hallis did?"

"I..." I'm trying to sound as calm and normal as possible, but I'm embarrassed that he witnessed me getting pushed into the pool, mad that I haven't heard from him and so happy to talk to him that I can barely even form a sentence. I don't know where to start. What I *should* do is hang up on him. But I've been waiting for more than two months for this call.

I need to know things.

"Can you come down?" he asks.

"Now? Wait—where?"

"Outside."

"I'm not at home," I say.

"I know."

"You— How?"

"Rose."

"I can't just—"

"Please."

Wow. I've never heard Jamie say *please* before. My stomach does a crazy little flip. It's hard to say no to Jamie Forta. But saying no to him when he says *please?* I wonder if any girl in history has ever been able to do it. Even as I'm thinking that there's no way he deserves to call me at 1:00 a.m. and have me get up and go outside simply because he wants to see me, I'm getting out of bed and putting on my wet shoes. I hate that he has this power over me.

But it's also sort of thrilling. Or…however you say it. Hot, I guess.

Yup. It's hot.

Which I know is dumb.

But I'm new to this whole *hot* thing, and I find it kind of irresistible.

"Okay, I'll try," I say. But he's gone, as if he knows that I'm already halfway out the door.

What am I doing? I saw the way he came to Regina's defense tonight. There's definitely still something between Regina and Jamie, no matter what Anthony Parrina thinks or says. But he also came to my defense.

I have to talk to him. To straighten things out once and for all.

Yeah, because that's how it works with Jamie Forta. All it takes is one conversation, and everything is suddenly super clear.

Uh-huh.

I know that I'll have no problem getting out of Tracy's room without waking her up, but I have no idea what it's like to try to get past her parents. Tracy does it all the time, but I don't know what her technique is. I guess if I get caught, I can just cry and say I've been sleepwalking ever since my dad died, and no one will even consider questioning my story.

Dad didn't tell the truth all the time—why should I?

I take two steps and realize that I shouldn't have put my shoes on yet. Not only are they loud on the wood floor but they're so waterlogged that my feet squish around and make weird sucking noises. I take the shoes off and leave them on the floor, tiptoeing out into the hall.

The front door is at the bottom of the staircase. I grab on to the banister and make my way down the steps, staying as far away from the center of each stair as possible, in case it's squeaky. I make it down without a sound, only to be greeted by the site of a glowing green light next to the front door.

The alarm system.

Once upon a time, the code to the alarm was Tracy's birthday—0729. But they could have changed it. And if I try to disarm the system with the wrong code, will it set off the alarm?

When my phone vibrates in my hand again, it nearly gives me a heart attack. I silence it and look at the screen. It's a text that says, "0729*."

I smile.

Tracy's not Jamie's biggest fan—and I guess she doesn't sleep as deeply as I thought—but she's helping me anyway. I'm sure she didn't even have to look out her window to know who called me.

I punch in the code, step outside, make sure the door can't lock behind me…and there he is. Across the street, leaning against the door of his green car, waiting for me.

He's beautiful.

I am not.

I'm barefoot in yoga pants and a T-shirt, also known as pajamas. I have no idea what my hair looks like, and I don't have on any makeup because I undid all of Tracy's expert work two hours ago with her expensive remover.

So what? A voice in my head says. *He's not your boyfriend.*

He could be—you don't know that he's not, says another voice.

Don't be an idiot. He didn't want anything to do with you all summer. Forget him. You shouldn't even be here.

Why are you so hopeless all the time? It's lame.

As if two warring voices in my head weren't enough, Caron chimes in, telling me to ignore the noise and just be present.

I hate to admit it, but it's good advice.

My feet carry me forward until I'm standing right in front of Jamie. He stares at me with those perfect gold-flecked hazel eyes that don't blink. Somewhere inside me I find the confidence to be quiet, to not fill the silence. He called me, he asked me to come out—he can talk first.

I stare right back, my arms folded across my chest. The silence goes on and on. He starts to look a little uncomfortable. It's kind of gratifying.

"Thanks—for helping Conrad tonight," he finally starts. I still don't say anything. I think it's the first time I've had any kind of upper hand with Jamie. Ever. "Rose, look, I'm sorry," he says with so much remorse that I have to bite my tongue to keep from telling him everything's fine and he shouldn't worry about it.

Instead, I say, "Why didn't you call?"

"You got my note?"

"The one that said you're not right for me? That you're *different*? That one?" I sound hostile. Jamie looks at the ground for a second and then up at the dark sky.

"Yeah," he says, shutting down. I don't want him to do that—when Jamie shuts down, he disappears, even if he's standing right in front of you, and there's no getting him back, no matter what. I've waited too long for this opportunity. I force myself to drop the hostility.

"You know Angelo gave it to me," I say as calmly and normally as I can manage.

"That's why I didn't call."

I shake my head and step closer to make my point as clear as possible. "If you don't like me, Jamie, just say it. You don't have to get all cryptic and write notes about how it's not me, it's you." The hostility is back. The voice that's coming out of my mouth is angrier and more hurt than I want it to be. But I can't shut it up.

"Who said I didn't like you?"

"*You* did. You sent me a note that didn't explain anything, and then you ignored me all summer. And tonight, you didn't even say hi. You pulled me out of the pool, but you looked mad. And on top of that, you still didn't talk to me. That means you don't like me. Actually, what it really means is that you don't respect me. And if you don't respect me, then I don't have any time for you."

The warring voices in my head are shocked into silence. I am finally telling Jamie what I've been thinking these past few months, and it feels so good to see that he wasn't expecting any of this from sweet little Rose, who is always so nice to him. Yeah, well, check it, Jamie Forta. Sweet little Rose has been replaced by new Rose, and she isn't going to let you jerk her around.

Turns out Jamie's not the only 2.0 in town.

My plan is to make a dramatic exit, to just leave without saying another word, but as I turn to go, Jamie catches my arm and pulls me back around to face him. He steps toward me, leaving about an inch of space between us. In a strange and exciting turn of events, even this doesn't intimidate me.

I like this 2.0 stuff.

"I was mad about Hallis—what he was doing to Conrad—and you getting pushed into the pool," he says. I can see that he's telling the truth, but only partly. There's something else going on behind his eyes, but I suddenly find that I have too much pride to ask him what it is. I'm not going to beg him to tell me his secrets. If he wants to be all taciturn and mysterious, that's on him.

"Oh, you were mad on my behalf? So, what are you? My bodyguard? My boyfriend who I'm not allowed to tell anybody about?" I demand. "Just make up your mind, Jamie, and stop messing with me."

Pain flashes across his face as if I've slapped him, and then suddenly his lips are on mine, hard and fast, knocking the air right out of my lungs. His kiss ricochets throughout my entire body in a nanosecond. He grabs my arms and turns me, practically lifting me off the ground as he backs me up against his car, pinning me to the driver's-side door with his body as his tongue flashes across my lips and into my mouth. It's like he's been waiting for this to happen again as long as I have.

But that can't be true.

I'm just a sometimes delusional girl who has a crush on a guy who...is currently kissing me as if his life depends on it.

His arms wrap around me, and they feel different now than they did the last time we kissed—it's not just that he's stronger, it's that he's solid and immovable, like a brick wall. And it feels to me like he is 100% committed to kissing me—he's not holding back. One hand is in my hair, the other sliding down my lower back. I literally feel my limbs going weak like some stupid fairy-tale princess. Once upon a time, I would have loved having weak, swoony limbs, but right here and now, in this moment, it pisses 2.0 off.

Jamie doesn't get to do this to me again. He doesn't get to just show up and take over my body for the time it takes to kiss me and then disappear. I think about what Conrad said—how Jamie shows up whenever he feels like it and kisses a girl so he can keep stringing her along.

Is that what he's doing right now?

I'm just about to make him stop when the hand on my back finds the bottom of my shirt and then slides under it and up, touching bare skin that he's never touched before. My head falls back against his car as my whole body starts to tingle. We both freeze for half a second when we realize at exactly the same moment that I'm not wearing a bra. I'm not sure if this is a good thing or a bad thing for a guy to discover—what does it say about a girl if she's not wearing a bra when she's making out with a boy against his car in the middle of the night? Anything? Nothing?

Slowly—with my body practically vibrating, begging him to touch every place he's not supposed to touch—he slides his hand back down and around to my waist and leans forward, burying his face in my neck. He still has that beautiful clean smell but there's something new under it—something that is just him, I guess. When he takes a step back and the weight of him leaves me, I lift my head and open my eyes. I can't catch my breath, but I see that he's a little out of breath, too—and when my eyes land on the front of his jeans, I can see why.

My face heats with embarrassment. I can't believe it. After all this time of thinking that there was nothing between us, that I imagined the whole thing, it turns out I was wrong.

Jamie is as turned on by kissing me as I am by kissing him.

I feel a rush of…something. Power? But the feeling drowns in confusion and fear. What do I do now? Am I supposed to do something about his…condition? If I don't, am I a tease? Or am I only obligated to do something about it if I'm his actual girl-friend? And if so, what, exactly, would that something be?

Wait—there is no obligation when it comes to this stuff, right? You're just supposed to do what you're comfortable with and nothing else?

That's what Ms. Masó drilled into our heads last year. It all made so much sense in health class. Now it doesn't seem so clear.

I realize that I've been staring at the front of Jamie's jeans for way too long to pretend that my gaze just fell there by accident.

I force my eyes up to his face, and I'm expecting him to be embarrassed or apologetic but he just gazes back at me with that same steady look, as if what's happening is totally normal. Which, I guess, it is. Although I can't imagine any of this stuff will ever feel normal to me. If anything, it feels like one big freak show.

He runs a hand through his hair and shakes his head as if, once again, he did something he shouldn't have. And 2.0 gets mad.

"Let me guess. You regret it already, right?" Right. Touching me was a complete and total mistake.

He shakes his head.

"Then what?" This roller coaster is making me insane.

"I wasn't gonna do that—"

"Don't bother, Jamie. You don't have to explain—"

"I do. There's a lot of stuff I gotta explain," he says, his eyes locked onto mine.

The fact that he knows he owes you some explanations means something. My anger starts to deflate. *But where the hell was he all summer? Did it take him months to come up with these explanations he claims he now has?* My anger balloons up again. *Well, so what if it did? Not everybody knows how to explain how they feel. You have to cut people slack sometimes.* Now my anger just sits still, not knowing what to do. Suddenly I find the entire situation…funny.

"Did you just say you're going to explain something to me? Seriously?" I tease. "You mean, I'm *finally* going to get some actual explanations out of Jamie Forta?"

After a moment of what looks like confusion, a little smile crosses his face, and I feel a shift. I don't know how to explain it in a normal way. It's like we've always been standing on two different levels, with him above me. But just now, the levels moved closer to each other and we're not so far apart anymore. We're almost—but not quite—on equal ground.

I guess another way to say it is that Jamie doesn't hold all the cards. I actually have a few of my own, and I like it.

"Next Saturday," he says.

Next Saturday. Next Saturday? As in, Saturday night?

"Dinner," he adds.

Last year, Jamie and I had covert conversations in his car in various locations, hidden away. But we never spent any time together around other people.

"Are you finally going to be seen with me in public?" I say, pretending to be astonished. "We better not tell anyone or we'll both end up in jail this time."

His smile gets a little wider and he actually laughs—that beautiful, delicious laugh that feels like a reward whenever it's let out.

It practically makes me giddy. And it dawns on me that Jamie likes it when I make fun of him. That's why the playing field is leveling out. Because I'm teasing him.

"I can't believe it," I say. "Jamie Forta and me, on an actual date."

"You don't have to keep saying *Jamie Forta,* Rose."

"Oh, sure I do. In these big moments, when explanations are being promised and public outings are announced, it's important to address you by your full name. The occasion calls for it."

His smile makes me want to get into his car and go anywhere with him. It's a little intimidating to feel that for someone. It makes you wonder if you're going to do something you don't really want to do, or shouldn't do. I mean, I haven't seen or talked to Jamie in months, and after one kiss and a couple of moments of me being really mad, I'm ready to have his hands on my bare skin again. Because that was amazing. That felt like…everything.

But I guess the point is, even though I'm feeling what I'm feeling, I'm *not* getting in the car with him. Although, why is that? Is that just because it's late at night and I'm staying at my friend's house and I don't want to get in trouble with her parents, or get *her* in trouble? Or is it actually because I have enough respect for myself not to drive off in the middle of the night with the guy who didn't bother to call me all summer?

I push off the car to show him—and myself—that I'm going back inside now.

"I'll call you," he says.

"I'll believe it when I see it," 2.0 answers. I feel all sassy as I walk past him, even though what I said doesn't exactly make sense—you don't really *see* someone call you. But I don't care. I look over my shoulder and Jamie's still smiling, looking at me like he's seeing me in a different way. A new way. A way he likes.

It was worth torturing myself all summer long just for that one look.

disinter *(verb):* to uncover or reveal
(see also: getting grilled in therapy*)*

4

"DO YOU UNDERSTAND THE ISSUE HERE, ROSE?"

What I want to say is, *the issue is that I should be eating Saturday-morning pancakes with my best friend and telling her about what happened with Jamie last night, not sitting on a therapist's couch with my mother for Saturday-morning therapy.* But I've already been told that sarcasm has no place here.

Caron's office is nicer than my mother's. The couch is squishier, the tissues are softer and the view of the backyard is more interesting. The room smells a little bit like wet dog, but I like dogs, so I don't care that much. Not that I've ever seen Caron's dog. I hear it snuffling around on the other side of the door every once in a while, but that's it. For all I know, it's just a tape of a dog, and the smell is some kind of weird incense—my mom says therapists do all sorts of things to their offices to make their clients feel comfortable. Even all the neutral colors serve a purpose—they're supposed to keep patients focused.

From my point of view, the only thing wrong with Caron's black-and-brown-and-cream office is what goes on inside it.

What *has* been going on inside it every other Saturday—or sometimes more often, depending on the level of drama in the house—since June.

"The issue?" I repeat, trying to prove to them that I've barely been listening.

"The *problem*," Caron says, stressing the word *problem* as if I need a synonym for *issue*. If she thinks I'm confused about the meaning of the word *issue* rather than just plain old baffled that we have to hash this topic out yet again, she's clearly forgotten my father, who she knew well. Dad started using vocabulary flashcards with Peter and me before we could talk.

Caron and my mother actually look like they could be sisters. They are both tall with dark brown hair and light blue eyes, and they're skinny and wear what I think of now as shrink clothes—earth tones that blend into the office furniture, with a colorful necklace or scarf. Maybe it's a kind of uniform. They both wear tortoise-shell glasses—my mom's spend a lot of time on her head functioning as a headband, but Caron's are always on her face. The difference between them these days is their energy, I guess you would say. Caron is calm; my mother seems totally wired, like she's fighting really hard to stay in control of things. Things like me.

"Do you understand why your mother has a problem with the memorial website?" Caron asks. "Why she wants you to take it down?"

I know that I'm supposed to say yes—after all, we've been going around and around on this topic all summer long. And I could just do that, because technically, I do understand the problem. I did something very public, and I did it without Mom's permission, using private family photos of Dad. But I don't understand why having a website in Dad's honor makes her so crazy. I thought she'd be happy when she saw all the photos I scanned and uploaded, and all the quotes I posted, and the Word of the Day section featuring his favorite words of all time.

But she wasn't happy. She was pissed. And when she realized that I didn't really care that she was pissed, and that if she wanted the website taken down she was going to have to figure out how to do it herself—all hell broke loose.

I think what freaks my mom out the most about the site is that it's an open invitation for people to express their opinions. I run the site, and I can make changes to it, but I have no say in how people respond. And it turns out that there are all sorts of people who knew Dad well, and they have things to say about him. Mom doesn't like that, because she can't control what they write.

Which, of course, is exactly why I *do* like it.

"Rose, are you still with us?" Caron asks. She usually gives me about three seconds to think before she makes a comment implying that I'm not paying attention.

"I guess I don't really get it, no," I lie.

"The problem, Rose," my mother says, her overt patience communicating just how impatient she is with this conversation, "is that you went behind my back after I specifically asked you not to, and you got Peter involved by using his credit card."

"Can you tell Rose how that made you feel?"

"Betrayed. Betrayed at a very vulnerable moment."

I'm tempted to roll my eyes, but I know that would probably also be betraying my mother at a very vulnerable moment. It's not that I don't care that she feels betrayed, it's just that I think her reasons for feeling that way are ridiculous.

Maybe that's the same thing as not caring. I'm not sure.

"It also scares me," she continues. "There are a lot of people out there who prey on those who are grieving. And Rose is now having interactions with people she's never even heard of before, who claim to know her father. It's dangerous in many ways, including emotionally."

"Can you explain to Rose what you mean by that?"

Once more unto the breach, dear friends, once more. That's Shakespeare for *here we go again.*

"Rose launched the website on the anniversary of her dad's death in June. Within a few hours, there were nearly fifty comments on the site about him. Some were nice, some were odd, some were from people who obviously didn't know Alfonso at all and just wanted to make themselves feel important and involved. It would have been extremely confusing and painful for anyone, but it was especially so for a teenage girl missing her father. Rose didn't leave her room for three days."

That's not entirely true. I left to use the bathroom and to eat occasionally.

"I was just reading the comments and writing back to people," I say. "It wasn't a big deal."

"That's part of what you were doing, Rose. You were also having an emotional breakdown as a result of being assaulted by all the information that didn't reflect back to you the person you thought you knew—"

"Kathleen," says Caron in her special voice. This is some kind of code they've established, because every time Caron says her name like that, my mother looks guilty and then stops talking.

So what if I'm in touch with people we don't know who knew Dad? So what if some guy he knew for, like, two days in Iraq posted about how they'd had a beer together and how he could tell that Dad was the "genuwine article"? Why is that less valid than my story about him showing me his twenty-volume Oxford English Dictionary for the first time?

I don't really know how Kathleen and I got here. I feel like things were fine, and then suddenly they weren't. We had this heart-to-heart conversation last year on my birthday and it seemed like everything was finally going to be okay between us. She apologized for "abandoning me to my grief," explained that she needed help and asked if I would come to therapy with her. I said I'd think about it.

What a mistake that was. Two months later, I launched my dad's site and when I refused to take a shower after sitting in front of the computer for a few days, she practically dragged me by my greasy hair to see Caron for the first time.

"So, Rose, when you hear your mother talk about feeling betrayed by you and scared for you, what do you feel?"

This question has come up before, but I guess I didn't answer it right. Maybe I'll try telling the truth today.

"I feel annoyed," I answer. This is a very different response from my usual *I feel bad.*

Caron's eyebrows shoot up.

"Annoyed?" my mother repeats very slowly.

"I don't understand why we have to keep talking about this. It's starting to get *annoying.*"

"We have to keep talking about it because you refuse to take the site down, even though you are unable to explain why you want to keep working on it when it clearly upsets you to be in touch with those people."

Those people. She means Vicky.

I just got an email from Vicky this morning, reminding me to have fun on my last free weekend before school starts on Tuesday. Vicky checks in on me from time to time, emailing me little inspirational sayings or pictures that she's scanned as part of her ongoing project to scan every photo she ever took with a pre-digital camera. She only sends me funny photos of herself, like from Halloween or from some party where she did something big and crazy with her hair. Vicky is from Texas, and she's a hairdresser, so she's had a lot of practice making big hair. Every time she sends me a new photo, it's the biggest hair I've ever seen. When I told her I had the lamest, flattest, straightest, most boring-est hair in the history of humankind, she said I needed to "hightail it on down" to Texas and let her take a crack at it. "When I'm done with you, honey," she wrote, "you won't even recognize yourself."

Vicky raised her son—the sergeant, Travis—and daughter alone. A "good, single Christian woman" is how she describes herself. She's never told me anything about the father of her children, although I read a letter Travis's dad wrote to him that she posted on the website. And she doesn't say much about her daughter. I kind of get the feeling that she and her daughter don't talk much. But she loves to write about Travis, and she always ends every email with, *Your dad is watching over you, just like my Travis is watching over me. God bless, honey.*

I was raised agnostic, bordering on atheist, but there's something about the way Vicky writes *God bless, honey* that makes me feel safe from all the awful stuff that goes on inside my head and out. When Vicky says she's praying for me, I believe it, and even though I don't think there's a god who pays attention to us, I like when she says it because I know she *does* think he's up there.

Of course I can't tell any of that to my mother.

"It doesn't upset me to be in touch with *those people*. Why do you hate Vicky so much, anyway?" I ask.

Kathleen sighs like she's the weariest person in history. "I don't even know Vicky, Rose. I just feel like you give her more than she gives you. And frankly, you don't need to take care of anyone but yourself right now."

"Rose, do *you* feel like you're taking care of Vicky?" Caron asks me. My mother looks at her sharply. Caron, to her credit, keeps her eyes on me and doesn't acknowledge the death rays that Kathleen is staring at her.

"We just email about stuff. She sends me funny pictures of her hair. Is that taking care of somebody—sending each other emails?"

"It is when she's sharing private details regarding how she's coping with the death of her son," my mother cuts in, sounding jealous and protective at the same time. "She's a grown woman. She shouldn't be burdening a child with her feelings under the guise of helping her."

"I'm not a child, Kathleen," I say.

I clamp my hand over my mouth. I had no intention of calling my mother "Kathleen" to her face. Well, no conscious intention, anyway. I can't imagine that it's going to go over well.

My mother's face changes color several times and I feel like steam is about to come out of her ears but she's doing her best not to lose it. I actually feel bad. I didn't do it on purpose. It just came out.

It probably hurts to hear your child call you by your first name, although I can't really say why.

But why do I have to worry about *her* feelings?

Because there's such a thing as basic human kindness, says one of the voices in my head.

Caron is watching my mother to see if she wants to address what just happened. When it's clear that my mother is taking the high road, Caron asks, "Is it easy to write to Vicky about how you're feeling, Rose?"

I don't like having to talk about Vicky in here like she's an *issue.* "I don't think about it—I just do it. She asks me questions and I answer them, and then I ask her questions. I don't see what's wrong with that. She's just a sad woman with a dead son. And I'm a 'depressed' girl with a dead dad."

My mother closes her eyes and twists her wedding ring on her finger. Then she finally says, "Please don't talk about your father that way."

"What way? He's dead, so I get to say that he's dead. Isn't the whole reason we're here so we can say whatever we want out loud?"

"It's the way you're saying it, Rose. You're saying it in a way that is disrespectful to your father and designed to shock and hurt me. And I know why you're doing it—"

"Kathleen," Caron says again, with a little more force than before.

This time my mother is the one to roll her eyes, which I think is pretty funny. I guess she's sick of Caron telling her what she can and can't say. She stares out the window into the backyard and looks…hopeless.

"Why do you keep stopping her from talking if we're supposed to be so open?" I ask Caron. Mom looks at me.

"Sometimes it's difficult for your mother to be a patient, which means things get a little uneven—"

"Rose, just tell me why it's important to you to keep that website up, even though it could send you into a tailspin at any moment," my mother interrupts, obviously not liking where Caron is going. I see a flicker of annoyance on Caron's face.

I know it seems to my mom and to Caron that I'm keeping this information from them, but I just haven't come up with the right way to tell the truth yet. For example, if I said, "Sometimes the site feels like my only connection to Dad," Kathleen might ask why *she* isn't that connection for me. I don't know how to answer that without hurting her. Also, when I was building the website, I liked that it was a way for me to connect with Dad directly, not through her or anyone else. And when I launched it and all those people started posting things, it became my favorite way to connect to him. And I definitely can't say that.

So I go with the easiest answer. "It's important to me to keep the site up because I'm learning things about Dad that I didn't know before."

My mother is so frustrated by this that she can barely stay seated on the couch. "What could you possibly learn about your father from people who barely knew him?" she snaps.

I snap right back. "Oh, I don't know, maybe the fact that he was going to stay in Iraq for a whole year."

Her irritation turns to shock. She shakes her head and then says to Caron, "See? This is exactly the kind of information Rose shouldn't be getting out of context."

"Kathleen, you're shutting Rose out of the conversation. Tell her, not me."

Mom stares at the ceiling for a few seconds before she turns to me and tries to ask very calmly, "Who told you that?"

"Not you. And not him," I mutter. "He told me he was only staying for six months."

"There wasn't time to tell you," Mom says, tears filling her eyes. "He made the decision right before it happened. Who told you?" she asks again.

"One of the guys he worked with. He wrote that he was glad when Dad said he'd signed up to stay for more time because playing chess with Dad was one of the only things that made life there bearable."

My mother starts shaking her head again. "He felt like it was worth it financially, Rose. Adults have to take all sorts of factors into consideration when making decisions."

I know that my mother feels guilty about encouraging my dad to take the contractor job in Iraq. And I also know that she encouraged him to do it because he'd lost his job as an engineer, the money in Iraq was really good and she'd been freaking out about their finances because of college tuition. The nice and smart and generous thing to do would be to let the matter drop.

But I can't. I just can't. I have to pour some salt in the wound. Actually, I have to pick up the saltshaker, take off the top and dump the whole thing on her raw soul.

"*He* felt it was worth it? Or *you* did?"

The tears that have pooled in her eyes spill down her cheeks and she stands up, pulling down the hem of her brown pencil skirt and straightening her peach silk shirt. It's the outfit Tracy always compliments her on, and which she wears whenever she needs help feeling good.

"I'm taking a break," she says to Caron, reaching for a tissue on the glass end table that is loaded with arty-looking books about photography. "I'll be back."

If my mother weren't a shrink, I'm pretty sure Caron wouldn't let her just walk out. I'd be forced to stay in the room for sure.

As the door closes behind my mother, I feel gross. Did I really have to say that to her?

Yes, Rose, you really had to say that. Or you wouldn't have said it. Clearly.

Caron gives me a sad smile and makes a quick note on her yellow legal pad. "So, school on Tuesday," she says, after some silence.

I nod.

"How are you feeling about that?"

I shrug.

"Are you worried about seeing Regina after the break?"

I'm surprised Caron is asking me this. She's sort of breaking protocol by talking about Regina during a family session when Kathleen's not in the room.

"Not really," I say. Caron tilts her head to express confusion, since last time she managed to get me to admit that I was nervous about seeing Regina. "I already sort of saw her."

"You *sort of* saw her? What does that mean?"

"At a party."

"You went to a party?" she asks, looking a little pleased even as she tries to be neutral. "How was it?"

"I got pushed into the pool."

Caron eyes me carefully, as if I might not be telling the truth. "Did Regina push you?"

"No. Matt did. Tracy's ex-boyfriend."

"That must have made you angry," she says. "Were you able to control your response?"

The question embarrasses me. She's asking if I was able to keep it together at a party. I guess I can't blame her, based on the way I went after Regina last year at track tryouts. Despite all my efforts to the contrary, I am now one of those "crazy" teens with emotional problems who I've seen going in and out of my mom's office my whole life. There's just no getting around it.

"Did you want to hit him?"

"Wouldn't you?"

Caron cracks a smile. "But you didn't?"

"I would have loved to punch him—for so, so, so many reasons—but there was other stuff going on."

She nods like she's impressed. I'm not sure if she should be. "More important things?"

"The swim thugs were trying to kill someone."

"Is that an exaggeration?" There's genuine concern on her face.

I shake my head. "They were literally trying to drown a freshman swimmer."

"And why is that?"

"Because they're psychotic," I say.

"Who exactly are the *swim thugs*?" she asks.

Something about this conversation is starting to feel like a trap.

"All the guys on the team," I answer, reluctant to name names. It's not that I want to protect those jerks, but I'm done whistle-blowing—that's what I've promised myself. No more running to the adults.

So how is it that I keep ending up in the position where the adults come to *me* for information?

My mother chooses that moment to return to the room. Her puffy eyes say something totally different than the fake smile plastered on her face. I can tell she attempted to fix her makeup and then gave up because she was just making things worse.

That's the problem with skin like ours—if you so much as look at it the wrong way, it gets red and blotchy.

"Kathleen, we were talking about how things have been going for Rose with regard to controlling her temper." My mother looks from me to Caron and back again, seeming to sense that she missed something. "So have you had any panic or rage attacks recently, Rose?"

"The new problem is insomnia," my mother says.

I don't like it when she answers for me. Plus, she's wrong. The problem isn't insomnia, it's the horrifying and freaky things that I can't stop imagining while I'm having the insomnia.

I have trouble shutting off my brain.

My dad always used to say that when I'd ask him why he looked so tired in the morning. "I have trouble shutting off my brain when I'm trying to sleep. It keeps going, even when I want it to be quiet." "You have insomnia?" I'd ask. And he'd say, as he scanned the headlines of the local paper, "More accurately, insomnia has me."

I never knew what he meant until recently. Now I spend half the night staring at the ceiling, trying to shut out the violent images that come into my head. But instead of telling Caron that, I stare at the espadrilles Tracy made me get for summer. I'd much rather contemplate my espadrilles than talk about my crazy imagination.

"The insomnia was a minor problem last year, but it got worse after the anniversary," my mother continues. "Before that, she was making a lot of progress."

I didn't realize I was being monitored for *progress*. But of course I am. If your mother is a shrink, aren't you constantly being monitored for progress?

"Rose, we have a few minutes left. Can you tell us what goes on in your head while you're not sleeping?"

"Just...stuff." I can feel my mother bristle. She hates vague answers.

"Can you clarify *stuff*?" Caron asks this without sounding condescending, but I still don't want to answer her. I don't know how those images got there, or what's causing them. I'll be thinking about something normal that happened during the day, like walking across the street to the drugstore. Suddenly, a huge truck will appear, and it'll smash right into me. Blood and guts and body parts everywhere.

But if I bring that up, I'll be coming to this office daily until I leave for college.

"Can she answer the question *I* asked before she left the room?" I say.

With what looks like a tiny bit of reluctance, Caron turns to my mother. "Kathleen? Can you answer Rose's question?"

Without any fanfare, she does.

"Your father made the decision." I can see on her face that it costs her to tell me this—she feels like she's betraying him.

That's how I know she's telling the truth.

"Dad *promised* that he was coming home after six months. He said he'd be back before I had to start high school."

My mother looks down at her ring and twists it again. When she looks up, the sorrow on her face makes my breath catch in my throat.

"Your father told me if he signed on for another six months, he would get a huge bonus. He asked what I thought, and I told him it was up to him. He said he wanted to stay for the good of the family." I watch her nervous hands as she slides her ring off and on without realizing it. "I think, up until that point, he'd felt...fairly safe there."

That's it for me. My brain refuses to take this in, and I am officially done with therapy for the day. I take my phone out of my pocket, pretending to check it so I don't have to have a reaction to what my mother just said.

"We can talk more about Alfonso's decision next time, Rose," I barely hear Caron say. I sense that they are waiting for me but I can't look at them. I just can't.

My mother reaches down to grab her bag and stands. "Thanks, Caron," she says. Usually when she thanks Caron, it sounds like she just had the best time ever and she is thrilled with everything we accomplished together. But today she sounds defeated and exhausted. Real.

"How's Peter doing?" Caron asks quietly, as if I suddenly can't hear just because I'm looking at a touch screen. Out of the corner of my eye, I see my mother glance to see if I'm paying attention, and then offer Caron a quick shake of her head.

Caron opens the door for us, and Mom and I walk out of the office without looking at each other.

When we get in the car, my mother just stares at the key in her hand for a minute.

"What's wrong?" I ask.

She looks at me, and I see my eyes. I never noticed before that our eyes are exactly the same. Cornflower-blue, my dad used to say about mine, with little white flowers in them. I wonder if he said it to her, too.

"He wanted to tell you himself. After he was gone, I didn't see any reason to bring it up because it didn't matter anymore. But I'm sorry if you feel I lied to you."

It's okay, I want to say. Sometimes I'm surprised by how hard it is to say things that should be easy to say. I don't really feel mad at her right now, but somehow, I still can't let her off the hook.

I don't like that about myself.

"Look, Rose, to change the subject for a minute, I don't want to put you in the middle, but have you heard from your brother?"

I shake my head. "No. But he hasn't been gone that long, Mom."

She thinks about this and then puts the key in the ignition. I wish that I were lying to her, but I'm getting nothing from Peter. Nothing at all.

A year and a half ago, we were a family of four. Now, it feels like Mom and I are the only ones left—a pack of two that is so twisted up in knots, we have to go to therapy in order to figure out how to untangle things.

As if she can read my thoughts, she gives my hand a squeeze and says, "We're all going to be okay, Rose."

She sounds about as certain as I feel.

FALL

potential *(noun):* the possibility of developing
into something good
(see also: the first day of sophomore year)

5

WHEN I WAS LITTLE, THE FIRST DAY OF SCHOOL WAS kind of great. Everything was new. You got to start fresh with new clothes, new pens and pencils, clean notebooks with no writing in them, teachers you'd never met—everything was about to happen, but nothing had yet.

This morning, as I get ready, I feel that buzzing excitement. It's clean-slate time, time for reinvention. Rose Zarelli is shedding her skin and everyone will see a beautiful new butterfly emerge—a butterfly who mixes her metaphors, but a butterfly nonetheless. Out with the semishy weird girl who mopes around carrying a French horn with running shoes tied to the case's handle; in with the unpredictable but exciting girl with the gorgeous singing voice who has all sorts of cool friends—and maybe a boyfriend who's a senior—and gets the lead in the musical. Yeah, maybe she's not the greatest dresser but her best friend is the most fashionable girl in all of Union High, so there has to be something cool about her. And yeah, maybe she did get into that really trashy fight with Regina Deladdo last year over Jamie Forta, but her dad died in Iraq, so people should just be nice to her because of that.

But wait, isn't she the girl who ended up in the pool at Mike Darren's party?

I almost laugh. Even while I'm daydreaming about what people say about me, I can't stay positive. I mean, who does that? Why bother having a daydream if it's not going to stay good?

I head down to the kitchen where my mother, who is already in her office with a client, has left me a note and a piece of toast with peanut butter. *Have a great first day!* the note says. When my mother still packed my lunch in elementary school, she used to put stickers on my napkins and write me notes. I would force myself to wait until lunch to read her message and check out what kind of sticker she'd chosen for me. It was my favorite part of the day.

Tracy honks outside, and I feel a little thrill of excitement. No more walking to school—my best friend has her own car.

I sling my new suede bag over my shoulder—Tracy made me promise never to use a backpack again—and the way it nestles under my arm makes me feel older as I make my way to her car. Tracy gives me the once-over and nods in approval at the outfit we discussed last night. So far, sophomore year is off to a pretty good start.

Five minutes later, at the traffic light right in front of school, that feeling starts to slip away. The massive building looms over us, no longer looking as harmless as it did whenever I passed it on my way to the Gap this summer. It now looks big, and kind of mean, if that's even possible. *Redirect your thoughts,* I tell myself, using a technique that Caron taught me for managing panic. *Focus on something simple and good.*

There's an old Patty Griffin song that I've been practicing lately. It's called "Moses," and it's the first song on her first album.

I think it's the most beautiful song I've ever heard. I was singing it last night, even though I should have been practicing for my *Anything Goes* audition. I don't sound like Patty at all when I sing it, and that bugs me, so instead I make up harmonies and sing along with her. It's weird how easy it is for me to sing harmony. I hear it in my head and it comes out of my mouth. And it sounds good.

When I sing, I totally lose track of time—an hour could go by and I'll think it was five minutes.

I love that.

The light turns green and Tracy goes right and then left, pulling into the lot that the school shares with the mall, where students are allowed to park. I'm wondering what teachers I'm going to have this year when I realize that the redirection technique worked. I'm not being besieged by dark thoughts in my head.

Note to self.

We drive around looking for a space—it's about 10 minutes before the first bell and the parking lot is practically full. Since I always used to walk to school, I've never been in this lot before the first bell. I didn't know it was such a scene.

No one is going in yet. Apparently everyone waits until the last second. There's lots of hair brushing, makeup applying, outfit comparing and texting on the part of the girls as they pretend not to check out the guys. The guys are either eating or throwing around a ball—or something that they took from someone to use as a ball—and they are pretending not to check out the girls. They obviously don't care that their faces are dripping with sweat and they've pitted out their shirts before they've even made it to homeroom. They still think they look hot.

It must be nice to be a guy—they don't seem to be as self-conscious as girls. Like, the other night, Jamie didn't seem even slightly embarrassed that he got turned on when we were kissing.

I turn my head so Tracy won't see me blushing.

I have to admit that one of the best things about starting the school year is that I'll probably see Jamie at least once a day. Maybe more, depending on what happens when we have dinner together.

When we have our *date*.

It's not a date, I remind myself. No one said *date*.

As Tracy pulls into what seems like the last available spot and I step out of the car into the most perfect September day ever, I feel another glimmer of possibility—good things could happen this year. Standing in this parking lot with Radiohead blasting out of a stereo and the sun reflecting off car roofs so intensely that everyone seems to be vibrating in time to the music in their own personal bubble of silver light, I feel like maybe—just maybe—I could actually make something of myself this year.

Rose 2.0.

"Trace! Rosie! Hey, y'all!"

Stephanie's squeal cuts clear through the parking-lot noise. Tracy and I haven't seen Stephanie all summer—she had to spend three months on her dad's farm in southern Illinois because of homecoming. At the time, her mother was feeling so guilty over the divorce that she hardly punished Stephanie at all for drinking to the point of passing out and ending up in the hospital. But when the summer rolled around, she packed Stephanie up and shipped her off to spend some quality time with pigs and cows. Stephanie was totally freaked out about going back there, claiming that there was nothing to do and no one to do it with.

Well, all it takes is one look at Stephanie Trainer to know exactly what she *did* do all summer: grow up, out and pretty. Way pretty.

Tracy is as dumbstruck as I am, but she at least squeals right back in delight at seeing our friend after what feels like months and months. I just stand there with my jaw on the ground, thinking about how yet another one of my friends is so much prettier than me that it's a small miracle she even wants to be seen talking to me in the parking lot on the first day of school. I should just fade into the background right now and not acknowledge that she's trying to get my attention. I'd be doing both of us a favor.

"Oh, my god! Hi-hi-hi!" She grabs Tracy and me, and pulls us into a group hug. My head seems to barely come up to Stephanie's chin. "I missed you girls so much!"

"Steph! Look at you! You look amazing," Tracy says, taking a step back so she can get a better view of the confident Glamazon that has replaced our once petite, once painfully shy friend. "What did your dad make you eat out there? You're, like, model-tall!"

"Oh, it's just the heels," she says, twisting around and lifting up one foot behind her to show us the crazy-high shoes she's wearing. "I'm not really this tall." When she turns back around, she immediately makes herself shorter by slouching. That's the kind of girl she is—she will actually make herself physically uncomfortable so someone else doesn't feel bad.

"Where did you get those wedges? They make your legs look ten feet long!" Tracy is now walking around Stephanie in a circle, as if Stephanie had been on a makeover show and this was her big reveal.

"Oh, shut up," Stephanie says, blushing so hard that her face matches her bright red hair.

"Canvas wedges are perfect this time of year. Are they designer?" As Tracy is talking, she takes her iPhone out of her bag and snaps pictures of Stephanie's shoes. Stephanie looks a little puzzled, but when she glances my way for an explanation, I just shrug and try not to regret wearing ballet flats that make my feet look like mini doublewide trailers. I'm also wearing jeggings, which don't do a lot for a short girl with runner's thighs.

It occurs to me that Tracy might have chosen an outfit for me that *she* would look good in, forgetting to take into account our very different bodies.

"Steph, how did you get out of the house in those things?" I ask. "I mean, if I even had those in my closet, my mother would freak out."

"Moms has a new job. She leaves before me and gets home after me, so I can pretty much wear whatever I want! In fact, these are *her* shoes—she'd kill me if she knew I was wearing them. But we're the same size now! It's awesome! Y'all should come over sometime and we'll go through her closet."

Tracy goes practically green with envy. Stephanie's mom is one of the few whose closet would actually be worth raiding, according to her.

The warning bell rings inside the school and we all start moving herdlike toward the main entrance, dragged forward by the gravitational pull of yet another school year. School is kind of like a conveyer belt in a slasher movie, I decide. You're strapped to it, and no matter how you struggle, you just keep moving toward the buzz saw that's ready to slice you into pieces.

See? Five minutes ago, the parking lot was an oasis of excitement and potential and possibility. Now I'm seeing homicidal buzz saws. Again, what the hell happened?

"So? What's up, girls? You both look so pretty and skinny and tan. Did you go to the beach, like, all summer long? I'm so jealous. There's nowhere fun to go swimming near the farm—there's nowhere fun near the farm, period! There are some swimming holes, but, you know, no ocean or anything like that. And the guys—oh, my god. You would not believe the guys out there. They smell like hay no matter how many times they shower or what cologne they pour on themselves. But you know what? Southern Illinois sure does grow 'em big!"

Stephanie giggles and does a perfect hair flip that gets the envious attention of a nearby cheerleader. I can see her sizing

Stephanie up, trying to decide if she should ask her to go to try-outs after school today. Wouldn't that just be perfect? As soon as I think Tracy might bail on cheerleading, cheerleading sinks its claws into Stephanie.

"Rosie, how's your mom? And how's Peter?"

I'm trying to compose a simple answer to those complicated questions when Mike Darren and Matt Hallis get out of what seems to be Matt's brand-new, white sports car. They're both looking as cocky as usual until Mike does a double take when he sees Stephanie and then trips over his own feet. He catches himself on the open car door and gapes at her before he pulls it together.

Stephanie looks panicked, immediately grabbing a section of her long red hair and twirling it around her finger. This gesture is practically the only thing I recognize about the person standing in front of me—the Stephanie I knew just a few months ago is long, long gone.

"Yo, Trainer, what's up? Haven't seen you in a few," he says, trying to cover his surprise and embarrassment. "How was Iowa?"

"Um, Illinois. It was fine. Did you have a good summer?"

"Oh, yeah, it was awesome. You missed an awesome party the other night," he says, as if the swim-team party and Con-rad's near-drowning were the highlights of his summer. I don't understand how Stephanie went out with Mike any more than I understand how Tracy went out with Matt.

"Yeah, it was killer. Rose had the best time of all," Matt says, his eyes plastered on Stephanie's bare, mile-long legs. Tracy lets out an annoyed sigh next to me. "You just love a good time in the water, don't you, Rose?"

"Did you go swimming, Rosie?" Stephanie asks.

When Matt practically falls down with laughter, Stephanie turns to me with apology in her eyes, knowing that she just took the bait but not understanding exactly how. Mike looks totally confused about whether he should laugh with Matt or take Stephanie's side.

I'm pulling Stephanie away to tell her what happened at Mike's party when I see Jamie's car. He slides into a space close to school that we somehow missed—it could have a reserved sign on it for all I know—and then Jamie, Regina and Conrad all get out of the car. Conrad slings a messenger bag crossways over his chest and gets away from them as fast as he can, walking toward school by himself. I feel bad, thinking of how much it would suck to have to walk into school on the first day of freshman year by yourself, especially after what happened to him on Friday night. But the pang passes when I remember all the stuff he said in Tracy's car.

I watch to see if Regina goes to catch up with Conrad, but she stays right by Jamie's side. She might as well be holding his hand, that's how close they are as they walk toward the school together.

I remind myself that I'm the one with a date with Jamie on Saturday night.

But maybe she's got a date with Jamie on Friday night.

As if he can feel eyes on his back, Jamie glances over his shoulder and scans the lot. When his gaze lands on me, he lifts his chin and gives me a half smile. I'm not sure whether to say hi or wave or what, and I miss my chance to do anything—he turns back around before I can decide.

Where is 2.0 when I need her?

"Jesus, Rose, are you still hung up on that asshole?" Matt says. "Wasn't he supposed to graduate last year?"

"Can you wait to start being a dick until lunch? Let's go," Tracy says to us. We follow her past Matt and Mike.

"Hey, Steph, thanks for all those emails and texts this summer," Mike yells after her.

Stephanie's ears turn red, but she calls back to him, "Yeah, Mike, right back at ya. You sure do know how to make a girl feel special." Then she executes a magnificent, conversation-ending hair flip, and Tracy and I struggle to keep up as she stalks away in her crazy heels.

"So what did I miss this summer?" Stephanie says with a grin. "Y'all have to catch me up before the bell."

I was busy imagining horrific events late into the night, pining after Jamie Forta and struggling to maintain my barely average attractiveness level, I don't say out loud. Tracy launches into her summer recap. We are swept toward the entrance of the building in the sea of high school humanity, whether we like it or not.

Everything goes to hell before first period even starts.

Tracy and Stephanie and I are sitting next to each other in our English room. Robert and Holly walk in. "Rose! Auditions are coming up! Are you ready?" she calls over the very loud conversations of our classmates.

I shake my head vigorously to indicate that no, in fact, I am not ready. I'm so far from ready it's not even funny. I may have been harmonizing to "Moses" over and over, but Patty Griffin doesn't exactly qualify as musical theater. I haven't picked sixteen bars of my favorite show tune, and I haven't watched the video that the drama teacher posted so people could familiarize themselves with some basic dance steps before the audition.

In short, I've been putting off getting ready. I guess my plan is to just show up and hope for inspiration.

Not the best way to achieve my goals.

As Holly is saying something about how she's totally sure I'm going to be great, Matt and Mike come in. Mike dives into the first free seat, doing his best not to look at Steph, and Matt stops in his tracks when he sees Holly. Robert sees Matt see Holly, and he quickly leans over his desk and takes her arm, pulling her gently backward. Holly, having no idea what's going on, starts explaining to Robert that they need to work with me after school so that I can "totally rock" my audition. Robert is nodding as he maneuvers her into a seat on the other side of him, away from Matt, who is still looking at her like she's edible.

"Who's that?" Tracy asks.

"That's Holly, Robert's girlfriend."

Tracy gasps, not even bothering to hide her shock. "Are you *kidding?* Where did she come from?"

"She moved here from L.A. Her dad is a *film* actor who's teaching at Yale. She met Robert in the summer show. She's nice," I grumble.

"Well, I guess you missed your chance," Tracy teases, referring to the fact that Robert has been asking me out on a regular schedule since the sixth grade. "Jealous?"

I am jealous, but not in the way that she means.

Holly's hair is perfect, her skin is perfect, her face is perfect, her body is perfect. I bet she doesn't hate mirrors. I bet she doesn't think about mirrors one way or the other. Life is probably really different if you look like Holly Taylor. Or Stephanie Trainer.

A bunch of cell phones buzz and ding at the same time and people quickly reach into their bags and backpacks to silence the devices that we are supposed to leave in our lockers during the day. Matt, still standing at the front of the room, manages to pull his eyes off Holly in order to check his phone. When he looks up, his face is weird. He turns to Tracy with a confused expression.

When they first got together in eighth grade, Matt looked at her adoringly. Then last year he looked at her like she was a parasite he couldn't shake. After they broke up, he stopped looking at her entirely. Now he's staring at her hard, like there's something he should say but he doesn't know how to do it.

Something about his expression makes me very, very nervous for Tracy. There's no way he suddenly feels bad about what happened last year. Something else is going on—something that is about to explode.

Yup, the fantastic potential of the first day of school.

Kristin—already dressed for cheerleading practice with her ponytail swinging madly and panic in her eyes—skitters over to Tracy and puts her iPhone on the desk.

"Just thought you should know about this," she says, eyes darting around the room, taking in everyone looking at their phones. If I didn't know any better, I'd say Kristin feels bad about whatever she's showing Tracy.

Matt ducks his head and takes a seat at the back of the room, and I start to feel sick to my stomach. Tracy looks at Kristin's phone and freezes.

I lean over her shoulder and see a photo posted on a Facebook page. The photo is of a list of names written on a bathroom stall door, and the date at the top is today's. The words "Top Ten Union High Sluts" are right underneath the date, followed by 10 names. Tracy, who has been with one guy in her entire life—one guy who is currently sitting at the back of our classroom, unable to make eye contact—is number 1.

I reach over and scroll up to see whose page it is. It belongs to the YouTube stalker, who posted Tracy's and Kristin's humiliating initiation dance after homecoming last year, but also captured on video what, at the time, I considered to be one of my proudest moments in my life: knocking Regina down at track tryouts.

The YouTube stalker must be a girl, since the caption under the photo reads, "fl. 3 stall 2 girls b-room." Or maybe it's a guy who's really crafty about getting into the girls' bathroom, which is creepy.

I find it ironic that the YouTube stalker needs a Facebook page. I guess not all social media platforms are created equal. Also, I'm stuck on how somebody could have written a list on a bathroom stall that has already been photographed and posted on Facebook. School hasn't even started yet.

"You're still coming to tryouts today, right?" Kristin whispers with concern. Tracy can't take her eyes off the phone. "We really need you there." When Tracy still doesn't answer, Kristin exhales. "It's just a slut list. It doesn't mean anything."

Tracy turns to me, her mouth hanging slightly open. Then she says, "Kristin, if it doesn't mean anything, why did you show it to me?"

Kristin gets a little defensive. "Like I said. I just thought you should know."

"That was *super* sweet of you. Did Lena think I should know, too?"

Kristin looks guilty as she snatches up her phone, wheels around and throws herself dramatically into an empty chair. "Just come today, Trace, okay? We need you. You're our best dancer."

Tracy slowly twists around in her chair, fixing her most withering stare on Matt. He actually looks sorry, which surprises me. She turns back and is about to say something to me when the bell rings and the famously cute Mr. Camber ambles in.

Every year at least two or three girls and the occasional boy get in trouble for writing Camber love letters on Valentine's Day. It's sort of a Union High tradition at this point. Last year I heard he got three, including a fake one that someone wrote him from Ms. Maso, who everyone wants Camber to ask out because they're both really good-looking and would make a great couple.

To keep his distance, Camber is generally a total hard-ass who doesn't waste a second on being chatty or friendly. He cuts right to the chase with us—no welcome speech, no "this is going to be a great year, kids," no nothing. As he writes his name on the board, he leads off with, "If you forgot to leave your phone in your locker, give it to me now or risk getting detention the second it rings. And I do mean the *second* it rings."

When Camber turns around to grab a stack of books off his desk, Tracy turns to me, wide-eyed. I mouth, *Are you okay?* She mouths back, *Are you?* I give her my best confused look. She gives me hers back. Then she points to herself and holds up one finger, and points to me and holds up two fingers.

For a second, I have no idea what she means. And then, in a moment of soul-crushing clarity, I do.

Number 2 on the Top Ten List of Union High Sluts?

Me.

Camber slams a book from the top of his stack onto my desk. It's called *As I Lay Dying*.

My phone—which I forgot to silence because it's my first day with a cell phone in school—dings in my bag, alerting me to the presence of what I am sure is a text from my mother supplementing the note she left me earlier, wishing me a great day.

Camber looks around for the culprit and seems surprised when he sees that I'm the one with a guilty look on her face. "Off to a fantastic start, Ms. Zarelli. See you after school for the first detention of the year. Welcome back."

Thanks. It's just *great* to be here.

Detention is supposed to be forty-five minutes, but when Camber holds up my phone and asks me—the only student in all of his classes who managed to get a detention on the first day of school—why I brought "this stupid thing" to class, I explain that I've never had a cell phone before and I'm not used to Union High's rules. He hands the phone back to me and tells me I can go.

"I hear good things about you, Ms. Zarelli," he says, sounding drill sergeant-y, just in case I might think he's being nice to me. "I hope they're true. See you tomorrow."

It *is* the nicest thing anyone has said to me today. Of course, that's no surprise, given that I've been called "Slut #2" multiple times by Union High's most notorious jerks—with the exception of Matt. Matt has been strangely silent and unwilling to make eye contact with me or Tracy, which, as far as I'm concerned, means that his girlfriend, Lena, is behind the list.

The thing is, Kristin actually has a point—it *is* just a slut list. Every high school has them, and they hardly ever have anything to do with reality. They're usually written by girls who are trying to ruin other girls' reputations, or trying to break up a couple by making a guy think that his girlfriend is messing around with the whole football team. Don't get me started on that double standard. Guys get to do whatever they want but a girl gets called a slut for, well, in my case, kissing.

I'm sure Lena put me on that list for all the wrongs I committed against Regina. Although really, she should be thanking me. I'm the reason she's the captain this year. Without me, she'd still be just another cheerleader.

It sucks to be on the list. It's already generated a nickname that could potentially stick with me for the rest of the year. But to be honest, after being called "911 Bitch" for half of last year and seeing it written on every desk I sat at, hearing "Slut #2" in the halls a few times doesn't really feel like a big deal to me.

"Slut #1," however, is apparently a huge deal.

Tracy spent the day with her head held high, ignoring the chant of "Number One! Number One!" that followed her through the halls. But I did take her into the bathroom a few times to cry. And when I tried to tell her that the list doesn't matter, she freaked out, saying, "Of course you think it doesn't matter, Rose. You haven't slept with anyone. If you had, you'd be way more upset, trust me."

I have no idea if that's true or not. Maybe it is. Or maybe my perspective is just different because of what I went through last year. But either way, I decided to keep my mouth shut for the rest of the day. I didn't even jump for joy when she said that there was no way in hell she was going back to cheerleading now.

I turn on my phone as I leave Camber's room and see a text

from Tracy telling me to meet her at the car if I want a ride home after detention. I head to the stairs, and through the huge glass window, I see the playing fields beyond the tops of the teachers' cars, impossibly green and covered in sports teams. I see the cross-country team running warm-up laps around the track and I wonder if maybe I'm supposed to be out there—if my dad would want me out there, especially since I didn't make it last year.

I feel a twinge of guilt about the fact that I'm not running anymore, and then I think of Vicky's email wishing me good luck on the first day of school. "Be what you want, not what anybody else wants," she wrote. At the time, I figured it was just cheesy advice she'd gotten from the inside of a first-day-of-school Hallmark card. But I kind of get her point now. It's easy to keep doing things just because other people want you to, even if you don't want to anymore.

I can't stop looking at the emerald-green fields. They look like they should be in a movie about the world's most perfect high school. The people on them are living perfect high school lives, in their perfect-fitting team uniforms. They are exactly where they are supposed to be, doing exactly what they are supposed to do. And me? I already had my first detention of the school year *and* made the slut list. What is it exactly that *I'm* supposed to be doing?

Singing.

But if a singer only sings when no one is listening, is she really a singer?

I go down the stairs and push the door open just in time to see Jamie and Regina heading through the teachers' lot to the mall parking lot—together, again. Frustration washes over me—I haven't heard from Jamie since he showed up at Tracy's.

There have been about fifty different moments in the past few days when I was going to text him. But I worked super hard to distract myself, and I didn't do it. If Jamie wants to take me out, he's going to have to call me and tell me what the plan is.

I watch as they stop walking and face each other. It used to be that when I saw Jamie and Regina together, I would get so jealous I couldn't even see straight. And I do still get jealous, but it's different. Because something about Regina is different. She seems…defeated or something. She can still kick ass and intimidate people, but I can tell something is wrong.

At first, it looks like Jamie and Regina are laughing together and I almost turn away. But they're not laughing—they're arguing.

Then I realize something else. I'm not the only one watching them.

Conrad is so engrossed in what's going on between Jamie and Regina that he doesn't notice me standing ten feet away, watching him watch them. He crouches down and gnaws on a fingernail as bits of their conversation drift over to us. It's just a word here, a word there—not enough to figure out what they're actually talking about.

Regina takes off in the middle of something Jamie is saying, stomping through the lot and up the hill to the mall, leaving him standing there. His hands ball into fists and he looks at the car next to him as if he'd like to punch it. I wonder if Anthony is up there, waiting for Regina, and it's driving Jamie crazy with jealousy.

But that doesn't feel right, either—jealousy is not what I'm seeing. I wait to see if he goes after her, but instead of going up the hill, he turns and heads toward the fields. I know he's not going to practice, since he was officially banned from all Union High sports teams two years ago. I have no idea where he's going.

I look at Conrad again, and I see that he's watching Jamie, not Regina. I expect Conrad to follow him, maybe give him a few choice words, but he stays right where he is until he can't see

Jamie anymore, and then he stands up and leans back against the car he was hiding behind. He closes his eyes, drops his head, takes a few deep breaths and then starts in my direction, toward the pool. I duck down and he walks right past without seeing me.

Conrad looks like a different person than the one who was scowling and spewing venom in the back of Tracy's car the other night. He's wearing blue jeans, a blue T-shirt and red Converse— nothing that would call attention to himself in any way, like fancy loafers. And he looks so sad, it's almost painful.

Maybe he's worried about what's going to happen when he shows up late for practice on the first day of school. To be honest, I'm sort of impressed that he's going. I don't think I would, after what happened at the party.

I wonder what Jamie's relationship with Conrad was like when he was living with the Deladdos. Conrad was pissed at Jamie the other night, but Jamie took it like it wasn't a big deal, like he knew he just had to wait it out. Maybe Jamie is like a big brother to Conrad, and it bums Conrad out that Jamie and Regina aren't together anymore.

Once Conrad is out of view, it takes me about half a second to make the decision to go after Jamie.

"Jamie," I call, out of breath because I ran to catch up to him, and I haven't run anywhere since spring. When he turns, he looks angry at first, then his face sort of relaxes and he smiles. He actually smiles. The bright sunlight picks up the gold in his hair and his eyes, and I imagine I can burn the image of him into my memory and look at it whenever I want.

"Hey," he says.

"Hey," I say back. "Happy first day of senior year."

"Thanks," he says, sort of surprised, like the fact that it's his senior year hadn't occurred to him.

His eyes wander over my face, taking me in, and it makes me think about what it felt like when he pushed me up against his car to kiss me. I shake my head to clear the thought, worried that he can tell just by the look on my face that I'm thinking about the sexiest thing that has happened to me in my entire life thus far.

"Um, I saw you and Regina back there. It looked like you were having a fight."

"Just talking," he says after a pause.

"I didn't…hear anything. If you're wondering."

He doesn't tell me whether he's wondering or not.

I think maybe it's time to start using the direct approach with Jamie Forta.

"What's going on with her?" My phone dings in my bag. "Sorry," I say as I grab it and look at it quickly. It's Tracy. **Gotta tlk 2 u.** I stuff the phone back in my bag. Jamie looks around like he doesn't want anyone to hear us. I lower my voice. "You don't have to tell me now, if you don't want to. You can tell me on Saturday."

I could punch myself in the eye. I wasn't going to say *anything* about Saturday—not a single word. Now it sounds like I was reminding him. Or fishing for information.

"Rose, look…I gotta work on Saturday."

The disappointment that settles in my chest is heavy. I'm not sure why my first instinct is to pretend that I don't care, to act like he didn't just bail on me—again. I think about all the truth-telling I'm learning how to do in therapy and I wonder why the hell I can't apply that here.

"You have a job?" I ask as casually as I can manage.

"Yeah. And I gotta work almost every night for a while. But I'm gonna get a Friday or Saturday off soon."

I look down at my feet, squeezed into my flats, and imagine that if I'd just worn my boots, this wouldn't be happening. As I'm making a pact with myself never to wear the flats again, Jamie's hand comes into my line of vision. I feel his warm fingers lifting my chin to make me look him directly in the eye.

"I gotta pay my dad back from when I got arrested."

I wonder if my parents would make me pay them back if I ended up in court for something. I also wonder what would happen if I just kissed Jamie right now. Obviously, those two thoughts have nothing to do with each other. I'm finding it very difficult to work my brain because my skin is still buzzing from where Jamie is touching me.

"I'm sorry," he says.

"Wow, two apologies in four days." I'm trying to channel that sassiness I found the other night, but it's not easy in the light of day. I feel like I'm trying too hard. "To be honest, I didn't really think we were going to have dinner, anyway."

"I just need a few weeks," he says.

My phone dings again. "I have to go." Half of me wants to take the words back—Jamie interactions are infrequent enough that I almost feel like I shouldn't cut it off first. The other half of me is proud of myself.

Jamie nods. "See ya, Rose."

I walk away from him before he can walk away from me, and as I go up the hill toward the student lot, I make myself count to thirty before I turn around. He is walking past the far side of the track, where Regina and I had our showdown last year. Thanks to him, I didn't get suspended. Thanks to her, I have scars on my forearms and shins.

When I get to Tracy's car and there's no Tracy, I text @ the car, and hop up on the hood. As I'm waiting, I hit "Photos" on my phone—my brain needs a distraction from trying to figure out what just happened. I'm now more than halfway through deleting my brother's pictures. When I first started, I really looked at each photo but now I just fly through them. Delete, delete, delete.

I'm just about to delete number 503 when I pause, unsure about what I'm actually seeing.

In the photo, Peter and Amanda lean over opposite sides of

a coffee table with straws in their hands, like they're about to start drinking out of the same glass. Except there's no glass, and the straws are half as long as they should be. It's not really clear what they're doing—their faces are partially covered by someone's arm reaching into the photo—but anyone who has seen a movie or two can fill in the blanks.

Without even stopping to think about it, I call Peter. I'm freaked out and worried, and I need to hear his voice. The phone rings and rings, and right before it's about to go to voice mail, Amanda answers.

"Hi, Rosa, it's Amanda! How *are* you?" she gushes. I can hear Peter in the background, telling her what my name is. "Ooh, sorry. Rose. What's up, cutie?"

God, I hate this girl. I try not to hate people, but I *hate* her.

"Can I talk to my brother?"

"He can't really talk right now," she lies.

"He's right there. I can hear him."

The phone gets all muffled for a second, like she covered it with her hand. I hear them laughing, and then, there he is. It's weird to hear his voice after not talking to him for a while.

"Hey, Rosie."

I suddenly don't know how to bring up the photo. I want to, but the words just won't come. What if I'm not seeing what I think I'm seeing, and I make a total ass out of myself?

Amanda is singing along to something that I can't make out in the background. She's off-key, of course.

"How's it going?" Peter asks. He's talking carefully, like he's trying hard to sound normal. The phone gets a little muffled again, and then I hear him exhale and say, "Thanks, babe." He's smoking something.

"First day of school," I blurt out, for lack of anything else to say.

"Oh, right. Awesome. Amanda, it was her first day of school

today," he says to her, and she makes that annoying "Awwwww" sound. "How's it going?"

"Um…it's over. It was fine."

"Cool."

I don't know why I need courage to talk to my brother about this. I wonder what my dad would want me to do. He'd want me to just say it out loud, just ask Peter what is going on. I'm about to, I think, but Tracy is suddenly in front of me, bouncing up and down with excitement. Her happiness is confusing since I saw her cry more than once today.

"Who are you talking to?" she asks.

"Peter."

Her eyes get huge and she grabs the phone out of my hand before I can stop her.

"Peter! It's Tracy!" she squeals. I can hear him laughing, which makes her laugh. "Oh, my god, it was the craziest first day. You wouldn't even believe what happened." She keeps giggling as Peter says something, and she takes a few steps away from me and walks in a little circle as she plays with her hair. Then she looks up at me. "I will, I totally will. But she's good. You don't have to worry about her—or me—anymore. We're sophomores now. Although we *were* both on the slut list today."

"Tracy, why are you telling him that?"

"It's totally fine," she adds, ignoring me, "because I have a se-cret weapon. I can't tell you what it is, though. You'll find out soon enough. Okay…okay, bye, Peter."

She finally hands my phone back to me.

"Hey," I say again into the phone. "Peter?" There's no one there.

"Oh, sorry, Rosie, were you still talking to him? I think he thought you were done."

I should call him back and ask him about the picture, but I can't. I just can't. Because what would I say? What would he say?

And if he told me the truth—which he probably wouldn't—then what would I do?

Tell my mother?

Tell Tracy?

I don't want her to think less of him.

I don't want to think less of him.

"What were you talking about?" I ask her.

She holds up her phone and shows me what looks like a fashion website. Across the top, it says, "The Sharp List." Underneath that is a super-glam picture of Tracy that I've never seen before.

"What is that, Trace?"

"It's the project you've been helping me with. And it's going to launch my fashion career."

Muse *(noun):* something or someone who provides inspiration
(see also: the wise and insightful Holly Taylor)

6

"WELCOME, WELCOME, WELCOME TO AUDITIONS FOR
Anything Goes, people! I know you're excited, but if you could
just tone it down a wee bit, we can get started and all be home in
time for *Glee.*" When nobody stops talking, Mr. Donnelly adds,
"Okay, kiddies, 'Tone it down a wee bit' is nice-speak for shut
your mouths!"

That works—everybody stops talking. Stephanie is so nervous
that she's shaking. She met me at my locker after seventh period,
said, "I think I'm going to audition! Can I walk with you?" and
then literally talked nonstop the entire way to the auditorium.
When we got here, she kind of shut down and that's when the
shaking started. I can feel her through my chair. I reach over and
squeeze her hand to try to calm her down, but she keeps staring
at Mr. Donnelly like he's a serial killer.

I had no idea that Stephanie was planning to audition today.
I don't even know if she can sing. But then, I guess I don't know
if I can sing, either.

I mean, *I* think I can. But what if no one else does?

I can. I know I can.

And I'm as ready as I'll ever be. I watched the video of the tap-dancing steps and I stopped singing "Moses" nonstop and practiced my sixteen bars of "Be Italian" from *Nine* not just in the shower but in front of the mirror. I stopped doing that when I realized it wasn't helping my relationship with mirrors at all.

Does anyone look normal when they're singing? Or maybe the question is, is it normal to look weird when you're singing?

Thanks to Holly, who offered to be my personal coach via email—probably after Robert told her that she shouldn't be spending her valuable preparation time helping me—I even have a backup song, just in case I get called back on the spot and asked to do something different. Holly says that happens a lot.

Of course, it probably happens to Holly a lot, which is different than it happening a lot to, say, *me*.

But if I'm really, truly honest with myself, I'm going to say that I think I sound pretty good. And I feel good, too.

Weirdly, I have the slut list to thank for that.

Tracy's secret project is no longer secret, and it's totally amazing. It's a fashion blog, and it was originally going to be called "Très Chic/Tracy." But after the slut list insanity happened, instead of going back into the bathroom to cry some more, Tracy had a brilliant idea. She went to see the business and marketing teacher to get a tutorial on PR. The teacher told her that the best thing to do in situations like hers was to "take charge of the spin" and "make the story hers." Tracy told her about the website, and the teacher helped her come up with "The Sharp List," which is a play on the slut list.

The blog is awesome. Tracy takes photos of outfits she likes on people at school and analyzes how each individual piece contributes to the whole look. And then she uses all those photos we scanned from magazines to show why the pieces were good choices. So, for example, the photo she took of Stephanie is right next to a scanned photo of a *Vogue* model wearing super-expensive shoes that have a resemblance to Stephanie's. She uses the work of professional photographers and stylists to show how fierce her friends' fashion instincts are. It's genius.

I helped Tracy with the technical part and I told her that she had to use photo credits, saying where she got each photo from and who the photographer is, so she wouldn't get in trouble. And now I have a credit on the site as "Editorial Director/Designer."

Tracy launched the site with announcements on Facebook and Twitter and an email blast to our entire class. The subject line was, "From Slut #1: There's a New List in Town." I helped rewrite her email, adding in some choice words that would send most of Union High to Dictionary.com. The final version said:

Announcing The Sharp List, a site designed to commend those with delectable fashion sense, and to remind those with brains that there is more to life than a slut list—like fashion! Art! Beauty! Self-expression! Every day, The Sharp List will call out the stylish, the fabulous, the rebellious. Who knows? Maybe one day it'll even be YOU...

Questions? Email me. But don't ask me to put you on my site. Just get on with your fashionista selves—I'll find you.

Haters, you will get no reply.

Click here NOW for the inaugural Sharp List.

Welcome to chic, Union High.

The first post on The Sharp List featured Stephanie and her awesome shoes and Holly and Robert in head-to-toe black. People went crazy.

Within a few hours, The Sharp List inbox was overflowing with emails from people telling Tracy she should look out for them tomorrow because they were going to be wearing something totally awesome. There was even one from the YouTube stalker that said, "Let me know when you're ready for your own show. I know people."

Not a single email said anything bad or mean—or mentioned the slut list. Not one. It was like the thing never existed.

Tracy had pulled off a PR coup of epic proportions. She had gone from Slut #1 to Union High's coolest celebrity overnight. Now, upperclassmen say hi to her in the halls just so she'll notice what they're wearing. And I'm proud that I played a small role in her success.

So yeah, I'm feeling pretty good today. You might even say I'm ready to rock this thing.

"All right, people!" Mr. Donnelly says, clapping his hands. "We're going to sing, then we're going to act, then we're going to dance." He looks down at his clipboard as he shoves a pen behind his ear. "Mitchell Klein? Are you ready?"

Mitchell climbs the stairs to the stage, where he sings a chunk of a song from *Anything Goes* called "It's Delovely." I immediately freak out—it's my backup song. I twist around in my seat to look at Holly, who is so excited about auditions she's practically bursting out of her seat. She just gives me a wave and a double-thumbs-up, her white teeth gleaming like she's on a gum commercial.

Robert, who's next to her, is slumped in his chair, a red scarf wrapped around his throat, his eyes focused like laser beams on Mitchell Klein. He looks my way for a split second and gives me a little nod, and then goes back to staring at Mitchell, who turns out to have a nicer voice than I would have predicted.

Mitchell looks extremely satisfied at the end of his song and he shoots Robert a smug look at he sits back down. I can practically hear Robert's teeth grinding as he takes a swig of his electrolyte water. It suddenly occurs to me, as Robert tightens his scarf, that I haven't seen him smoking any cigarettes this year. He must have quit.

Funny—I never thought Robert would quit smoking for anything. Or anyone.

After a few people who don't make it through their sixteen

bars—either because they are giggling or they lose their place or they just sort of freak out and melt into silence in front of everyone—Mr. Donnelly calls, "Stephanie Trainer."

A hush seems to fall over the room as Stephanie stands up looking supermodel tall in her platform shoes, her red hair gleaming, a nervous blush on her cheeks. She stumbles a bit because her legs are shaking, but she stops to take a deep breath and in an instant, she snaps out of her jitters. I literally see it happen. It's like she just decides that she is done being nervous, and the nerves disappear, leaving behind a supremely confident being who happens to be wearing a super-cute outfit that looks like it would be right at home on an ocean liner, which is where *Anything Goes* takes place.

I look down at my cut-off jean skirt and Feist T-shirt and realize that I did not dress for success. Unless Mr. Donnelly happens to be a Feist fan.

Stephanie climbs the steps to the stage, clears her throat and without introducing herself or even letting Mr. Donnelly ask, "What are you going to sing for us today?" she launches into an a cappella version of "Mine" by Taylor Swift.

And she sounds amazing.

Completely, shockingly amazing. It's not that she sounds like Taylor Swift—just the opposite. She sounds like herself, and like the song is hers. I'm sure you can hear her out on the street, never mind outside the auditorium. She looks so happy, so natural, that Mr. Donnelly forgets to stop her after sixteen bars, and she just sings the chorus over again. When she's done, the whole auditorium whoops like the real Taylor Swift is standing on the stage.

When she makes it back to her seat after fielding high fives from almost everyone, I lean over and say, "I didn't know you could sing like that!"

She giggles, flips her hair over her shoulder and says, "Me neither!"

I have to fight really hard against being annoyed at my friend who magically transformed into a goddess this summer while I was helping residents of Union choose between original, skinny and loose fit.

When the applause dies down, Mr. Donnelly cheerfully calls, "Holly Taylor to the stage, please." Holly pops up, looking perfect in a flowery dress with black boots that button all the way up to her knees. She walks onstage and says, as if she's done it a million times, "Hi, everyone! I'm Holly Taylor and I'm new at Union. I just moved here from Los Angeles. Today I'll be singing 'All Through the Night' by Cole Porter, which the character Hope sings in this show. I hope you like it. It's one of my favorites."

And then, of course, Holly opens her mouth and a beautiful, mesmerizing sound comes out as she sings the famous ballad. Mr. Donnelly sits up straighter, a gleam in his eye, no doubt thrilled beyond belief that he has found not one but two brilliant singers in the first half hour of auditions.

When Holly sits back down, Robert puts his arm around her, kisses her on the cheek and smiles at everyone, beaming with so much pride it's almost embarrassing.

What's it like to have the guy you're with think you're the greatest thing in the world?

Mr. Donnelly stands up and looks at his list, and I know what's going to happen before it happens—he calls my name.

I get to sing after Stephanie *and* Holly. Fan-freakin'-tastic.

I make my way to the stage and everything goes a little wonky. My vision blurs on the edges and I feel like I'm going to puke. Holly told me that if I got nervous I should just imagine that I'm in my bedroom, singing by myself. But suddenly I'm having one of my freak-out moments, and I'm seeing the balcony falling on top of all those people sitting in the seats out there, crushing them into nothing but puddles of gristle and blood. I shake my head to clear the image and I hear Mr. Donnelly ask, "What are you singing today, Rose?" I manage to answer and he says, "Ah, *Nine*. An excellent choice! Go ahead whenever you're ready."

Nobody ever really means, "Whenever you're ready." Because if I waited until I was ready, I would be standing here for the rest of my life.

I look down at the floor in case my classmates are still crushed under the balcony, and I start the song. I start it too high and I have to begin again. Mr. Donnelly says, "It sounds nice, Rose. Just take your time." I start lower this time, and I get a few seconds in and then forget all the words.

I look up and I can see Holly, a smile frozen on her face as if she's trying to stay positive for me but really, she's mortified by what's happening. She starts mouthing the words to me but I'm distracted by Robert, who can't even watch. He's staring up at the theater's high ceiling. Mr. Donnelly gives me the lyric and tells me to start over one more time. I make it through this time, but I have no idea what I sounded like or if I was off-key or anything.

When Mr. Donnelly smiles and says "Thank you," I can't read his tone. Instead of going down the steps to my seat like a normal person, I just walk off stage and exit through the backstage door to the hall. I don't care that I've left all my stuff in the auditorium—it doesn't matter because I'm planning on abandoning my identity and taking up residence in a new city anyway.

I can't believe I thought that singing could be my future. Clearly, I don't have a future. Because I suck.

I slide down the wall and sit on the floor, putting my hands over my ears so I don't have to hear anyone else's audition. I close my eyes.

I'm not sure how long I've been sitting there when I feel someone tap me on the shoulder. I open my eyes and Ms. Maso is standing above me.

Ms. Maso has dark skin and brown eyes, and if Tracy had her way, I bet she'd feature Ms. Maso on The Sharp List every single day.

"Do you want to get up, or should I come down there?" she asks. When I don't answer, she sits next to me, holding a bunch of posters that say, "Practice Tolerance, Union High! No excuses!" in bright red, and underneath that, "School assembly on Monday, attendance required. Report to the auditorium with your homeroom."

"What are those?" I ask.

"You were at Mike Darren's party, weren't you?"

I lose track of the question for a second because I can hear Robert singing a song from *My Fair Lady*. He is belting his heart out—no way is he going to let Mitchell Klein play opposite Holly. Not a chance. I admire that.

"Yeah, I was at that party," I finally say.

"I heard you ended up in the pool."

"It was fun," I say as drily as I can manage.

"Tell me, what are you doing out here in this hallway?" she asks.

"I blew my audition for the musical and I didn't feel like going back in."

"Are you sure you blew it?"

"Yeah," I say.

"You don't sound sure."

"I had to start over three times so I'm pretty sure that means I sucked."

"Rose, do you know what I've noticed about you since I met you a year ago? You're mean—to yourself." I can feel her looking at me but I'm not up for eye contact right now. "You're a language person, right? Think about all the negative words you just said in reference to yourself in one short conversation."

I sigh. "You sound like my mom's shrink."

Ms. Maso doesn't miss a beat. "Well then I hope she's yours, too."

I shrug.

"Stop being mean to yourself, Rose. It can be as self-destructive in the long-term as doing drugs or starving yourself or cutting or... Would you like me to go on?"

I shake my head. "I get it."

"Good." She stands up, brushes off the seat of her jeans and holds up a poster. "Listen, the school is looking into what happened at that party, in part because Conrad Deladdo—who apparently is one of the best athletes the school has seen in years—quit the swim team and won't tell anyone why. Since you were the one in the pool with him, you might find yourself in Principal Chen's office soon. Just a word of warning, okay?"

Well, that's delovely. I haven't chatted with Principal Chen since the last scandal I was a part of. Can't wait.

"Go back in there and finish the audition, Rose. Even if you don't feel good about it, at least you can say you saw it through to the end."

Ms. Maso tapes a poster above my head, reaches down to touch my shoulder and disappears up the stairs, her clog boots echoing in the hall. As I watch her go, I think about how she always gives great advice that I never want to take.

I'm worrying about how to get my bag out of the auditorium without seeing anyone when the stage door opens and Holly leans out.

"Rose! We're about to start the scenes! Hurry!"

I shake my head. "I'm not going back in."

Holly steps into the hallway and lets the door close behind her quietly. She holds out a hand to help me up.

"So what if you had to start over? You sounded great. Your voice is so cool—it's different, you know? It's like a... I don't know..." Holly takes a second to think, looking up at the ceiling and spinning the bracelets on her arm. "Like an old-school rock star's or something."

And there it is.

A compliment on my singing.

It's the first one.

I don't know exactly what she means, but the compliment is out there now, in the universe. And I feel it inside me, expanding to fill up all the empty spaces that I haven't known what to do with lately. I get so lost in the feeling that I can't even acknowledge what Holly said, or make any move to take the hand she's offering. She misinterprets what's going on and kneels down in front of me, her button-up leather boots creaking.

"What's wrong?" Holly asks, putting her hand on my arm. Tears well up in my eyes. And then tears well up in her eyes, just because they're in my eyes. She laughs, maybe a little embarrassed by the fact that she's crying with me though she doesn't know what we're crying about. I don't know how to tell her that what she said was awesome, so naturally she thinks that something is really wrong.

"Rose," she asks, "is this, um, about a guy?"

Something about the way she asks is weird. She's looking at me like she already knows the answer but wants to see if I'm going to tell her the truth. So instead of trying to explain to her that she, a real singer, just called *me* a real singer, I nod. It's easier than figuring out how to tell her what I'm feeling right now.

"Is it Robby?" she asks, her eyes huge and round and watery. And guilty.

Oh, no. No, no, no. I know exactly what Robert did without even having to ask. But I ask anyway. "What did he tell you?"

"Well, I don't mean to make you uncomfortable but Robby told me that you're, um, in love with him, but that he thinks of you like a sister. And so, I was wondering, does it bother you that we're together? I mean, I hope it doesn't, Rose, because I really like you. But if it makes you feel bad to see us together or to talk to me—"

I hold up my hand to get her to stop. "It's not Robert." *It was never Robert,* I want to say just to spite him. But I have a better idea. I'll just take one for the team now, and Robert can owe me—big-time—later for using me to seem extra desirable to his girlfriend. Maybe one day, when the right time presents itself, I'll tell Holly that she's dating a pathological liar.

That's a really nice way to treat the guy who helped you through your father's funeral and the girl who just gave you your identity, one of the voices in my head says.

I tell it to shut up.

The stage door opens again and this time Mr. Donnelly sticks his head out. "Ready for your close-up, ladies? It's time to *act,*" he says, looking at Holly expectantly.

"We're ready, Mr. Donnelly!" Holly says. She leaps up and holds out her hand again. I take it and she pulls me up with surprising strength for someone who is the size of a pixie. Before I can make a decision about whether or not a girl with an old-school rock star's voice should bother continuing with an audition for musical theater, Holly drags me into the auditorium and the door behind us closes with an appropriately dramatic thud.

Conrad is waiting for me at my locker before homeroom the next morning. My stomach instantly feels like it's tying itself into a really complicated nautical knot. I know how much he doesn't like me, so I'm pretty sure that whatever this is, it's not going to be pleasant. It irritates me to be nervous about talking to a freshman, but this isn't just any freshman. This is a freshman with the knife-sharp confrontation skills of a Deladdo.

"This should be fun," Tracy says as she holds up her phone and snaps a photo of Conrad, ignoring the people around us who are pretending not to pose for her but totally are. I swear, she takes about fifty pictures in the time it takes to get from one class to our lockers to our next class. When we walk down the halls now, Tracy basically navigates through the lens of her phone as she snaps a continuous stream of photos, and she never bumps into anyone because the sea of humanity just parts for her. She's mastered the art of making her way through a crowd of people clamoring for her attention without making eye contact but still managing to seem gracious and charming.

I guess you could say she's a natural.

As we get closer, Conrad pushes off my locker and turns to face me like we're about to have a showdown. I half expect him to reach for a pistol on his belt. Fortunately, he just crosses his arms.

"Did you do this?" he demands.

"Good morning, Conrad!" Tracy chirps. "How are you? 'Oh, I'm fine, Tracy, thanks for asking. Nice to see you. Oh, and hey, thanks so much for driving me home from that party a few weeks ago—I really appreciate it.'"

Conrad looks at Tracy for a solid five seconds. "Are you done?"

"I think I made my point," she answers.

"Did you do this?" he repeats, looking back and forth between both of us.

"Do what?" I ask as I reach past him to spin the dial on my lock. He juts his chin toward one of Ms. Maso's posters announcing the tolerance assembly as my locker door pops open and two textbooks fall on my foot, capturing exactly what it's like to have a conversation with Conrad Deladdo first thing in the morning.

"If you're asking if we told anyone what happened to you at the party, then no, we didn't," Tracy replies.

I pick up the books and swap them for the ones I need. When I slam the door shut, I see that Conrad is waiting to hear what I have to say. He looks too skinny, and he has big circles under his eyes.

Tracy is checking out Conrad's clothes, and that's when I notice that he looks different than he's looked recently. He's not doing the blending-in, jeans/T-shirts/sneaker thing he was doing on the first day of school. His outfit is more like the one he wore to the party—blue polo shirt with the collar flipped up, red skinny jeans and those loafers Tracy was so worried about.

"Ask Ms. Maso about the assembly. It's her deal," I finally answer.

"How do you know that?"

"I saw her putting up the posters yesterday."

"Did she say anything?" He's being so intense that I take a step back.

"Hey, you guys!" Kristin comes bouncing down the hall toward us as if we are her dearest friends in a cool-looking floral shirt and super-dark jeans with white stitching. It's the first time I've seen Kristin in anything other than a cheerleading outfit— aside from her demonic fairy costume last Halloween—in over a year. She stops right in front of us and puts a hand to her hip as she twists slightly away from Tracy's camera, to make sure she looks as thin as possible in the photo.

"Ooh, nice one, Kristin. Is that shirt Rodarte?" Tracy says, genuine excitement in her voice.

When Kristin shrugs, Tracy reaches behind her to check the label, then circles her, continually switching the orientation of her phone to get different shots. I have to hand it to Tracy—she is an equal-opportunity photographer. If she likes the clothes, she'll take the picture—it doesn't matter who the person is. Although I haven't seen her take any pictures of Lena or Matt yet.

Conrad gives my shoulder a sharp little shove. "Focus. Did she say anything?"

His attitude is supremely annoying, like we're all just here to serve him. But in a weird way, I'm sort of impressed. He's trying to take charge of what's happening to him, which is a pretty far cry from what I did last year.

Conrad is never what I think he's going to be.

"She said there are rumors going around about the party—" Before I can finish, he cuts me off.

"I can tell by the look on your face that that's not all she—"

I cut him off right back. "You want to know or not?"

A few people turn to see what's going on. Conrad looks at the staring faces of our fellow students and for a second, I see the kid he turned into when his mother was holding open the door, waiting for him to come inside, wondering why her son had come home early soaking wet when he was supposed to be having fun at a party. Conrad mutters an apology, but just as quickly, he makes a sarcastic little gesture to indicate that I now have the floor.

"Chen wants to find out what happened at the party because you quit the swim team." I hesitate for just a second before adding, "Even though people are saying you're the best athlete the school has seen in a while."

I recognize the look on Conrad's face. I think I probably looked pretty similar when Holly said I sang like a rock star.

If you're not used to compliments, they can really mess you up for a minute.

"Fuck," he says to his loafers.

Tracy chooses that moment to take a step away from Kristin and snap another picture of Conrad. He spins around. "What are you *doing?*"

"It's for The Sharp List," she says, in an isn't-it-obvious voice. "You've got style, Conrad, whether you want to admit it or not. I want to feature you—"

"Do. Not. Even. Think it."

"It would be a great way to revamp your—"

The warning bell, followed by the sound of locker doors being slammed in unison, drowns out her last words, which is just as well because Conrad was about to unleash some ugly fury.

"Don't say *anything* to Principal Chen if—"

Conrad spots someone behind me and shoves past me. He literally uses the back of his hand against my upper arm to get me out of his way. "Did you get my text?"

I turn to see who Conrad ditched me for in midsentence, and there's Jamie. It's the first time I've seen him in his army jacket since last spring. I love that jacket on him—I want to check all the pockets for clues. He doesn't even have to be in it.

Although that would be nice.

"Yeah, man. What's up?" Jamie says to Conrad, sounding confused. Before Conrad pulls him off to the side so they can have a private conversation, Jamie spots me and winks. It throws me off guard. I try to be all 2.0 and I wink back, which a) is not what you're supposed to do when someone winks at you and b) looks super lame if you can't actually wink. Which I can't, I just found out.

I end up blinking at him. Fortunately, he doesn't see because he's already deep in conversation with Conrad, who is jabbing a finger at Ms. Maso's poster on the wall.

"That boy is rude," Tracy says as she opens her locker and slips her phone into the chic little leopard-print holster she affixed to the inside of the door.

"He's just freaking out."

"That doesn't give him a reason to be rude." She checks her makeup in the mirror above the holster, slams the door shut, loops her arm through mine and starts pulling me along to class when Jamie calls out, "Rose, wait up for a second."

I turn around just in time to see fury overtaking Conrad's face. He shoots a disgusted look at me, smacks the locker behind Jamie's head, snarls, "Thanks for nothing" and stalks off. Jamie runs a hand through his hair as if he's at a loss. Then he starts toward me.

Tracy disentangles her arm from mine. "Maybe you're finally going to find out when His Highness has time for you," she whispers, and then she's heading to Camber's class, which is what I should be doing if I don't want to get another detention from him.

"Hey," Jamie says.

"Hey, yourself." Lame. So very, very lame.

"I'll walk you," he says. We start off down the hall and I feel my face getting red before I realize why. It's not like we're holding hands, and no one is looking at us or anything, but this is the first time that I've been seen with Jamie Forta in school.

I have to act like it's nothing or I'm going to end up being the biggest dork in history.

"Is Conrad okay?" I say.

"He thinks that assembly is about him."

"What does he want you to do about it?"

Jamie shakes his head and shrugs. He turns into the stairwell to the second floor and I follow him.

"I thought...I guess I thought Conrad didn't really like you, or that he was mad at you."

"Conrad's always mad at me."

"But he still texts you when he needs something?"

"Yeah."

"Lucky you," I joke.

Jamie says nothing.

We're outside Camber's room before I realize that I never told Jamie what my next class was. He turns to me with such a serious expression on his face that I have no idea what's coming next. "I have Saturday off," he says.

"You do?"

"You free?"

"Yes!" I say.

Jamie cracks half a smile. "Don't you have to check your schedule or something?"

"Yes. I do. I'll check my schedule and get back to you." I try to pass off embarrassment as sass, which is about as easy as winking when you don't know how. The last bell rings, and Camber comes to close the door.

"Mr. Forta," he says by way of greeting, looking from me to Jamie.

"Hey, Camber."

"Ready for today?" Camber asks him pointedly.

Jamie nods. "Yeah."

"Good," Camber replies. "You joining us, Rose?" I must have a weird expression on my face because Camber says, "Yes, Ms. Zarelli, I am not the sole property of sophomore English. I do teach other students." Camber gazes at me over the top of his cool glasses to emphasize the point.

I've become suspicious of Camber's glasses recently. I think he wears them to try to be less appealing to his students, but based on the group of hot seniors who just cruised by and waggled their fingers at him—eliciting only a scowl, which just made them throw back their flat-ironed hair and laugh—I think it's going to take more than glasses for him to be less appealing.

"Take your seat, Rose," he says a bit more urgently.

Jamie heads back down the staircase. "Text me about Saturday," he calls over his shoulder.

Camber raises an eyebrow at me and I blush so fiercely I feel like I'm covered in sunburn.

As I walk into the classroom, I replay how uncool I was with Jamie. I might as well have said to him that I have no life, and I'm always free, just sitting around, waiting for him to call.

But I'm too excited to really care about my dorkiness.

It's finally happening.

All will be revealed.

Saturday.

superfluous *(adjective):* unnecessary, unneeded, unessential
(see also: me, Rose Zarelli)

———————

7

SITTING ACROSS THE TABLE FROM JAMIE AT MORTON'S is a surreal experience for a bunch of reasons. First, we're on a date, I think. That's the weirdest thing. Second, we're on a date in public, which means that people can see us—together. Third, Robert is our painfully attentive waiter, which wasn't supposed to happen because last I heard, he got fired over the summer when the owner got busted for hiring underage servers and undocumented workers, and paying them all under the table.

But the most surreal thing of all is that tonight is the night I've been waiting for, when I will finally have the opportunity to ask Jamie questions—about Regina, about the summer, about us.

If there is an *us.*

I just need a little more…confidence, I guess? I'm having trouble getting the words out. Probably because Jamie's quieter than usual.

And that might be my fault.

I told Jamie that he didn't have to pick me up, and I asked Tracy to drop me at the restaurant. It didn't have anything to do with him—I just didn't want to deal with Mom. She's known for a while that I like Jamie but she and I are in a weird place now, not the halfway decent place we were in when she agreed to let me go to the junior prom. Back then, she was so happy we were talking to each other again that she didn't dare say no, especially since I'd just gotten in that fight and I was in a somewhat "precarious emotional state," I believe is how she put it.

I didn't lie to her, exactly. I told her I was spending the night at Tracy's, which is true—I'm going over there later to help with the redesign of The Sharp List site.

It's just that I'll be out with Jamie first.

So far, my attempts at conversation have yielded a few three-sentence discussions—with two of the sentences being mine—on the beginning of school, and how nice the weather has been. His one sentence, which consisted of a single word, probably doesn't even qualify as a sentence. So I've temporarily given up on conversation, and now I'm pretending not to watch him as I try to decide if I should apologize or just not say anything.

Robert keeps interrupting my decision-making process by coming over every minute or two to fill our water glasses, check our bread basket, take our order, double-check on our order and swap out a perfectly clean knife for a less clean knife, so he can come back later and swap it out again.

Watching Jamie Forta is never a bad thing—he looks really handsome tonight in a dark green shirt that kind of matches his hazel-gold eyes. But I did not come here tonight just to watch him. I came to talk to him.

Rose 2.0 gives me a sharp kick and tells me to get off my ass—apologize or ask him a question, but *do* something.

"Remember last Thanksgiving, when I was here with my mom and we saw you?"

He nods.

"That was after Peter told me he'd asked you to look out for me."

Robert arrives with our burgers. "Need anything else?" he asks, directing the question at Jamie. When Jamie shakes his head, Robert turns to me. "Everything okay here?"

He sounds like he's playing a detective in a black-and-white movie, talking to a damsel in distress who needs to be rescued from the man she's with.

"I'll let you know after I have a chance to *taste* it," I answer, trying to subliminally convey to him that yes, I am on a date with Jamie Forta of my own free will, and yes, he should please *leave* now.

When Robert finally does tear himself away, Jamie takes a bite of burger. While he's chewing, he unbuttons his cuffs and rolls up his sleeves like he's about to take on some big, heavy task. "That was when you found out I knew your mom," he says.

I freeze with my burger midway to my mouth. Out of the corner of my eye, I see Robert standing near the bar, watching. I ignore him, and put my burger down without taking a bite, trying to figure out exactly what I should say next to make sure I don't blow this.

"Is that what you wanted to explain tonight?" I ask. "Why you had to see my mom?"

Jamie runs a hand through his hair and stares at the table for a few seconds. "Yeah. Well, no. I wanted to tell you about mine."

I wait. I wait some more.

"That note I wrote. About being different. I was talking about her."

The noise level in Morton's is rising by the second as people fill up the bar to watch some game. The sound makes it hard for me to keep up with Jamie, which involves trying to fill in all the blanks. Sometimes when Jamie talks, his sentences have big, giant gaps right where information should be.

"So, it's your mom who makes you different?"

He picks up his fork and presses it into the tablecloth, making an indentation pattern as he tries to figure out what to say. "She was sick. She had some things wrong with her."

Last Valentine's Day, Jamie and I sat in his car up on the golf course, and he told me that his mother had died in an institution of some kind. He never told me anything more than that—at the time, I thought it was obvious that he didn't want to, so I didn't ask. But now I think maybe you're supposed to ask, so that the other person knows it's okay to talk about it.

I'm sitting as still as I possibly can as if any sudden movement would stop what's happening. "What kind of things?"

He pushes the fork into the tablecloth a little harder, then picks it up and turns it ninety degrees and does it again. "She heard voices and stuff. Growing up, she did weird things. That's why my dad sent her away. He thought she was gonna do something. To me. That kinda shit, it makes me different. From normal people. Like you."

He turns the fork one more time. I look down and see that Jamie has made a little house using the fork-tine indentations. The first time we ever talked, he was drawing his dream house on the back cover of his notebook. I watched his hands as he drew, thinking how beautiful they were. They still are—that hasn't changed. What has changed is my idea of how Jamie sees himself.

"You think *you're* the one who's not normal? Seriously?" I ask. He gazes at me steadily, as if daring me to tell him differently. "There's nothing normal about me, Jamie. I'm totally weird—"

"That's not the kind of normal I mean."

Robert appears and looks down at my plate with the intact burger. "Is something wrong with your food?" I shake my head, hoping that if I don't use words, he'll just disappear. There's a long pause, and then he says, a little grudgingly, "You sounded good yesterday." He turns to Jamie. "Did she tell you about her audition?" He sounds like he's accusing Jamie of something, of not knowing something about me that's super important.

Jamie looks at Robert like he dropped in from another planet.

"Robert, we're in the middle of something," I say, trying to politely tell him to get lost. I am finally—*finally*—really talking to Jamie. The last thing I want to do is talk about musical theater.

Jamie stands up. "I'll be back," he says to me.

I want to throttle Robert. It's like he could tell that Jamie and I were having a totally crucial moment so he came over specifically to mess it up. He fills up our water glasses for the seventh time and hovers. Having no desire to make anything easy for him right now, I don't look up.

"Rose, what are you doing? He's still seeing Regina," Robert whispers. "I see them together all the time."

I want to smack the bottom of the pitcher and send all that ice water flying, even though I'm supposed to be keeping my violent urges firmly under control.

"Robert, why did you lie and tell Holly that I loved you?"

He looks down into the pitcher and swirls the ice around, and for a second it seems like he's going to try to deny it or put some kind of spin on it. But maybe Robert's been working on keeping his lying under control the way I've been managing my violent urges.

"I don't know," he admits.

"She's, like, a once-in-a-lifetime kind of girlfriend."

"No, *really?*" he says.

"You tell her, or I will."

"Tell her what?" Panic crosses his face.

"That I was never in love with you and that you have a problem telling the truth if it doesn't fit into your version of how you'd like the world to be."

Robert's blue eyes narrow at me. "In my version of how the world should be, you're going out with someone who doesn't already have a girlfriend."

I clench my jaw. "They're not together anymore."

"So why is she always with him?"

"If you would just—" Jamie is heading back from the bathroom. "Please, Robert. Leave us alone, okay?"

"I don't want you to get hurt, Rosie," he says.

It's not lost on me that Robert hasn't called me Rosie in a long time. But that doesn't change the fact that I still want him to leave.

"Go. Away."

Robert fills up Jamie's glass so high that Jamie won't be able to pick it up without spilling water everywhere. When Jamie arrives, he stands next to his chair, waiting for Robert to go.

Robert says, "Ask her about her audition."

Jamie gives me a questioning glance and I shake my head as if to say it's not worth discussing. Which it isn't, in the context of what we've been talking about.

When it seems that Robert plans to stay indefinitely, Jamie says, "Is it legal for you to work here?"

Without another word, Robert takes his pitcher and heads off to refill glasses somewhere else. Jamie watches him and then sits.

"You auditioned for something?" he asks.

"I probably didn't get it," I say, trying to shake the horrifying memory of the dance audition. Apparently, watching a video of dance steps doesn't actually qualify a person to perform those steps in an audition. Who knew?

"What was it?"

"Just the school musical. So—" I start, trying to figure out how to get us back to where we were.

"You're a singer?" he asks. Surprise lights up his eyes and a real, unguarded smile spreads across his face before he can stop it. It takes everything I have not to tell him how beautiful he is.

"Um, I...am?" I answer. "Holly Taylor says I am. She's Robert's girlfriend, and her dad is a real actor, so I guess she would know. She says I sound like an old-school rock star."

I'm embarrassed telling him all this, but there's something real about saying out loud, "I am a singer." It's like it came true the instant I said it, and I feel different by, like, ten degrees. Maybe even fifteen.

"Cool, Rose," Jamie says. I watch the surprise in his eyes dim, and it's replaced by sadness—I don't get what's happening. The people at the bar suddenly cheer—someone just scored in the game—and the noise level is overwhelming for a minute. Jamie turns to look at the TV but I don't think he really cares about the game.

"Jamie? Can I ask you a question?"

He turns back and lifts his glass, managing to take a sip of water without spilling any. My stomach tightens into a little knot. Here we go.

"What's the deal with you and Regina?" I ask the question as purely as I can, with no anger, or jealousy, or judgment. I just want to know the truth.

He answers as if he's been waiting for this question. "Nothing."

I tilt my head. "Really?"

"She's with Parrina." A shadow crosses Jamie's face. "You know that."

"You two aren't…?" He shakes his head. "Conrad said you were in summer school together and that…you…"

"That I what?" he asks, sounding mildly amused by the prospect of hearing what Conrad said.

"That you wanted her back."

"He's just messing with you."

"So you don't?"

"No."

"Does she want *you* back?" He shrugs like it doesn't make a difference one way or the other. "I mean, she's with Anthony just to piss you off, right?"

Jamie looks surprised—maybe it never occurred to him that

I spend almost as much time thinking about Regina's motivations as his—but I'm on a roll and I'm not going to stop now.

"Jamie, what did Anthony say to you at that hockey game?"

Thinking about it makes him angry. His jaw clenches like he's grinding his teeth. "Something about my mom. She'd been gone a month or something. I lost it."

I think back to that moment, which I remember thinking was sort of exciting. I'm not sure what that says about me. Jamie was flying across the ice toward the goal with Anthony right behind him. Suddenly, Jamie just spun around, lifted his hockey stick and hit Anthony in the neck. Anthony went down, sliding across the red centerline frozen into the ice. I can still hear the sound of the whistle and the ref throwing Jamie out of the game. Anthony had to be carried off the ice, and he went to the hospital in an ambulance. I learned that day from my dad that professional hockey players have been killed by what Jamie had done to Anthony. If you do it with the intent to cause injury, you're out of the game—and in this case, off the team.

"Parrina's shit," Jamie says.

"Why's she with him?"

Jamie starts making more indentations with his fork on the other side of his plate. "I don't know. But I gotta keep an eye out."

My inability to understand is frustrating me. "After what she did to you, why do you care?"

Jamie drops the fork. "I owe the Deladdos."

"Because they let you live with them?"

Jamie leans forward. "I'm gonna tell you something that's private." He lowers his voice—I can barely hear him over the bar. He waits until I understand that I'm not ever supposed to repeat what he's about to tell me. I nod. "Mr. Deladdo hit Conrad and Regina and their mom. This summer, I made him stop."

Everything turns upside down in an instant.

I close my eyes.

I picture Conrad and Regina getting beaten by a man whose face I can't see.

I see Jamie lifting his stick to hit Anthony; Anthony grabbing Regina; Conrad getting shoved into the pool.

I see my dad on the desert floor, fractured like a broken mirror dropped from a great height.

The last thing I see is a girl, flying across a track and crashing into another girl, knocking her to the ground with every ounce of strength she can muster.

It's me. I did that. I did that to someone whose father hits her.

It's in me, too.

I push my plate away and watch my hand as it slides across the table to touch Jamie's fingers. "How did you make him stop?" I whisper. I don't understand how Jamie could make a grown man—an abusive man—just up and leave his family.

"I held a gun on him."

"You…" My mind goes blank and I can't finish the sentence.

"He was looking for an excuse to leave—it didn't take much."

"A gun?" I gape like a moron.

"My father's."

"Does he know?"

"He handed it to me himself after I told him what was going on over there."

"Your *dad* gave you…? Was it— Were there bullets in it?"

"I don't know."

I'm freaked out about a lot of things, like the fact that Jamie's father would just hand over his weapon to his son, loaded or not. But somehow, I'm not freaked out that Jamie has held someone at gunpoint. He looks so guilty, I want to put my arms around him right in the middle of the restaurant.

It's the guilt that makes all the pieces of the Deladdo puzzle finally fall into place.

"Jamie, is that why you think you owe them? Because you don't. You *helped* them—"

He cuts me off without looking at me. "You deserve someone who's there for you. And that's not me. Not now."

I pull my hand back before I know I'm going to do it. As soon as my fingers leave his skin, he slides back in his chair and crosses his arms, his eyes searching my face. "I like you," he says. "I wanna make sure you know that."

The sad thing is, I've played this version of events in my head as many times as the other version, because in the daydreams that my brain cooks up, things don't always go my way. I pictured myself handling Jamie's rejection with maturity, grace, blah blah blah. But I never imagined it would come at the end of what I thought was our first official date.

I say the first thing that comes into my head, even though it's pathetic. "Should I wait?"

He hesitates for maybe half a second. "No, Rose."

Robert comes over and slaps the bill down on the table without asking if we want dessert. "Have a great night," he says and walks away.

Neither of us looks at him.

Jamie waits, but I have no response to what he said.

He stops waiting and reaches for the bill.

"How many of you people sitting here today know who Matthew Shepard is?"

It's Monday morning, and Ms. Maso looks super intense standing on the auditorium stage next to Principal Chen, speaking to the entire school. Some other faculty members are solemnly sitting in chairs behind the podium. There are a few seats off to the side of the stage, filled with some people I don't recognize, and one I do—Caron.

Great. My mom's shrink is a spy for the Union High administration. That must be why she was asking me all those questions about the party. So much for patient-shrink confidentiality.

I thought about calling Caron yesterday. She always said I could call her whenever I needed to, day or night, and yesterday, for the first time, I thought maybe I might need to. I had a dream at Tracy's after my non-date date with Jamie. It started out as the movie dream about my dad, where I'm sitting in a theater watching him on the screen. The movie always starts out fine, and then he gets blown up. But this time, he didn't get blown up. Because Jamie was there with the gun, and he was shooting it at my dad. The image played in my head all day.

The one thing that helped was singing—I could just close my eyes and drift away. So I got in the shower and sang myself hoarse until my mother knocked on the door and told me that while I sounded nice, it was time to turn off the water.

I didn't call Caron because I didn't want to tell her about the dream, or what happened with Jamie—especially the part about him saying he doesn't want to be with me. Or he can't be with me. I'm not sure which it is. Or if it matters.

"Union High, are you awake out there?"

Ms. Maso is in full-on fierce mode, which is what I like to call it when she uses her superpowers to get a bunch of dumb adolescents to listen up and learn something important and possibly even life-changing. She's sort of like a rock star when she's in fierce mode.

But people are sleepy. It's first thing in the morning and they probably haven't had their bagels or coffee yet. The last thing they want to do is learn about some guy. I happen to know that Matthew Shepard isn't just *some guy,* and I also know that the student body's general indifference to learning about him is just feeding Ms. Maso's burning desire to school us. If we don't settle down and give her our undivided attention, she'll figure out a way to give the entire school detention and extra homework.

She stares at us for another second, and when some of the rustling around subsides, she picks up a clicker from the podium. She presses a button and projects onto the screen above the stage a picture of a young blond man in a sweater with light eyes and just the suggestion of a smile, standing in front of a window. She turns to look up at him.

"This, Union High, is Matthew Shepard."

Even from where I'm sitting at the back of the auditorium with the other students from my homeroom—which is basically everyone else in school whose last name begins with a "z"—I can see that Ms. Maso is moved by this photo.

Movement near one of the auditorium side doors catches my attention and I see Conrad being escorted in by a teacher who has his hand on Conrad's shoulder, as if he thinks Conrad might bolt at any second. The teacher directs him to an empty seat and makes him sit down. It's not until Conrad sits that he looks up and sees Matthew Shepard above the stage. I can sense his panic from two rows away.

"If you don't know who Matthew Shepard is, then you haven't been paying attention in your civics class. Recently, our president signed a major piece of civil rights legislation named after this young man that makes it a federal crime to assault people based on sexual orientation, gender or gender identity."

She presses the clicker again and Matthew's face fades to an image of a split-rail fence adorned with flowers, out in the middle of a beautiful, wintery prairie.

"But just so we're all on the same page, I'll assume you don't know, and I'll tell you a little bit about him. Matthew Shepard was a 21-year-old University of Wyoming student who was planning to major in political science with a focus on human rights." She waits a few seconds before continuing to make sure that this information has registered. "In 1998, he was kidnapped from a bar, beaten and tortured for being gay. His two attackers—young men who were about the same age as Matthew—tied him to this fence that you see here, and they left him there, battered and bleeding, in the freezing cold. Matthew was discovered there eighteen hours later with so much damage done to his face and head that he was unrecognizable. He died several days after that in a hospital. Today is the anniversary of his death."

Ms. Maso turns back to us and seems to make eye contact with every single student sitting in our huge auditorium.

"So why am I bothering you with this on a beautiful sunny October morning, just a month into the school year?" she asks. It gets so quiet that I can hear my own pulse. "Principal Chen and I, and the rest of the faculty, are extremely concerned. We feel that we have not been doing our jobs, that we have not taught you to the best of our abilities. Because if we had, you would know about Matthew Shepard. You would know about hate crimes. You would know what tolerance means. And you would not have allowed your classmates to throw a party during which a student was called 'faggot,' 'fag' and 'homo,' and thrown into a pool multiple times, once while he was choking on water that had been forced into his mouth from a hose!" she says, pounding on the podium.

No one is rustling around anymore—I don't think anyone is even breathing. Conrad sinks lower into his seat.

"I can't begin to tell you how disappointed I am in all of you. But I'm just as disappointed in the grown-ups in your lives, including the ones up here today. If we had been doing our jobs, you would have stepped up to stop this reprehensible behavior. From what I understand, only one student—*one* of you—tried to help, and she got pushed into the pool for taking a stand."

A few heads swivel around, and that old familiar feeling of wanting to sink into the floor surfaces. But this time—unlike last year, when I was called out for supposedly saving Stephanie's life—I want to sink into the floor because I feel shame.

I am not proud of what I did, because I was not taking a stand. I wasn't trying to stop a hate crime. In fact, I didn't even understand that what was happening could be considered a hate crime. So in the context of what Ms. Maso is talking about, I didn't do anything at all.

I was just trying to stop Conrad—who I can no longer see, he's so low in his seat—from drowning.

"Think about it, people. Who do you want to be? Do you want to be the coward who is so afraid of people who are not like him, who is so narrow-minded and small, that he attacks out of fear? Is that what we are teaching you to do here? Because if it is, then we are failing you miserably and you should hold us accountable!"

At this point, Ms. Maso has left the microphone behind and is yelling at us from the edge of the stage, leaning forward as if she wants to leap into the crowd and shake us until we come to our senses.

"Now. Am I comparing throwing a fellow student in the pool and calling him 'homo' to the horrifying crime that was perpetrated against Matthew Shepard?" She thinks for a second. "They are not the same thing, no. But they *are* on the same spectrum. It's the spectrum of hate. And you know what, people? This spectrum of hate includes all sorts of terrible things, including a crime you may remember from your studies of post–Civil War America, known as lynching. All of these things that we are talking about today are related."

She clicks the clicker again and an old black-and-white photo of a man hanging from a tree by his neck appears. Students gasp, unused to seeing evidence of lynching anywhere other than in textbooks, as small photos barely big enough to show the person's lifeless face frozen in terror or agony. Ms. Maso's photo seems about twenty feet tall and provides plenty of inescapable detail—the man's hair showing from underneath his round cap; his hands bound so tightly that the rope cuts into his flesh;

shockingly beautiful dappled sunlight shining on the trunk of the tree that holds him; the stain on his pants.

The collective gasp of the student body causes Principal Chen to look over her shoulder to see what's on the screen. When she turns back, she shoots Ms. Maso an exasperated look, calmly takes the clicker away from her and turns off the projection screen. Ms. Maso is not pleased, but she takes a few steps back and gives the principal the stage.

"Thank you for making that connection for us, Ms. Maso," Principal Chen says drily as she leans into the microphone, sounding like she's already composing a letter to angry parents in her head as she talks. "Let's get back to present-day Union High. Here's the thing, folks. That party happened before school started and it didn't happen on school property, so we have no recourse. However, it still provides a great opportunity to have a dialogue about tolerance. This dialogue will take place publicly—in assembly and in classrooms—and privately, in my office. Over the next few days, some of you will be paying me a visit so I can better understand what went on at that party, and what we need to do to ensure that nothing like it ever happens again, okay?"

She takes a look at her watch, confers with the assistant principal, and then says, "Mr. Donnelly would like to make an announcement before we end."

Mr. Donnelly walks to the podium slowly, as if buying himself some time before he has to speak. When he gets there, he pauses as he looks out at all of us.

"Good morning, people. I have a special announcement that is relevant to what we've been talking about. In honor of the commitment to tolerance we are making here at Union High and the new federal legislation, the spring play will be *The Laramie Project,* a theater piece based on interviews with people who knew Matthew Shepard. It's a beautiful, difficult piece of theater that asks hard questions, and I think it is very fitting, given what we are currently trying to accomplish. On a personal note," he says, pausing, then exhaling into the microphone, "I have experience with intolerance, and I would like to invite anyone who has suffered discrimination or harassment as a result of their sexual orientation to come talk to me whenever they'd like. Thank you."

Mr. Donnelly steps away from the podium, ignoring a few surprised looks from faculty members as murmurs ripple through the auditorium. Suddenly, he leans back into the microphone and adds, "I almost forgot. The cast list for *Anything Goes* is now on the board next to the theater."

I can barely even process the announcement about the cast list—or the fact that Mr. Donnelly basically just outed himself in front of the whole school—because my head is spinning. Did I witness a hate crime? Am I doing something wrong by not talking about it? I didn't think it was that big a deal—I mean, I thought it was a big deal because Conrad was in danger, but I guess I didn't understand how big the danger was.

But I vowed not to embarrass myself again this year by running to the principal to tell on someone. Even if that someone is Matt Hallis.

The murmuring in the auditorium increases as students sense that the assembly is about to end. Should I go look at the cast list before first period or just wait until somebody tells me who got what, since I'm sure I'm not on the list?

The nice thing to do would be to go look at it with my friends and congratulate them.

Do I feel like doing the nice thing today?

I'm focusing on the wrong issue, asking the wrong question. The question should be, am I going to do the *right* thing today? Do I even know what that is?

Principal Chen comes back to the podium. "Proceed to period one, which will end at the regular time. And thanks for your undivided attention!" she yells with a sarcastic twinge as the din becomes a full-on roar—the student body is officially no longer listening.

I stand and look for Conrad. I need to see him before I get dragged into Chen's office—I need to know what he wants me to say, and not say. But he's already gone.

This school sucks. Don't they realize that they are making the situation worse for Conrad by doing stuff like this? First of all, even though they didn't say his name, everyone knew Maso and Chen were talking about him. Also, it's not like the swim thugs are now going to apologize and beg Conrad to rejoin the swim team. If anything, they'll go after him more for possibly getting them into trouble.

Dumb. Adults can be so dumb when it comes to stuff like this. They should be able to figure out a better way to handle these things.

I throw my bag over my shoulder and leave the auditorium with the rest of the herd just in time to see Jamie. He lifts his chin at me to say hi, and although I'm relieved that we're not ignoring each other, I have a hard time smiling. He points in the direction he's going, and I see Conrad slipping out a door to the courtyard. Jamie goes after him, but he's having trouble getting through the sea of students. We get swept along in different directions and he's gone before I can make a decision about whether I should go with him or not.

We hardly talked on the drive from Morton's to Tracy's. I was too confused—I wasn't sure what had just happened. It wasn't until later, when I was lying awake on Tracy's trundle bed listening to her breathe the oh-so-peaceful slumber of a beloved high school celebrity, that I started sorting through everything he said and realized that it didn't all add up. Jamie thinks he owes the Deladdos, so he's made them his priority. But for how long? Forever?

And why does Jamie feel guilty about Mr. Deladdo, given what he was doing to his family? If he was hurting them, aren't they better off without him?

What am I missing?

I get to the bulletin board by the theater, where Stephanie and Holly are holding hands and jumping up and down with excitement as Robert, a giant grin on his face, talks to a glum-looking Mitchell Klein. When Holly and Stephanie see me they suddenly stop jumping and the smiles slide off their faces, which tells me everything I need to know. I wave at them and say "Congratulations!" as genuinely as I can manage and I keep walking toward the list even though I know I'm not on it.

There's a crush of people around it, and it takes me a while to work my way to the front of the pack. When I do, I see that Holly, Stephanie and Robert are the leads, and Mitchell has a small but funny part playing a gangster. Then, as my eyes travel down the list, I get a little jolt. My name *is* there.

Rose Zarelli, it says. *Passenger #3.*

At first, I don't feel anything. Then I think, well, okay, at least I'm in the thing, right? That thought is quickly followed by a wave of disgust. I look at the list again—does it really say *Passenger #3?*

Yes. Yes, it does.

I look to see who Passengers #1 and #2 are. I don't recognize the names, which probably means that I'm playing third fiddle to two freshmen. My face turns bright red just as I hear, "Rose, would you come with me, please? I'll give you a late pass."

I turn around to see the crowd scattering to get away from Principal Chen as she motions with one finger for me to follow her.

revelation *(noun):* an enlightening surprise
(see also: the future gets a little clearer)

_____

8

PRINCIPAL CHEN'S OFFICE IS DECKED OUT IN A FALL theme that goes with her painfully bright, industrial-orange carpeting. There are strands of fake, multicolored leaves hanging from the ceiling and pumpkins and gourds on every flat surface. The principal herself has a plastic witch pin blinking on and off on what Tracy would say is a fall-appropriate, rust-colored blazer. Even though Halloween is still more than two weeks away, there's a black plastic cauldron full of candy corn on her desk, with foil-wrapped Frankensteins and Draculas wedged in it like tiny tombstones. When the principal picks up a little metal scoop attached to the cauldron to help herself, a spooky Halloween theme plays.

"Candy corn, Rose?" she offers.

"No, thanks. I don't touch the stuff before 9:00 a.m.," I say in a weird character voice. I'm trying to make a joke but I'm nervous and I end up sounding rude, like I'm saying she shouldn't be eating candy, even though she weighs about a hundred pounds and could probably use the calories because she burns more energy in one day than everyone at Union combined.

"Breakfast of champions," she says with a grin, dumping the contents of the scoop into her hand. "So, Rose, how is sophomore year treating you so far?"

"Fine," I say.

"You just got cast in the musical?"

"Not really."

The principal tilts her head, confused. "'Not really'?"

"I'm Passenger #3. It's not a big deal."

She nods thoughtfully. "There are plenty of people who didn't make the cut, you know."

I shrug.

"Have you ever heard the saying, 'There are no small parts, only small actors'?"

I do my best to avoid rolling my eyes as I nod.

"Well, I don't believe that. But I do believe in paying your dues. This year it's Passenger #3. Next year maybe it's Maria in *West Side Story*. The word around school is that you have quite a powerful voice."

Wait—what? Did Mr. Donnelly tell her that? Is it true?

I think another person just called me a singer.

"All right, enough chitchat," she says, ignoring the scoop and grabbing a handful of candy corn directly out of the cauldron. "You know why I want to talk to you?"

The last time I got called to the principal's office was after I called 911 at homecoming and the YouTube stalker posted the video of Tracy and Kristin's cheerleading initiation. Apparently, I am now going to be called to the office once a year because of someone's initiation gone wrong.

The intercom on the principal's phone buzzes before I can answer the question. "Principal Chen, I have Conrad Deladdo out here for you."

The principal puts her candy down on her giant desktop calendar and presses a button on the phone. "Thank you. Tell him it'll be just a few minutes."

She leans back and waits for my answer.

"I'm guessing you want to talk to me because of the party."

She nods. "You're the only one who tried to help."

"That's not true," I say.

"That's news to me. Who else stepped in?"

"Jamie Forta."

"Jamie Forta," she repeats. "Well, that's encouraging." She makes a note on the corner of her giant calendar, and I realize that I just won Jamie a trip to the principal's office.

"So are you willing to tell me what happened, and who the instigator was?"

"I won't tell you who did it," I say.

"Rose, listen—"

"It's not me I'm worried about."

The principal starts shoving the candy around on her calendar, putting a piece on every other day of the month. Then she says, "For now, why don't you just tell me what happened."

I spend the next few minutes explaining what I saw when I first showed up at the party, and how I ended up in the pool. But I'm pretty sure I'm not telling Chen anything new. When I'm done, she takes a second to slide the last piece of candy into place on her calendar and then presses the intercom button.

"Would you send Conrad in, please?"

Of course. Of course it would come to this. I hope she's not too disappointed when she finds out that Conrad does not see me as an ally, no matter what I did for him at that party.

The door opens and Conrad comes in, hesitating when he sees me. His glare could stop a freight train.

"Conrad, thanks for joining us. Have a seat. I was just asking Rose here how she ended up in the pool at the swim-team party."

Conrad doesn't say anything. He doesn't even nod to acknowledge that the principal is speaking. Slowly, he sits down.

"Would you tell me how *you* ended up in the pool?"

Conrad crosses his arms over his chest. "If *she* told you how she got there," he says, making a point of not saying my name, "you already know how *I* did."

"I'd like to hear it from you," she replies. "And I'd also like to know what made you quit the swim team."

Conrad stares hard at the orange carpeting. For some reason, the spooky Halloween theme plays even though no one touched the scoop. Principal Chen picks up the plastic cauldron and switches it off.

"It's not an easy team to make, Conrad, and the coach says you're one of his best already. Why would you give up a spot you worked so hard to win?"

After a painful moment of silence, the principal leans forward in her chair, folds her hands on her calendar without messing up her candy-corn art installation, and looks from Conrad to me and back again.

"This event—what happened at the party—is bigger than both of you. It's about more than your concerns about what people will think of you if you talk to me. Now, that's a lot to put on you, I know. But I want all students to feel safe here at Union High, and I can't make that happen without you two stepping up."

Conrad lifts his gaze to her, his voice cold as ice. "Sure you can."

The principal raises an eyebrow, fixing Conrad with her best authoritarian stare. "Excuse me?"

"You don't need me to tell you who was calling me a faggot because it doesn't matter *who* was doing it, just that someone *was* doing it. Oh, and also? While we're looking at the big picture, wanting the students at Union High to feel safe, what about *my* safety?"

Principal Chen looks taken aback by the fact that Conrad

didn't fall in line after her standing-up-for-what's-right speech, and I can see her shifting tactics. Slowly, she gets up, walks around to the front of her desk and leans on it, so that she is less than a foot away from us both. She's barely five feet tall but somehow she manages to tower above both of us anyway. Despite the flashing witch pin, she's intimidating.

"Conrad, in situations like this, it helps to talk to the perpetrators, whether punishment is involved or not."

"Helps who?" he snarls, standing up out of his chair so suddenly that he startles both Principal Chen and me. She stays very still, probably trying to gauge whether she has a truly violent student on her hands or just one who's temporarily super pissed off.

"Everyone," she says calmly. "Including you. Now I'd appreciate it if you'd spend some time thinking about that and come back to see me tomorrow. You're excused for the rest of the day."

Conrad is confused—he seems to be waiting for the other shoe to drop. When nothing else happens, he grabs his black messenger bag, slings it across his chest, and is out the door in a flash.

The principal turns her attention to me. My heart is already pounding in my chest—being around Conrad is like waiting to see if a bomb was defused properly or not. And Principal Chen's laser-beam stare isn't helping my nerves.

"It would be great if you would tell me who the ringleader was," she says, all business now. "I have my suspicions, but confirmation from someone who was actually there would make my life a lot easier."

"It won't do any good," I mumble.

"I know things were tough for you last year. Not to diminish your experience, but what's happening with Conrad is harassment on a whole other scale. It is evidence of a major problem. You would be helping to solve that problem."

My resolve is deteriorating. I try to defend myself. "It's just going to backfire on me. And him."

"Making things better requires risk," she says. "Sometimes the moral imperative to speak up outweighs personal need. I know you have it in you. Whether you like it or not, you do what's right, even when it's hard, Rose."

The intercom buzzes again. "Ms. Maso has arrived."

The principal closes her eyes and takes a deep breath as if today is one of the longest days of her life. She walks around her desk, sits back down in her chair, presses the button and says, "Tell her I'll deal with— I'll be with her in just a moment."

Then she fixes that stare on me once again. My face starts to get hot. "I need you to trust me here, Rose." I don't answer, but I can't look away from her. "So. Matt Hallis?" she asks quietly, as if the walls have ears.

I look up at the ceiling, thinking about the assembly this morning, and the spectrum of hate. The photo of that fence. Conrad, who's important to Jamie.

I nod once, quickly, without making eye contact, as if that somehow makes me less responsible.

Without acknowledging what I've done, Principal Chen says, "Thanks for coming in, Rose."

As if I had a choice.

She stands and opens the door for me. Ms. Maso is right there, arms folded across her chest. Principal Chen waves her in like she's a student who has gotten herself in trouble for shooting off her mouth yet again.

As Ms. Maso passes me, she pats me on the shoulder, somehow knowing I caved without anyone having to tell her.

"Rose, blend, okay? Take that big voice of yours and *blend!* I'm begging you."

It's the third time Mr. Donnelly has stopped rehearsal because I am unable to *blend*.

Whatever that is.

We're sitting in chairs on the auditorium stage learning a really complicated song with lots of harmonies and people singing different things at the same time. I have no problem coming in at the right time or hearing my part, and for a while, before the blending issue, I was actually having fun. There's something cool about being on a stage looking out into an auditorium—even an empty auditorium—singing in, like, four-or-five-part harmony while the pianist plays her heart out. Being inside music like that can make you feel like nothing else in the entire world matters except what's going on right then.

Unless you can't blend.

Which, apparently, I can't.

"From the chorus, one more time!" Mr. Donnelly shouts. Then he turns and stage-whispers to me, "Ears, Zarelli. Use your ears!"

Mr. Donnelly cues the pianist, and I decide to mouth the words this time just to see if he is really hearing what he thinks he's hearing. Because how could he possibly hear that I'm doing something wrong over everybody else?

He stops us again and points at me.

"Now you're not singing at all," he says.

Everyone is frustrated by having spent the past twenty minutes on this one part—passengers #1 and #2 look like they want to punch me.

"Do you know what I mean by blend?" Mr. Donnelly asks.

When I finally shake my head, he clasps the sides of his music stand like he's going to fall down, and gives me a look of extreme exasperation.

"People, if you do not know what I am talking about, ask me! There's no shame in asking questions—that's what rehearsal is for. Who wants to tell Rose what blending is?"

Mitchell Klein is the only one who raises his hand, which makes me suspect that there are other people in the dark here.

"Blending is making sure your voice fits in with other people's, so you don't stand out."

"Thank god for Mitchell Klein!" Mr. Donnelly cheers. "That's right, Mitchell. Rose, you have a unique voice, and that's great. But in a song like this, every voice has to work together to create one sound. If one person stands out, the balance of the song gets thrown off and the audience ends up listening to an individual voice rather than the whole piece of music. Any questions?"

I don't want to look dumb again, but at this point, I just need information. And based on the way a few people are looking at me, it seems like everybody else needs me to have information, too.

"So how do you do it?" I ask.

"Ah, an excellent question." Donnelly grabs his ear and tugs at it ferociously. "You listen. Listen to what's happening around you, and try to match the quality. Try to fit in. Okay?"

I nod as if what he said made sense.

"Again!" Mr. Donnelly says happily, as if the problem is finally solved. He cues the pianist and we all start singing. I listen as hard as I can, and I try to imitate the alto next to me—her voice is thinner than mine, and calmer.

Mr. Donnelly doesn't stop us again.

So I guess the way to blend is to make yourself sound like someone else?

If so, that's fitting, because lately I've been thinking maybe I should just *be* someone else. If I were, then maybe I could, oh, I don't know, have the guy I like and not cave when the principal grills me and get cast in a good role and sing the right way.

When we finish the song, Mr. Donnelly says, "All right, people, go home and learn your parts *and* your words! It's not enough to just know the notes. You must also know the lyrics! Get off book by next week or I will hurt you," he jokes. "Rose, come see me, please."

Great. I grab my bag and walk over to Mr. Donnelly.

"Listen, I know you feel like I'm singling you out," he says, "and you're right. I am. You have a nice voice—it's just a little contemporary for what we're doing. Do you know what I mean?"

"You mean it's wrong for the show."

"No, no, nothing like that. I wouldn't have cast you if it were wrong for the show," he says, sounding like he's chastising me for even thinking such a thing. "You just need to rein it in. Let it rip on your solo lines in other songs, but in this one, it's all about the balance. You'll get it," he says, patting me on the shoulder, trying to be reassuring but basically just making me feel like I'll *never* get it, and I'm going to ruin the show.

Singing by myself is *way* more fun than this. Although it's hard to harmonize with yourself.

I pull on my sweater as I walk to my locker. Less than a minute later, Holly shows up with Robert.

I really don't feel like talking to her right now. I know she just wants to make me feel better but I don't want to hear her being all positive about my singing when I just got my ass kicked for about half an hour in front of the entire cast.

And I definitely don't feel like being around Robert. He's been staring at me at rehearsals since Morton's. Now, standing next to Holly, he wears this sort of pleading, imploring look on his face, like he thinks I'm going to tell Holly the truth about him at any second.

I guess I did sort of give him the impression that I might.

"A bunch of us are going out for a slice. Do you want to come?" Holly asks.

"Thanks, but I have to go home and study. The PSAT is tomorrow."

Holly looks confused. "You're taking the PSAT already? Are we all supposed to be doing that?"

"No, I'm just doing it for practice. I want to qualify for a National Merit Scholarship next year."

"God, Rose, you're so smart," she says. "But are you sure you can't come? Even just for one slice?"

"I'll come next time. But I think the cast of *Anything Goes* could use a break from my *unique voice* for a while."

"Rose, don't worry about the blending thing—Mr. Donnelly was after me for the same thing all summer during *Damn Yankees*." I can tell by the way Robert suddenly looks at Holly like she's crazy that she's making this up for my benefit. "Your voice is just too interesting for the chorus. Which is why, next time, you'll get a lead! So this is a *good* thing!"

I'm getting tired of words like *interesting* and *unique* and *unusual* being used to describe my voice. At first I thought they were compliments, but now I think they're just synonyms for *weird* and *irritating* and *too much*. I can feel myself getting angry about being embarrassed at rehearsal, and that's a bad place for me to be. When I'm mad because I'm embarrassed, all sorts of mean things come out of my mouth that shouldn't.

Like this.

"There isn't going to be a next time. Musical theater sucks."

Holly and Robert both jump like I've just used an electric cattle prod on them.

"What—what do you mean?" Holly asks. The pain on her face makes me feel like I just said the most hurtful thing I ever could have said to her.

But does that shut me up? Nope.

"I think the choreography and the style of singing are totally forced, and the music itself bugs me. It's cheesy."

This is only marginally true. I do sort of think those things, but I also really like the dancing, even if practicing choreography is so repetitive I could cry. And I love singing harmony. Even if the music is cheesy, I enjoy it. I just don't feel like admitting any of that to these two right now.

Holly's big brown eyes are full of apology. "Oh, my god, Rose, I'm sorry. I really thought you'd like working on the show. That's why I wanted you to do it."

"It's not all bad. I love watching you and Stephanie—you're both amazing."

Holly sneaks a quick glance at Robert. It's not lost on her that I left him off my short list of people who are *amazing* in the show.

I doubt it's lost on him, either.

And then, because I'm already in bad-behavior mode, I add one more thing for good measure: "I just think the show is lame."

And there it is. I have successfully offended them as much as humanly possible.

After another stunned silence from two of the three people who have to carry the show that I just called lame, Robert says in an ice-cold voice, "First of all, it's Cole Porter—it's literally impossible for it to be *lame*. Second of all, if you had a lead role, you might see things differently. But not everyone is lead-role material."

"Robert!" Holly gasps. She's probably never seen Robert be mean before.

Come to think of it, I haven't, either.

The tears in my eyes surprise me. I know I totally deserve what he just said, but that doesn't make it easier to hear.

"You might want to rethink being a jerk to me." I sound calm as I raise my eyebrows to remind him that at any moment, I could just open my mouth and tell Holly that he lied. He turns bright red.

"I'll meet you at Cavallo's, Hol." Robert leaves without looking at me. Holly watches her boyfriend go, and when she turns back to me, I see bewilderment in her eyes, mixed with something that I've never seen in her before: suspicion.

Holly is very still as she watches me, and then she says, with some steel in her voice, "I don't understand what just happened. Are you and Robert in a fight?"

I try to figure out what I'm doing and why before I say anything. I don't want to blow up Robert and Holly's relationship—they have something real, and nice.

They're lucky.

So basically, I'm just being a bitch.

"I'm in a bad mood, Holly. That's all."

She takes a second to look down at her fuzzy vintage sweater and button one of the shiny heart-shaped buttons before she asks, "Rose, are you sure you're okay with me going out with Robert?"

"Yes!" I grab her arm for emphasis. "I am. Totally. You two are good together. I'm sorry about what I said. Will you tell him I'm sorry?"

"Come with me and tell him yourself," she says. "And he could apologize, too. He shouldn't have said what he said to you."

"It's okay. I— He was just mad. But I'll come next time. I promise."

Holly leans in and gives me a quick hug, her bracelets jangling. When she pulls back, I still see suspicion in her eyes, which makes me feel guilty for not telling her the truth.

"Good luck tomorrow. Tell me how it goes, okay? I want to know what those tests are like."

She gives me a little wave and then heads off down the hall. I get my stuff from my locker and check my phone, looking for a text from Tracy offering me a ride but feeling relieved when I don't have one. I need the walk home—there's a lot of crazy in my head right now.

When I leave the building, it's starting to get dark. I can smell fall. The leaves of the maple trees glow bright orange and red against the purple sky. They make me wish I could paint. I wonder if painting is easier than singing.

My dad always said that nothing easy is worth having. I think probably every dad in the history of humankind has said that to his kid at one point or another. I never really knew what it meant before, but I think I do now.

When I decided I was going to be a singer last year, I didn't think it was going to be so complicated. Or uncomfortable. I always figured that finding your thing was the hard part. But once you found it, everything else would fall into place, because if you were destined to do something, then it wouldn't be hard, right?

Maybe I don't understand the whole concept of destiny.

Because I'm thinking such deep philosophical thoughts as I walk home, and because it's nearly dark, I almost miss Regina and Anthony entirely. They're under the overpass a few blocks from school, kissing. Regina is up against the concrete wall, and Anthony has his arms braced on either side of her, like he doesn't want her going anywhere. She turns her head to the side and he moves with her, making her kiss him again. Her arms are behind her, and she's leaning back on them—she and Anthony aren't touching at all except for their lips. He's so big he looks like The Hulk next to her.

It's the first time I've seen Regina since Jamie told me about her father, and she looks different to me now. Or I guess maybe it's that I see her differently.

It used to be when I looked at her, I was afraid. I couldn't help but think of all the awful things she said and did to me, and the way she loved trying to scare me. Now when I look at her, I imagine her dad hurting her.

What exactly did Jamie mean when he said that Mr. Deladdo *hit* Regina? Did he…smack her? Punch her? Throw things at her?

What is it like to have a father like that?

And what is it like to see your ex-boyfriend—who you're still in love with—pointing a gun at him, threatening him, making him leave? What did she feel when Jamie did that? Did she want her father to go because she was sick of being hurt, or did she want him to stay because he's her dad?

I get a weird little shock up my spine every time I think about Jamie with that gun. It still seems impossible to me that he could hold it and point it at a grown-up, and tell him what to do.

I wonder if he was scared when he did it.

And what kind of father—what kind of *cop*—just hands his gun to his son and tells him to go do something like that?

I watch Anthony and Regina for another second, and then I start to feel creepy. I pick up the pace so I can be long gone by the time they come up for air.

When I get home, I close the door and head straight up to my room as quietly as I can. My mother's light is on in her office—either she's still with a patient or she's doing paperwork. My phone chimes while I'm on the stairs and I clutch my bag to my side to try to muffle the sound. I don't want to have to talk to my mother right now.

When I'm safely in my room, I root around in my bag for my phone and see a text from Tracy, telling me that she's emailing me the next Sharp List. As "editorial director," I look over her posts before they go live. But she hardly ever gives me time to do it—she just sends endless texts and emails marked "urgent," and I'm supposed to drop everything I'm doing and give all my attention to her blog.

I open my laptop, but instead of checking my email, I click my Broadway cast recording of *Anything Goes* and start trying to blend. I have no idea if I'm doing it right or not. All I know is I get so paranoid about sounding like myself that I'm sitting totally still, barely moving my mouth at all and not even inhaling deeply to get a good breath, which makes my throat hurt.

Blending can't possibly mean "hold your breath and hurt yourself."

I stop the music and open my closet to grab a pair of sweats.

On the back of my closet door is the full-length mirror that I took down over the summer—I put it back up when school started for obvious reasons. It's partially covered by old backpacks Tracy won't let me use anymore and jackets she says are too big for me that are hanging from bright blue hooks my dad installed to help me keep my room neat. But I can still see myself in the mirror, in the middle of all the stuff hanging there.

Instead of closing the door to get away from the mirror like I usually do, I stand there and take a good look. It's weird. I'm disappointed when I look in the mirror but it's not because I don't like what I see. I mean, I don't, but that's not what bugs me. What bugs me is that what I see in the mirror doesn't match what I see in my head. In my head, I'm prettier than I am in real life, so when I look in the mirror and see what I see, I feel let down. And also a little crazy. Where did I get that image in my head if not from the mirror?

I think about Holly and Stephanie, who are so pretty they cause whiplash in the halls. I think about Tracy, who is Union High royalty—she's more on the map with The Sharp List than she ever was when she was just another cheerleader. I wonder again about that question Conrad asked—which I'd been asking myself—about what Jamie saw in me.

I know he saw something—maybe he still does. I mean, he did say that he likes me. But…the time isn't right? I think that means that it's not personal. Except it's hard not to take it that way.

Robert always said I was pretty but he clearly doesn't think that anymore. Either he didn't know what he was talking about, or he just didn't know what pretty was until he met Holly. My dad always said I was pretty, too. But what if he just said that to make me feel good about myself? Isn't that what parents do for their kids—build them up even if they don't deserve it?

I close my closet door and force myself to check my email.

There's Tracy's message—subject line: "URGENT!"—and a message with a photo attachment from Vicky.

There's also a message alerting me to a new posting on my dad's site.

When I see that, I get excited—there have been no new postings on Dad's site for a long time. But when I click on the link, the post is just a bunch of gibberish code. That's never happened before. I wonder if I got hacked. I log in with my administrator password and delete it.

It pisses me off that no one's posting on Dad's site. Has everyone forgotten him? One-year anniversaries are a big deal but after that, life goes on, I guess.

When I open Vicky's message, "Monster Mash" blasts from the speakers and the photo pops open. It's Vicky with a huge beehive hairdo, a fake mole above her lip and cat-eye glasses. Underneath the picture it says, Just getting ready for Halloween. What are YOU going to be, Sugar?

I write back, Not doing Halloween this year. I already feel like enough of a freak show. You look AWESOME though! I hit send.

Then I open Tracy's email. The post is a big one—she's been building buzz about it on her site for days. It shows Tracy's top three favorite designers and the top three most fashionable students at Union High, rocking looks that Tracy feels have a lot in common with her favorite designers. As I'm looking at pictures of Kristin, Holly and a pretty freshman who I've never even talked to, I realize that I haven't ever been on The Sharp List.

Not once.

All our friends have been on it at least once if not two or three times—and Tracy herself is on it all the time—but I haven't made it on. Not even when I'm wearing an outfit that she put together herself.

Maybe the reason I haven't made it onto The Sharp List has

more to do with my face—and my status at Union High—than my clothes.

I double click on the PSAT program and try to concentrate on a practice test, but there's just too much happening in my brain.

Screw the stupid PSAT. I'm not taking the test tomorrow.

I crawl onto my bed, grab my phone and jam my headphones into my ears. I'm listening to Adele—who has a totally *unique* voice—and I have what might be called an epiphany.

Opera singers don't have to blend.

Rock stars don't have to blend.

And after I finish this musical, I don't have to, either.

WINTER

reprisal *(noun):* retaliation
(see also: Conrad's surprise*)*

9

"DIRK TAYLOR?" MY MOTHER EXCLAIMS, BLUSHING TO the roots of her hair. She awkwardly tries to juggle the winter coat draped over her arm and the bag on her shoulder as Holly's dad shakes her hand and gives her his million-dollar megawatt smile. "I certainly didn't expect to meet you at the opening night of a high school musical." She shakes her head a little in disbelief. "I'm such a fan of your films."

It annoys me that everyone insists on referring to Dirk Taylor's movies as *films.*

Also, what *films* are we talking about? He doesn't even look familiar to me.

Well, maybe he does, a little. He's probably one of those actors who gets small parts in everything and so while he's totally recognizable, no one can name a single movie he's ever done.

"I really thought you should have won for *Rain in Spring.* Or for *Getting Out Good.* Or actually, for any of the movies you were nominated for," my mother gushes.

Okay, so women my mother's age can name his movies.

Wait—nominated? This guy is an Oscar nominee?

"Look at your mother," Tracy whispers in my ear. "She's totally blushing—so cute! How awesome that she's wearing her favorite outfit today."

As Dirk Taylor stares appreciatively at my mother's pencil skirt with his camera-ready, piercing blue eyes, I wish she'd chosen to wear something different.

"Do you live here?" my mother asks, clearly puzzled by the presence of a movie star in Union, of all places. I notice that he is still holding her hand and she's not making any attempt to get it back. Holly—who is standing next to her dad, holding the biggest bouquet of flowers I have ever seen in my life—notices my mother's response, too, and she grins at me in a conspiratorial way that I find alarming.

"Dad and I moved here this summer, Mrs. Zarelli," Holly says. "He's teaching at the Yale Drama School this year."

"Well, talent certainly runs in the family, Holly. Your performance was extraordinary. What a lovely voice you have!" my mother says.

My mother is complimenting Holly on her performance without having said a single word to me about mine. So what if Passenger #3 only had two solo lines? No small parts, only small actors, right?

Of course, she didn't really get a chance to say anything at all before she was blindsided by Dork Taylor, who, by the way, is *still* holding her hand.

"Holly's amazing, isn't she?" Robert says as he comes out of the boys' dressing room, his red scarf carefully wrapped around his throat as if he might "catch a chill" in the hallway. Tracy takes out her iPhone and snaps a picture.

"Are you kidding?" I whisper.

She solemnly shakes her head. "That thing is three-ply cashmere."

"Robert!" my mother exclaims. "I had no idea you were so talented! You were just magical up there!"

She's not wrong—he is pretty amazing in the show. Robert looks so happy I think he might burst. "Thanks, Mrs. Z.," he says, giving her a little bow.

I'm still waiting for her to say something to me.

"Great show, son," Dirk says, finally letting go of my mother's hand to shake Robert's. Robert's voice drops about an octave. He gives Holly's dad the manliest handshake he can manage and says, "Thanks, Dirk," as if he's been calling Dirk Taylor by his first name for years. "I couldn't have done it without my leading lady," he adds.

Robert gives Holly a kiss on the cheek. My mother watches for just a second too long, then looks at me.

My mother has always liked Robert, despite his history of lying. I think she was probably hoping that someday he'd get his life together and we'd end up dating. But I'm sure she's thinking now that I missed my chance. Because of course there's no way I could ever compete with the daughter of Dirk Taylor.

"Honey, you did a great job," she finally says to me, giving me a hug with one arm and squeezing me against her. "You looked like you were really having fun."

"A show is nothing without a good supporting cast," Dirk adds, nodding.

For a split second, while the charm and charisma are directed at me, I feel all warm and gushy and…special. But I know it's an act and I refuse to fall for it like the group of mothers that is now standing around us, desperate to be part of our conversation, edging in closer and closer, making me feel claustrophobic.

"Excellent dancing, Rose," Dirk continues. "And you have a great ear for harmony and a remarkably strong voice. I could pick you out in every number."

So much for blending.

Holly jumps in. "What he means is that you sounded fantastic."

Dirk looks puzzled. "Well, of course that's what I mean! It's an amazing thing to have such an unusual voice. Why would you want to sound like everyone else?"

I don't want to sound like everyone else, Dork. And as soon as this musical is over, I won't be trying to sound like everyone else ever again.

"Mr. Taylor? A photo, please?" says a reporter from the *Union Chronicle*. He must have been tipped off about the Taylors. I don't think the *Chronicle* has ever cared about an opening night at Union High before.

"Actually, this is my daughter's night, so I'd prefer not to," Dirk replies, sounding oddly proud of himself considering all he's doing is turning down an opportunity to be photographed for a small-town newspaper.

"How about you and your daughter together?" the reporter asks. He isn't about to miss out on the biggest scoop to hit town in, oh, probably twenty years.

"It's okay, Dad. I don't mind," Holly tells him quietly.

"Are you sure, honey?" he asks, looking concerned.

"It's fine," she assures him with a hint of disappointment in her eyes that her father misses because he's too busy looking for his spotlight.

And he's not the only one. Robert turns toward the camera like a heat-seeking missile, oblivious to the fact that his girlfriend might not want to have her picture taken just because she's Dirk Taylor's daughter—especially after she just performed a lead role in a show totally brilliantly.

"Okay, then, let's do it," Dirk says. My mother and I step back as the reporter moves in. Dirk puts his arm around Holly, trapping her beautiful hair. She reaches up to free it and suddenly

I remember how my dad used to tell me I was lucky I got my mother's hair and not his, like Peter did.

My dad would have loved seeing me play Passenger #3, no matter how I felt about the whole thing. If everything had gone according to his plan, he would have been back by now, and he and my mother would probably be talking to Dirk Taylor together, in a welcome-to-the-neighborhood way.

Instead of Dirk talking to my mother in an I-like-your-pencil-skirt way.

Dirk holds up a hand as the reporter gets ready to take the picture. "Kathleen, Rose, please join us. The photo will be so much nicer with you lovely ladies in it."

This guy's good—he and Holly have the same classy manners. But if you're paying close attention, you can see just how calculated his are.

After some more cajoling from Dirk, my mother steps into the photo. I stay on the sidelines, though Tracy tries to shove me forward, whispering in my ear something about a once-in-a-lifetime photo op. Dirk pulls my mother close and puts his arm around her waist, making her blush again, which makes him laugh. Robert positions himself between Holly and Dirk with his arms around both of them. Holly smiles her picture-perfect smile, but as the surrounding crowd gets bigger and more camera phones are pulled out of pockets and purses, her smile starts to look fake. It's not an expression I'm used to seeing on Holly, who seems so comfortable all the time.

Dirk Taylor is seriously an idiot. He has no idea how Holly feels right now. He's too busy thinking about himself.

I back away and start toward the dressing room to get my stuff.

"Rose freakin' Zarelli! Whatup, Sweater?"

I turn around, and even though I'd know that voice anywhere, I barely recognize Angelo—he looks like a different person now than he did last year.

Angelo is Jamie's best friend. He calls me Sweater because when I first met him in study hall at the beginning of freshman year, I was wearing a sweater even though it was still, like, ninety degrees out.

I was actually scared of him. He looked like he was about twenty and he had long, greasy hair, and every day he wore a different metal-band concert T-shirt drenched in Axe. But one day, he showed up in a Neko Case shirt—she's only the best singer-songwriter ever—and things changed. We started talking about music. I found out he was in a band called Fuck This Shit—which he renamed FTS when he realized how much easier it was to get hired without the F-word on his fliers—and Angelo and I became friends.

Angelo and his band went on a six-month tour that they put together themselves right after graduation, and now the long, greasy hair is gone. There's no concert T-shirt under his slick black leather jacket. He's wearing blue-black jeans, Doc Marten's and a gray sweater with a big industrial-size zipper down the front. Considering that the last time I saw him, he was wearing a tuxedo that was at least one size too small for him and his hair probably hadn't been washed in a week, I would say that being a real musician agrees with Angelo.

He grabs me in a big hug and spins me around and around. I can't stop laughing even though I'm getting so dizzy I might throw up. I've missed Angelo.

When we finally stop spinning and he puts me down, he has to hold on to me for a few seconds so I don't go crashing into the wall. But I'm not so dizzy that I can't see Jamie coming through the door at the end of the hall near the girls' dressing room.

Every time I see Jamie after not seeing him for a while, I feel like I'm in seventh grade again, watching him play hockey, unable to take my eyes off him. But I feel something different now, on top of the thrill and the attraction, and it takes me a second to figure out what it is.

It's fear.

Not fear of him—fear *for* him.

I'm worried about Jamie. There's so much I don't know about his life, and what exactly he's doing for the Deladdos.

"Good job, Rose," Jamie says. Before I know it, he leans forward and kisses me on the cheek, and I can smell that clean-laundry scent I love. I reach up to hug him but he's already pulling away by the time I get my arms around his neck. We both sort of freeze, and awkwardly disengage and step back from each other. I notice he's got his phone in one hand, and he's turning it over and over.

"Yeah, good job!" Angelo whacks me on the shoulder and grins. He moves closer and whispers too loudly, "But musicals? Come on, man! You gotta get a band!"

"Wait, really? You think I could—"

The crowd that has gathered around the Taylors laughs at something Dirk says, and Jamie and Angelo look past me to see what's going on.

"Hey, that's that guy...that guy from...that thing," Angelo says. "What's he doin' here?"

"He's Holly's dad," I answer. Angelo looks at me blankly. "Holly, with the dark hair, who was in the show?"

"Oh, yeah. She was hot," Angelo says thoughtfully, as if he is the first person to make this observation. "But where's the redhead? She was, like, *smokin'* hot."

He looks around the hallway for Stephanie, who is for sure still in the dressing room. No one takes longer to get out of costume than her. It's her first starring role and already she's learned the art of making her public wait.

"You mean Steph?" Clearly Angelo has no idea who he was

watching during the show—I'm guessing he's not much of a program reader. "You remember her from last year, right?"

Angelo looks blank again for a second, and then his jaw practically hits the floor. *"That* was Steph?"

More camera flashes go off.

"Your mom knows that guy?" Jamie asks.

I turn to look at Mom again. Dirk's arm is still wrapped around her waist. Whatever he's saying now is just for her, and it makes her laugh.

The truth is, I haven't seen my mother have fun in a long time, so part of me is happy for her, but it gets squashed by the part that is super annoyed that she—along with every other woman in the hallway—is buying Holly's dad's act.

I can't believe that my mother is so susceptible to this cheeseball.

"No, she just met him," I answer, turning away so I don't have to watch anymore. "What are you guys doing here?"

"Whaddya mean, what're we doin' here? We came to see *you!*" Angelo says. "You totally rocked that one line they gave ya."

I roll my eyes. "Two, Angelo. I had two."

"Seriously!" Angelo insists. "You got killer cords. And you been holdin' out on me."

"Angelo Martinez?" says Tracy, extracting herself from the throng of adoring fans surrounding the Taylors. "There's no way *you* are Angelo Martinez."

"Yo, Trace, up high!" Angelo grins, putting his hand up for a high five. "Hey, where's that awesome little cheerleader outfit you used to wear?"

"I've moved on from polyester-spandex blends," Tracy says, giving Angelo the high five he's waiting for and then reaching out to inspect the funky zipper pull on his sweater.

"Whoa, Trace, you gotta take me to dinner first," Angelo says, looking down at her with amusement as she tests the zipper, sliding it up and down.

She doesn't even hear him. "Can I take your picture? The Sharp List is doing a special post on transformations. You would be perfect, if we can find pictures of you with that crazy hair from last year," Tracy says.

"My hair last year was rad!" Angelo looks both offended and confused. "What's a Sharp List?"

"Have you been living under a rock?" Tracy scolds as she pulls out her phone to show Angelo her website. She gives me a quick look that means I should take advantage of the opportunity to talk to Jamie in semiprivate.

Since the conversation a few weeks ago that left Jamie and me in a weird limbo, I've been driving Tracy a little crazy. She keeps asking why Jamie and I aren't together, if we had as nice a time on our date as I keep telling her we did. I tell her that he said it's just not the right time, and she tells me that I need clarification—what exactly did he mean by that?

I can't tell her that I already have clarification. Once again, I'm in a situation in which I have to keep a secret from her, even though we aren't supposed to be keeping secrets from each other anymore.

But Jamie asked me not to tell anyone about Mr. Deladdo, and I won't.

This past Thanksgiving, Mom and I went to Tracy's house with Stephanie and her mom. Before we ate at the beautiful table that Tracy's interior-decorator mom set with crystal and china—and a centerpiece made of real leaves from the maple trees in their backyard—Tracy's dad said grace.

I usually get nervous when people do religious stuff because we never do it at home, but I can handle saying grace at Thanksgiving. Mr. Gerren asked us all to think of something we were grateful for, something we couldn't imagine our lives without, and

I immediately thought of Jamie. And then I wondered, if Jamie is the first person I thought of, why am I keeping my distance just because he said I should, when maybe he could use my help?

"Rose?" Jamie says. He smiles but his eyes look tired. He's flipping the phone over in his hand faster now, and I realize that he's waiting for a phone call. Probably from Regina. "You sounded good up there."

I scoff. It's embarrassing to have people tell you that you were good when you were in the chorus. I mean, who watches the chorus?

"What, you don't believe me?"

I shrug. "It's nice of you to say, but, you know, I just have a small part."

"Yeah, but I could hear you."

I almost tell him that that means I didn't do it right, but instead, I move closer to him and angle myself so that no one will be able to hear what I'm about to say.

"I can't stop thinking about what you told me, Jamie."

His gaze scans behind me before his eyes settle back on mine, giving me what I assume is permission to continue talking about this.

"Were you—were you scared? When you did what you did?" His eyes seem to soften a tiny bit, but he doesn't answer. "It's just, I'm worried, about you, and about what you're doing. Shouldn't you maybe not be so close to the Deladdos—"

I don't get to finish the question. "Things are bad for them."

"How could things be worse for them now than before you did what you did?"

"Don't worry about—"

When Jamie's phone rings, he steps away from me so fast it's like he got an electric shock or something. He holds up his hand in apology as he listens. Then Angelo looks up, and Jamie nods at Angelo over my head, waving him over. He puts his phone back in his pocket and says, "I gotta go. You were great, Rose."

"Yeah, man, you were awesome," Angelo says. "And Trace, if I'm gonna be, like, the star model on your blog, email my agent. He's gonna want his ten percent."

Angelo winks at Tracy, and he and Jamie go down the hallway. I have a bad feeling about whatever it is they're going to do. A really bad feeling.

"Hey, Rose!" Angelo yells when they get to the door. "Tell the redhead I say she's totally hot. Tell her I'm gonna be on Tracy's thing, okay? And give her my number!"

"Where are they going?" Tracy asks as they disappear through the door.

I shake my head. It used to be exciting when Jamie walked away from me without answering my questions. Then it became annoying. But tonight, it's actually scary. Jamie and Angelo have some sort of plan, and I'll bet anything it has to do with Regina and Anthony.

"Girls," my mother calls to Tracy and me. "The Taylors have invited us all out for dessert at Morton's. Would you like to go?" she asks, looking directly at me, clearly hoping that I'm going to say yes.

The idea of spending any more time watching Dirk Taylor get his picture taken just to inflate his ego and impress my mother while Robert inserts himself into every photo op sounds so gross that I might throw up right here. I want to say no, but Tracy throws an elbow into my ribs and answers for me.

"That sounds great, Mrs. Zarelli. Thanks, Mr. Taylor," she says graciously, trying to make up for the scowl on my face. "We'll just go get Rose's stuff and meet you at Morton's in a few minutes. Let's *go*, Rose," she says before I can open my mouth.

I gape at Tracy but she doesn't have to utter a word for me to hear her saying, *Your mother deserves some fun. Don't be a bitch.*

Robert tightens his scarf around his throat, buttons his jacket and takes Holly's mittened hand in his. Dirk makes a show of bending over to pick up the leather glove my mother dropped and then escorts her out the door—his hand on her elbow—into the cold December night. I've never seen any man but my father take my mother's arm, and it's hard not to give Dirk Taylor a shove that will send him sprawling onto the icy sidewalk, and tell him that the last thing in the world my heartbroken mother needs is some movie star messing with her head while grief for my dad obviously has her so confused she doesn't know what's real and what's fake.

If my dad could see her right now, what would he do? What would he say?

Can he see her right now?

I hope not, for his sake.

Just as I feel tears coming, Tracy slips her arm through mine and says, "She's a big girl. She can handle it."

Well, I'm glad somebody can.

"*You* told her we would go, Trace. I didn't. I didn't say anything about having dessert with Dork Taylor."

Tracy pulls up to the stoplight at the parking lot exit and puts on the right-turn signal. "Rosie, don't be like that. He's not that bad."

I see the dessert caravan about a block away, heading to Morton's. I suddenly know that I am not going. Even if I have to open the door and throw myself out of a moving car.

"He's not that *bad?* He's so cheesy, it's embarrassing."

"I think he's kind of charming."

Of course you do. Because he's going to look great on your blog. I pointlessly kick at the bunched-up floor mat under my feet, trying to flatten it out, even though I know there are magazines living under there.

"Rosie, your mom will be hurt if we don't go."

"Mr. Hollywood will make her feel better. Oh, my god. You don't think he named Holly after Hollywood, do you? Because that would be pathetic."

"Let's just go to Morton's for a few minutes and then leave, okay?"

"Trace, I don't want to watch my mother flirt with that asshole."

Tracy is quiet—my swearing probably surprised her. Swearing is not my favorite mode of expression—my dad drilled into our heads the concept that there is always a better, more expressive word than a swearword—but I have to admit that swearing feels good sometimes. And if you do it sparingly, it really gets people's attention.

After a pause, Tracy says with that annoying calm that she seems to have mastered this year, "Your mom wasn't doing the flirting. Dirk Taylor was."

"It takes two," I grumble.

"You know what, Rosie? You're being selfish."

Tracy might as well have just slapped me. "*I'm* being selfish? My dad's been dead for a year and a half! That's *eighteen* months! And she's already…she's already…"

I can't finish the sentence or I'll start crying.

Usually when I get into irrational mode about my mother—or crying mode over my father—Tracy is helpful and nice and knows just what to say.

But not this time.

"She's already what, Rose? Talking to a guy? Letting him pick up something she dropped? Going out for dessert with him and a bunch of other people?"

"Getting her picture taken with his arm around her for everyone in the world to see!" I snap.

I grab the iPod that's plugged into the car's sound system and start scrolling.

Willow...Sugarland...Neon Trees...

Tracy's taste in music drives me crazy sometimes.

Ke$ha...Enrique Iglesias...

Eminem with Rihanna. Perfect.

There's nothing like Eminem when you're pissed off. His fury reaches through the speakers and jams itself down your throat. You can practically taste it. He always sounds like he's half a second away from punching someone. I like that.

That's the kind of singer I want to be—not some stupid chorus girl in a musical going "la la la" in harmony.

I wonder: Can a girl sing the way Eminem raps?

I turn the volume up so loud it feels like my ears are going to bleed. Tracy uses the volume control on the steering wheel to turn it down, but she leaves it just loud enough.

She's about to turn right out of the parking lot and start toward Morton's—and I'm trying to figure out the safest way to launch myself out of a moving car—when Jamie's car flies by, heading in the other direction.

I lean forward, watching his taillights. Before I can say anything, Tracy looks at me in disbelief. "You can't be serious."

"*You* wanted to know where they were going."

"First of all, you're the one who wants to know where they're going. I couldn't care less. Second of all—"

A car behind us honks, annoyed that we're sitting still at a green light.

"If you follow them so we can find out where they're going, I'll come to Morton's," I lie.

"We shouldn't be anywhere near wherever they're going."

"What's that supposed to mean?" I ask.

I resent the implication that Jamie and Angelo are automatically up to no good, just because of who they are. Although in this case, I know Tracy's right—something's going on, and we *should* stay away from it.

The car honks again, longer this time.

"They've both been arrested at least once. That's all I'm saying."

"Five minutes. Then Morton's."

Tracy sighs dramatically, like I'm asking for the moon. Then she switches her turn signal and guns the Prius, flying out into the intersection.

I calm down as the possibility of dessert at Morton's gets farther and farther away in the rearview mirror.

I grab the iPod again and turn up the volume, leaning back into the seat as the angriest voice on the planet drills into my brain. Caron says I'm not supposed to indulge my anger without trying to understand it.

Caron can go F herself.

For a while, Tracy just looks bored and annoyed as we follow the guys into the rich part of town. She's just about to say she's not going to follow them anymore when we turn onto Matt Hallis's block.

That's when things get interesting.

Jamie and Angelo pull up in front of Matt's house. It's a beautiful, huge colonial with white lights in the pine trees on either side of the front door and garlands stretched across the top of the portico. There's a massive Christmas tree in one of the front windows, and the colored lights reflect off the hood of Matt's white sports car, which is sitting in the driveway. There are a bunch of other cars I sort of recognize—it looks like the swim team is hanging out at Matt's tonight.

Without talking, Tracy turns off her headlights and we idle in her silent Prius by the curb a few houses away. I sink a little lower in my seat as we watch Jamie and Angelo get out of their car, but they're focused on someone with a backpack who comes out to meet them from behind the bushes separating the Hallis property from the neighbors.

The three of them talk for a few seconds, and then Jamie holds up his hands and shakes his head as if he's disagreeing with something. He and Angelo step back as the figure drops the backpack to the ground and starts to rifle through it. When the figure stands up and moves out of the shadows, the overhead streetlight reveals Conrad, holding a can of spray paint.

He shakes the can hard for a few seconds and motions to Jamie and Angelo. Jamie crosses his arms and looks down at the ground, then slowly turns to face the house. Angelo faces the street. It's like they're standing guard.

Which—I realize as Conrad takes the top off the can and starts to spray-paint Matt's car—is exactly what they're doing.

"Oh, my god," Tracy says. "They are going to kill him this time—*for real* kill him."

We're far enough away that we can't see what Conrad's doing, but whatever it is, it must be elaborate because it's taking a long time. When a minivan turns onto the street, Conrad ducks down behind Matt's car while Angelo lights a cigarette and pretends to be having a normal conversation with Jamie. When the minivan passes, Conrad jumps back up and grabs another can of spray paint from his backpack and the guys go back to their posts.

Conrad climbs onto the hood of the car to work on the roof, leaning forward and lying on the windshield to reach every inch of it. The light from the streetlamps illuminates him in his black sweatshirt, his hood pulled up over his head, his arm working furiously—a pissed-off graffiti artist trying to finish before he gets caught.

When he's finally done, he jumps off the hood and jams everything in his backpack. He heads toward Jamie's car with Jamie and Angelo, then stops short, runs back to Matt's car, climbs on the hood and jumps up and down until the car alarm goes off.

Jamie and Angelo freeze for a second and then sprint to Jamie's car and climb inside. Jamie starts it up, yelling out the window at Conrad who leaps off the hood of Matt's car. Conrad is barely in the backseat before Jamie hits the gas. I see him struggling to get the back door closed without falling out as they round the corner.

"Go, Trace," I say, my voice barely more than a whisper.

As we zoom past Matt's driveway with the headlights off, we can see—in huge, black block lettering on the hood, the roof and the sides of the once-perfect, shiny white sports car—the words *faggot*, *fag* and *homo*.

novice *(noun):* beginner
(see also: first time for everything*)*

10

"ROSE, WOULD YOU PASS THE WINE TO DIRK, PLEASE?"

I'd rather pour the wine directly on my mother's beautiful white linen tablecloth and watch it spread like a bloodstain in a mob movie than pass it to Dirk. But I fight the urge to mess with this dinner that my mother—who pretty much hasn't stopped smiling since she met Mr. Hollywood—has been planning for days.

My mother invited the Taylors to Christmas Eve at our house under the guise of being a good neighbor. "They probably don't know a lot of people in town yet and it might be nice for them to celebrate with new friends," she'd said by way of explanation, as if half of Yale University hadn't been clamoring to spend the holiday with a movie star.

But—lucky us—Dirk chose to accept my mother's invitation.

I pick up the bottle and try to hand it to Dirk, who is sitting to my right. Robert—who apparently is now part of the Taylor family and goes wherever they go—is sitting on the other side of Dirk. He reaches across Dirk, nearly knocking over a candle, and takes the bottle from me. He pours, because, of course, Dirk can't possibly be expected to pour for himself.

"Jingle Bells" plays on the iPod dock in the living room.

If I weren't so tired, I'd be way more annoyed than I am. But I was awake half the night, freaked out, depressed, frustrated and furious—freaked out about Conrad, who I think, based on what I found online at three in the morning, may have committed a felony; depressed about Jamie, who hasn't called me back even though I've left him two messages saying that I know what happened and I need to talk to him; frustrated that no one has posted any comments or messages on Dad's site for weeks now; and furious that my brother still hasn't called or emailed to say whether he is going to bother coming home for Christmas.

One of those alone would be enough to keep me awake. All four nearly drove me insane. And now I feel like I might just crash right here at the table. Or under it.

"Rose," Dirk says in that baritone voice that makes me all itchy, "are you interested in film at all?"

I consider saying no so that the conversation will end before it even starts, but when Robert's head snaps up from his plate in sheer panic, I suddenly want to find out what Dirk is talking about.

"I like movies," I say noncommittally, stifling a well-timed, completely spontaneous yawn.

"Ooh, Rose, you should totally come to our film club! That's a great idea!" Holly says, looking perfect in a cranberry-red sweater with extra-long bell sleeves that Tracy would take a picture of in a heartbeat. "You, too, Mrs. Zarelli! It's so fun."

"Holly, please, call me Kathleen." My mother smiles uncomfortably. I guess hearing her married name doesn't go that well with making dinner for a man who's not my dad.

I don't know how long I'm going to be able to stand all this. I yawn again.

"What a great idea! Kathleen, you and Rose should come. Every Thursday night my students and I watch an award-winning film and discuss it."

Dirk smiles hopefully at me as if he actually cares whether I join the film club, and because of all that oozing charisma, I almost fall for it. But I know he's just thinking that if I join, my mother's more likely to join, too. And then he'll have the perfect excuse to spend even more time with her.

Robert, on the other hand, looks totally freaked by the possibility that I might join the film club. In a moment of Christmas spirit, I see things from Robert's point of view and feel sorry for him. The Taylors are the closest thing Robert has had to a family in a long time. I'm sure the last thing he wants is to have someone around who could potentially destroy that for him.

Well, luckily for Robert, my desire to keep my mother away from Dirk is much stronger than my desire to get back at Robert for lying about me.

"So what do you think, Rose?" Dirk says.

"Would we be watching your movies?" I ask, trying to sound as innocent as possible. My mother gives me the sternest glance she can muster without being obvious, but Dirk just laughs.

"If we only watched my award-winning films, Rose, the club would have ended after one week."

"That's not true, Dad. You've been in movies that have won Oscars, BAFTAs and Palme D'ors," Holly says, beaming at Dirk, looking genuinely proud.

I've never seen Holly look at her dad like this, and it surprises me because I thought she found the whole Hollywood thing to be a bummer. As I watch Dirk put his arm around her and give her a squeeze, loss crushes me.

I haven't felt this in a while. I haven't had the chance. Thinking about Dad has usually meant fighting off horrific images in my head, so I haven't let myself think about him that much. But grief for the man who should be sitting next to me at the table—where Dirk Taylor is sitting instead—is about to fill up my lungs and drown me in front of everyone.

I stand up to bail just as we all hear the sound of a key unlocking the front door.

My mother freezes. I can see her taking mental inventory of the family and realizing that there's only one person who could be unlocking the front door on Christmas Eve. Her face lights up with hope.

I get to the door about five seconds ahead of my mother, just in time to see Peter standing there, looking like he hasn't eaten all semester.

Tracy is next to him, fidgeting.

I blink. I don't understand why Tracy's here. Next to Peter.

"Peter!" my mother exclaims, sounding happy, mad and worried all at once.

"Merry Christmas, Mom," he says, leaning over to give her a hug. He's still got the super-dark shadows under his eyes that he had this summer, but at least his eyes aren't glazed over. They're surprisingly clear.

Over Mom's shoulder, as he continues to hug her because she won't let him go, Peter is studying my face in the same way that I've been studying his. "Hey, Rosie. You look like you're falling asleep standing up."

My head is going to explode. How can he just talk to me like that, after totally blowing me off since September? I ignore him and turn to Tracy.

"What are *you* doing here?"

I sound way angrier than I intend to, and she looks taken aback. "I just… I was on my way over to talk to you and I ran into Peter in front of the house."

Peter looks down at her and gives her a small smile. "It's good to see you, Trace."

What? I look like I'm falling asleep standing up but it's good to see *her?*

"Hello, there. You must be Peter," comes Dirk's voice from behind us. "I've heard a lot about you." He extends his hand into our happy little group to offer one of those manly handshakes of his.

Peter's expression goes from confusion to recognition to surprise and back to confusion as he shakes Dirk's hand. "Uh, hi," he replies eloquently.

"Peter, this is Dirk Taylor. He and his daughter, Holly, are new to town and they're having dinner with us tonight. Holly is one of Rose's classmates," my mother explains, leaving out the whole movie-star thing. "We were just about to have dessert. Why don't you two come sit down?"

My mother says this as if it's the most normal thing in the world to say "you two," meaning Peter and Tracy.

"Actually, Mom, I need to talk to you," Peter says. "You, too, Rose."

"Kathleen, we'll clear the dishes and get dessert ready. Take your time. Nice to meet you, Peter."

"Likewise, Mr. Taylor," Peter says, looking slightly awestruck. Barf, barf, *barf.*

"Here, take off your things," my mother says. When Peter takes off his hat, his crazy hair springs out and he suddenly looks more like Dad than ever. I practically have to step back from him. My mother also sees it—I can tell by the way she stares before she takes his coat and hat.

Nothing wrong with my mom being reminded of Dad while Dirk Taylor is washing dishes in her kitchen.

Tracy, still next to Peter, is now shifting from foot to foot, her high-heeled boots clacking on the floor, her long, striped scarf tied in a perfect knot around her neck.

"I came to talk to you about something, Rose, but I'll just call you later," she says hesitantly, obviously not wanting to leave.

"No, Trace, it's okay. Stay." Peter gives her another one of those smiles and I suddenly know that whatever bad thing Peter's about to tell us, Tracy already knows.

I realize that the hard pinch I've been feeling in my stomach since the front door opened is jealousy.

I've been mad at my best friend, and I've been hurt by my best friend, but there's something about this that feels worse. Way worse.

The four of us go into the living room, my mom still oblivious to the fact that Peter's about to run her over with a freight train.

"Mom, I have to take a semester off," Peter says before she's even sitting down.

Her smile slides right off her face.

"No, that's not a good idea, Peter. Structure is good for you right now."

I nearly laugh out loud. What *structure* is she referring to, exactly? The structure of partying every night and then sleeping through class? The structure of doing serious drugs with his girlfriend? *That* structure?

"It's not…optional," Peter says.

My mother looks puzzled but I get it instantly. I wait to see if Peter is going to elaborate but he's too chicken to do it so I step in.

"What he's saying, Mom, is that he got kicked out of school."

"That is not what I'm saying," Peter replies, irritated. "I've just been asked to take a semester off."

"Why?" my mother says.

"Because he's been partying instead of studying," I answer. I can't help myself.

"Rose, stop answering for your brother."

"Tell her I'm wrong, Peter," I challenge, not looking at my mother.

For a second, it seems like Peter's going to tell me to F-off, but he shakes his head slowly.

"You're not wrong," he admits.

"Rose Zarelli," my mother says, turning on me. "You lied to me."

He just got kicked out of school and she's mad at *me*?

I jump up off the couch, outraged. "*I* lied? What are you— How do you even—"

"You've been telling me for months that you haven't talked to Peter!"

"She hasn't, Mrs. Zarelli," Tracy says in my defense, even though it's not true. "I know she hasn't."

The sound of Tracy's voice in the middle of a private family conversation infuriates me.

"Why are you even here?"

"She's defending you, Rose," Peter says. "Don't be such a bitch."

"Peter!" my mother shouts.

Our resident movie star leans into the room from the doorway. "Kathleen? Is everything okay?"

He looks at her with an expression of grave concern that he's probably perfected over the years by practicing in a mirror.

My mother, horrifically embarrassed, swallows and smiles. "Fine, Dirk. We're just settling a disagreement. I'll be there in a minute."

With another perfectly executed look, this one of sympathy, Dirk disappears into the kitchen, where it sounds like Holly and Robert are loading the dishwasher.

The exhaustion-rage combo is making me feel wired— everything seems surreal. My eyes land on my phone, which is sitting on the coffee table where I left it during the excruciating hors d'oeuvre course.

"If you haven't been in touch with Peter, how do you know what happened?" my mother asks.

If Peter hadn't called me a bitch, I might not be so ready to show her what's on my phone.

But he *did* call me a bitch.

I grab my phone and see that I missed three text messages from Tracy earlier. I go straight to the photos. I sit down next to my mother and show her the one image of Peter's that I kept. Her face goes pale.

Peter, recognizing his old iPhone, jumps up. "What are you doing?"

He grabs my hand and twists the phone toward him so he can see what I'm showing her.

It's the photo of Peter and Amanda leaning across a coffee table toward each other with those weird little straws in their hands.

Everything goes quiet while we all process what's happening.

Peter sits down on the other side of my mother, staring daggers at me over her head.

"I asked you to erase my photos."

"Why would you give me your phone with *that* on it?" I shoot back.

My mother's hands fly to her mouth and she closes her eyes.

"Everything's going to be fine, Mom. I just have to take some time off, but they'll let me go back. Don't worry about it."

"Don't worry about it?" she says. She snatches the phone out of my hand and shoves the picture in Peter's face. "Are you addicted?"

Peter scoffs. "It's college, Mom. Don't be ridiculous."

"Don't call her ridiculous!" I say. "You don't think we knew what was wrong with you when you were home this summer? You've been going out with that junkie for—"

"She's not a—" Peter stops himself. "God, Rosie, sometimes I forget just how young you really are. Go help in the kitchen, okay? I need to talk to Mom alone."

Steam practically comes out of my ears.

"*Young?* You're the one who's doing drugs just to impress a girl who is out of your fucking league!"

"Rose!" my mother says, unaccustomed to hearing me drop the F-bomb. "It's Christmas Eve!" she adds, as if this has some relevance.

Right on cue, the Christmas carol playlist goes back to the beginning and "Jingle Bells" starts again.

Peter looks over at Tracy, who stands up as if he has just communicated with her telepathically.

"I have to talk to you, Rosie. Please?" Tracy pleads.

Without answering her, I grab my phone from my mother and stomp up to my room, knowing that Peter somehow enlisted *my* best friend to help him deliver this news, and that she is on *his* side. Tracy follows me and stands in the doorway looking guilty. It's all I can do not to slam the door in her face.

"Why do you know about this? Have you been talking to him behind my back?" I demand.

"I came over because you weren't answering your phone," Tracy says slowly, like I could snap at any second. "When I got here, Peter was getting out of his car. We talked for a few minutes."

She hasn't answered either of my questions. She's also not telling me to stop being paranoid, which is what she usually says when she thinks I'm out of control.

"What did he tell you? Or are you not supposed to say anything?" I spit out angrily.

"He said that Amanda's dad pulled her out of school and sent her to rehab, and told the dean that Peter needed help, too."

I turn away and smack my computer keyboard to bring up the screen—anything to shut her out. My email pops up and there's a new message from Vicky titled "Reindeers Rock!!!!" I click on it, and there's a picture of her with huge fuzzy antlers on. They stick out of the mass of gigantic curls piled on top of her head at crazy angles. Her message is just two lines long: *Tried to post on your site. Did it crash cuz there were lotsa holiday messages for your pops?*

My site's not down—is it? I type in the URL and it comes right up.

"Rose," Tracy says, exasperated, trying to get my attention. "Matt called me."

I'm still trying to figure out why Vicky thinks my site is down when Tracy's words sink in. There's only one reason Matt would call Tracy right now, and it's not to wish her a Merry Christmas.

"He saw us?" I ask, turning around.

"I don't know. But he said to tell Conrad that he's dead."

"How does he know it was Conrad?"

Tracy tilts her head at me. "Conrad might as well have signed his name."

The door to Peter's room slams shut with a bang, making both Tracy and me jump. Tracy looks over her shoulder at Peter's closed door.

"Girls! Dessert is on the table," my mother calls from downstairs, her voice tight with the strain of trying to pretend, in front of her celebrity guest, that her son did not just come home from a prestigious northeast college and announce that he's been kicked out for drug use.

"We should tell the police," Tracy says.

"That'll just get Conrad arrested, and get Jamie and Angelo in trouble, too."

"Conrad won't get arrested, not after he tells them about the party."

"It doesn't work that way," I snap. "Vandalizing a car like that? It can be considered a felony. *Why* he did it doesn't matter."

"Girls?" my mother calls again, slightly more desperate this time.

My head is starting to vibrate with exhaustion—I can't go back down there.

"Tell her to start without me. I'll call Jamie and tell him about

Matt." Tracy is about to argue with me but I cut her off. "Go check on Peter," I say, finally giving in to the urge to slam my door.

"Nice, Rose," Tracy says in the hallway.

I hear her clacking down the stairs and saying something to my mother. Then the front door opens and closes.

I guess she's not up for dessert after all.

I reach for my phone just as Vicky's name pops up on my caller ID.

"Rosalita! Merry Christmas, girl! Y'all having a white one up there?"

I love talking to Vicky. I don't even have to say anything most of the time because she's got enough to say for both of us.

"Hi, Vicky. No, no snow yet."

"You get my latest?"

"Nice antlers," I say. I sit down on the bed, and then fall backward, sinking into my comforter. It feels like the most comfortable place in the entire world.

"I worked real hard on those, honey. Made 'em just for you."

"Thanks, Vicky."

"You okay, hon? You sound blue."

"Holidays. You know."

"Oh, honey, the holidays can be meaner than a skillet full of rattlers," she says. "Hey, what's goin' on with your website? I couldn't post. Got one of those darn error messages."

"There haven't been any posts in a while. Everybody forgot."

"No way, honey. Not possible. You go on and give tech support a call. They'll tell you what's wrong. But trust me, no one forgot your daddy."

Maybe she's right. It could just be a technical glitch. Maybe so many people posted on the site that it just crashed. Although that kind of thing only happens when celebrities die and people go crazy, writing messages about how much they loved someone they never even met.

I wonder how many hits Dirk's website—which I was look-ing at around four o'clock this morning—would get if he died. Probably more than my dad's. If my dad had been a *film* actor instead of an engineer, the number of hits on his memorial site would definitely be higher.

And my mother probably wouldn't already be interested in someone else.

"Are you there, hon?"

"Yeah, sorry, Vicky."

"You missin' your pops?"

"Yeah. You miss Travis?"

"Every day. Every day. But we'll be okay, sweetie, you just re-member that. Even if it feels like you're movin' backward, time is still movin' forward and it heals all."

I can hear people at her house in the background—someone is making a racket with pots and pans.

"I gotta go fix my antlers and be nice to my guests. Now you go have yourself a good Christmas with your momma, okay? And remember that she's missin' your pops, too. God bless, honey."

By the time I hang up with Vicky, I can't get off my bed. I lie there listening to the Christmas carols playing downstairs, the clink of forks on dessert plates, and Peter on his phone in his room, probably telling Amanda what idiots my mother and I are. Dirk says something and Holly and Robert laugh, but I don't hear my mom. I try to picture her putting on a good face and entertaining them all when she's probably dying of em-barrassment that neither of her kids bothered to show up for dessert.

The mature, Christmas-y thing to do would be to go down-stairs and help her—with entertaining everybody, with clearing the table, with washing the dishes after everyone is gone.

That's what my dad would want me to do—even if she does have a crush on some other guy.

It's the last thought in my head before my eyes close without my permission.

I wake up with a start.

I forgot to call Jamie.

I grab my phone. It's 2:00 a.m. Too late to call.

But it could be an emergency.

I'll text. I write, **Matt called Tracy. He knows it was Conrad.** My finger hovers over the send button, and then taps it.

I watch my phone for a minute to see if anything's going to happen. When it doesn't, I tiptoe into the bathroom to brush my teeth and get rid of the taste of Christmas-Eve-dinner-gone-wrong. I'm halfway through when I hear my phone ping.

I run back into my room, toothpaste spilling out of my mouth and down the front of my shirt.

His reply says, **Not sleeping?**

Not really, I write back.

Can I come over? he asks.

Here we go again.

I look at my phone just to make sure I didn't read the time wrong.

I didn't. It's 2:13.

Outside? he writes before I can reply.

Back door, I text back.

Fifteen minutes later, after trying to salvage the makeup that I slept in and changing out of my toothpaste-stained shirt, I hear a car park in front of the house. I lift up the window shade a crack and see Jamie. My breath catches in my throat as I think about the last time I saw him in the middle of the night.

No way that's going to happen again.

I open my door and step into the hallway. I have no idea if

I can pull this off—the stairs to the first floor are right next to my mother's room, and I've never paid attention to whether or not they creak. I start tiptoeing down, and I'm happy to discover that these stairs are practically silent compared to the ones at Tracy's house.

I pause for a second to see if anyone else is up, but the house is silent. I slip through the living room and the kitchen to the back door, and there he is, underneath the brightest stars I've ever seen, wearing his army jacket and no hat or gloves, even though it's twenty degrees outside. He doesn't even look cold.

Carefully, quietly, I unlock the back door and hold it open for him. He doesn't move.

"I can come in?" he asks.

"Yeah," I whisper. "We just have to be quiet."

He still doesn't move.

"What's wrong?"

"I don't wanna get you into trouble," he says.

"It's fine."

"Not if you're having me come in the back door, it's not."

I shiver as the cold air pours in through the open door. "It's just, my mom wouldn't like you being here."

He jams his hands in his pockets. "That's why you wouldn't let me pick you up."

I'm puzzled for a second. The date—he's talking about the date.

When I see it through Jamie's eyes, I realize this is the second time I haven't let him into my house in a normal way.

I've hurt him.

But technically, he shouldn't even be here. He's the one who told me I deserve someone else.

"I didn't let you pick me up because I didn't know if it was a date," I say, forcing myself to look him straight in the eye. "And it turns out it wasn't."

There's no way he can argue with that, unfortunately for me.

Jamie looks like he has something else to say, but doesn't say it. He takes a careful step across the threshold, like he's expecting an alarm to go off. I lead him through the mudroom and into the warm kitchen.

"You're dressed," he says, looking at the thermal shirt I pulled on, which doesn't really go with the black skirt and patterned wool tights I was wearing at dinner. For once, I couldn't care less. "Thought you were trying to sleep."

"I fell asleep in my clothes for a little while."

I take two glasses out of the cabinet and fill them with water. When I turn to hand him his, he studies my face so carefully that I have to look away. When Jamie stares at me like this, I can only enjoy it for a moment before I start to feel sort of ashamed. I wish I were prettier, for his sake. I wish that he had a beautiful face to look at instead of mine.

I'm not one of those girls who walks around telling her friends how ugly she is. It's true, I don't like mirrors, and I do know that my closest friends are prettier than I am, but it's not really an obsession for me like it is for some people.

But when Jamie Forta is looking at me, I wish with every bone in my body that I were beautiful.

"I couldn't sleep last night," I say, conscious of the black circles under my eyes. "I guess I can't tonight, either."

He puts his glass down on the counter where we're standing side by side without taking a sip. Our silence is punctuated by the ticking of the clock hanging on the wall. Only the stove light is on, and I don't want to turn on anything bright, so I reach over and plug in the Christmas lights that my mother strung over the sink. The kitchen glows a little.

"Why can't you sleep?"

I shrug. "I can't stop thinking."

"About?"

"Everything. Peter came home tonight. He got kicked out of school for drugs. I sort of already knew, I guess."

"Did your mom know?"

"I think she's been trying not to, if that makes any sense."

"You worried?" he asks.

"I'm mad at him," I say, without caring how that sounds. One of the things I love about talking to Jamie is that nothing is a big deal, nothing freaks him out. He just stays calm and doesn't get worked up. It makes me feel like I can tell him anything.

Jamie looks over his shoulder at the Christmas lights above our heads. He reaches up and adjusts the one that's blinking on and off, trying to get it to stop. It does.

"So, like I said, Matt knows," I say. Jamie nods, as if to say he's not surprised. "Jamie, did you know what Conrad was going to do that night?"

"He said he was gonna need help with something. But he didn't tell me what until we got there."

"It looked like you tried to talk him out of it."

Jamie smiles a little as he reaches over and brushes a strand of hair off my face, surprising me. His fingertips barely touch my skin but I can feel the exact path they took as if they were tracing it over and over again. "You spy on me now?"

I blush a little.

"What were you doing there?" he asks.

"Following you."

"Why?"

"I told you—I'm worried. About you."

He watches me with that faraway look, like he's appraising me from a distance. There's a lot of silence in conversations with Jamie. Sometimes it means he's trying to figure out how to say something. Other times it means he has nothing to say at all. The only way to find out which it is, is to wait.

"I worry about *you*," he finally says, the words awkward in his mouth, like he's never said them aloud before.

Jamie takes my glass of water and sets it down on the counter next to his. Then he faces me, putting his hands on either side of me on the counter. He's so close I can see the gold flecks in his hazel eyes and smell December on his jacket.

A tingling sparks low down in my stomach and my breath gets shallow.

How does he do this? How does he get this reaction from me within three minutes of walking in the door without even touching me? All he's doing is just…being him.

I guess that's my answer.

I try to speak but my mouth is dry. I swallow and try again. "Why do you worry about me?"

"You're sad. Not always, but a lot."

Is he right?

At the beginning of the year, I had plans, plans to really be somebody, to find my thing and have friends and be liked and be sassy—Rose 2.0. I was happy about that. But it all just felt like too much to maintain.

Tracy has The Sharp List; Stephanie is basically a one-woman show, popular with the entire school at this point; Robert and Holly have performing, and each other. So where does that leave me?

Doing musicals didn't turn out to be my thing—I'm not sure what I'm supposed to do about singing now. I put all that work into the website and nothing's happening with it anymore. And I didn't even take the PSAT like I planned. I'm nowhere.

No. Not nowhere. Even though he's not supposed to be here for a whole bunch of reasons, Jamie Forta is in my kitchen in the middle of the night, looking into my eyes and telling me he's worried about me because I'm sad a lot.

That's something—that's more than something.

"Can I ask you a question, Jamie?"

"Yeah," he says, his eyes roaming my face and landing on my mouth. I feel my cheeks getting hot.

"Why do you feel guilty about Mr. Deladdo, when he was doing what he was doing?"

"Now they have nobody. Because of what I did."

I can't wrap my head around his logic. "Not because of what you did—because of what *he* did."

Jamie shrugs. I can't tell if what I said doesn't make sense to him or he just doesn't agree.

"I thought it would fix things, making him leave."

"He's not hurting them anymore."

He shakes his head. "But things got worse. Regina with Anthony, all this shit with Conrad. Mrs. D. won't leave the house."

"She won't leave the house? Like, at all?"

Jamie shakes his head slowly.

"What did you say to him, when you…had the gun?"

"I said I knew. And he had to go."

"And he did?"

"He's a chicken-shit coward, that guy." Jamie looks down, examining his construction boots. "I knew, for a long time. Regina made me promise not to do anything. I never shoulda listened to her."

"How did it go on for so long?"

"Guys like that hit only where no one can see."

"So how did you find out?"

He doesn't answer right away. Then he says, "I saw her bruises."

I know that I should feel sympathy for Regina, not extreme jealousy over Jamie, but it's so hard for me to think about him being with her.

I lean away from him—reaching for my water even though I couldn't take a sip right now if someone paid me—but he doesn't move his arms. I'm trapped.

"Rose."

I take a deep breath and give up on my lame diversionary tactics, meeting his eyes.

"It was a long time ago," he says, and then he leans in and kisses me so gently I can't breathe.

For a moment, only his lips are touching me, and I think that I can extract myself, that I can figure out a way to get out of this kiss that shouldn't be happening.

Then his arms close around me and I can't help myself.

There's something simultaneously great and awful about kissing a guy who can melt you in a heartbeat. It's exciting to be powerless when he touches you, but it also sort of sucks to be a slave to attraction. Suddenly you're going against decisions you thought you'd made, and doing exactly what you know you shouldn't.

This is one of the many things about all this that I haven't figured out yet. Why does being attracted to someone make it almost impossible to make smart decisions?

This kiss is different than the others. It doesn't feel totally out of control and reckless and on fire. It feels soft and sweet and warm and safe.

Which makes it even more dangerous.

There's no fanfare when Jamie slips his beautiful, warm hands under my shirt and slides them up my ribcage. I don't know what I was expecting—a voiceover announcing that I was about to go to second base for the first time? One moment his fingertips are grazing the bottom of my bra, and the next his hands are sliding up and over the fabric.

"Okay?" he whispers against my lips, his voice seeming to come from inside me somehow.

I nod, having lost the ability to talk as his fingers slide over my bra and then behind my back to find the clasp. It's happening so fast I have to brace myself on the counter so I don't slide to the floor.

When he unclasps my bra like it's nothing, like he's done it a million times, I tense up for a second. I thought there was a whole stage to second base that involved contact *over* clothing, before the clothing started to come off or get unclasped or whatever.

He senses my hesitation and keeps his hands on my back, giving me time to change my mind. When I don't, he slowly slides them around to my front to explore my bare skin.

And suddenly I don't care if Jamie's unclasped a million bras before mine. There just aren't any words for how good it feels to have someone you like—someone you love—touch you like this.

Love. Is this love? Do love and attraction feel like the same thing? How do you figure out the difference?

Wait, wait, wait. That's not the right question. The right question is, if we're not together, why is this happening?

Why am I *letting* this happen?

"Jamie," I whisper as he kisses my neck, his thumbs tracing circles on my sensitive skin, making it hard for me to speak. My head is tilted back and my eyes are closed. I can't seem to open them. "Why are you doing this?" I manage to say.

His hands go still, though they stay where they are. Then he laughs a little—I feel his exhalation hot on my neck.

"Guess I'm not doing it right."

I force myself to open my eyes and look at him. "No, it's… It feels… You're so…"

I'm breathless. I can't finish the sentence.

Jamie's hands slide down my stomach and out from under my shirt. He puts them back on the counter on either side of me but doesn't meet my eyes.

"I mean, I thought… You said… Did something change?" I ask.

"No, Rose. Nothing changed. I'm sorry—"

I put my hands on his chest to stop him. "Please don't. It'll make me feel like we…shouldn't have. I mean, I guess we shouldn't have, but it wasn't *wrong*. It didn't feel wrong, did it? It didn't to me."

Jamie leans forward and kisses the top of my head. "No wonder you can't sleep," he says into my hair.

Feeling self-conscious about how lumpy my unclasped bra looks under my thermal shirt, I reach behind me and adjust it. Jamie stays where he is, perfectly still against me, like he doesn't want to move.

Then he steps back and reaches inside his jacket, pulling out a thick, light blue scroll tied with a red ribbon. He hands it to me.

I take it from him uncertainly. "For me?"

He nods. "Merry Christmas."

A gift. He brought me a gift. I hold it in my hands, not wanting to open it. It's perfect just the way it is.

"You open it like this," he teases after a minute, pulling on one end of the ribbon.

As the ribbon loosens, the scroll unravels, and it turns out to be an old musical score of some kind. The cover says *Panofka: The Art of Singing, 24 Vocalises for Soprano.*

I open it, and on the inside page, in tiny, neat handwriting, is the name Sylvie Durand. Under that is a date from twenty years ago, with a list of notes that say things like "Mark phrasing" and "Practice with encyclopedias" and "Internalize tempo."

It's a book of increasingly difficult vocal exercises, and they've all been marked up with breath marks and phrasing. Someone worked very hard on these.

I'm not a soprano, but I don't care—it's still a cool gift.

Jamie reaches over and flips the pages back to the inside cover where the notes are written. "My mom was a singer, too."

I'm looking at the name Sylvie Durand for a good ten seconds before I catch on.

"Wait, is this— This is your mom's book?"

"Yeah. She took lessons when I was a kid."

"I can't—"

"Yeah, you can."

"Jamie, she would want you—"

"She'd want a singer to have it," he says, taking it out of my hands and putting it on the counter behind me so I can't give it back to him. I almost tell him that I'm not a singer like she obviously was, but I stop myself.

I *am* a singer—I can feel it. He can, too.

Somehow, instinctively, I know how important it is to say those words, and to believe them, and to trust that they're real.

As he leans in and kisses me on the cheek, he takes my hand in his and I feel his thumb lightly slide down my palm. His lips linger for a moment and I can feel his breath on my cheek. Then he heads for the back door.

"Jamie," I say, grabbing the sleeve of his army jacket to stop him. I have no idea how much stuff Jamie still has that belonged to his mother, and I really don't feel like I should have this music book with her handwriting and notes and thoughts in it. But I do know that when someone makes a gesture like the one Jamie just made, you are supposed to accept—you have to.

But I want to give him something, too.

My fingers slide down his sleeve and find his hand again. "I just want to tell you that no one's ever…done that to me. What you did. Before."

The surprise on his face is quickly followed by regret, and then he actually closes his eyes and drops his head. Not the reaction I was hoping for. I just wanted him to see how much it meant to me—how much *he* means to me.

"Wait—what's wrong?" I ask.

He struggles for a second, then says, "I didn't think… I shoulda…"

I wait for the end of the sentence but it never comes.

Although there are many things about desire that I haven't figured out yet, here's something I do know: it only takes a second for things to be misinterpreted and get really confusing when people are talking about touching each other.

"I loved it," I whisper, embarrassment heating my face at the sound of my very simple, innocent words.

After a moment, he brings my hand to his mouth and kisses it.

Jamie lets himself out and disappears into the dark as I stand in the quiet kitchen, listening to the ticking of the clock, memorizing what it felt like to have Jamie Forta's hands on a part of my body that no guy has ever touched before.

I feel like I'm his.

conflagration *(noun):* a big, destructive fire; inferno
(see also: therapy with my mother *and* my brother)

11

"YOU HAD NO RIGHT!"

"I had every right. You're a minor!"

Caron looks baffled by the intense argument my mother and I are having. Peter has sunk so far into the couch that he's practically a part of it, his head tipped back on the squishy pillows as he stares up at the ceiling, trying to pretend he's not in the room with us.

The new year is off to a great start for the Zarellis.

I took Vicky's suggestion and called the company that hosts my website to say that I'd gotten a weird post with code and nothing else in the comment-posting section for a long time. When the woman who was helping me suggested I talk to my mother about it, I knew exactly what had happened.

"You lied to them about being eighteen when you took Peter's credit card to set up that website—"

"I didn't take it—he gave it to me!"

"—and when I told them that you lied, they said I could shut the whole thing down. But all I did was shut off the posting feature. So consider yourself lucky that the website is still up."

I must look like a demon right now. I'm sure my eyes are beet-red, and the tears and snot are flowing freely. Caron is watching me closely, probably trying to decide whether to ask me if I'm struggling with any violent impulses right now.

Yes, Caron, I am. I'm struggling with my desire to jump over your lovely glass coffee table in a single bound and throttle my mother on your cozy couch.

It's all I can do to stay in my seat.

I sniffle loudly and Peter picks up a box of tissues on the end table between us and tosses it at me without saying anything.

I catch it and pull a tissue out to mop up my face. "What's the point of a memorial website if people can't leave comments, Kathleen?" I snarl.

"Rose, your mother told you she wouldn't engage in conversation if you called her by her first name. And if there's no conversation, there's no reason for us to be here," Caron says.

"Fine with me," I grumble.

"Is it fine with you, Kathleen?" Caron asks.

"No. There are several things we need to talk about." My mother doesn't look at either Peter or me when she says this, and Caron gives her a nod. Obviously there's a predetermined agenda for this session.

"Rose, is there anything else you'd like to say about the website?"

Yeah. How about, why don't I get any privacy? Why does she get to monitor everything I do? And why is she being so insane about something that actually makes me feel connected to my father? Or it used to, anyway, back when people could still post on it.

I throw my tissue in the trash with as much force as a person can possibly throw a soggy tissue.

"Let's revisit the website issue at the end of the session." Caron nods at my mother again.

My mother smoothes her skirt. "We need to talk about going back to school in the fall, Peter. The dean of students says that if you complete an outpatient rehab program, hold down a part-time job and make up some credits, you'll be welcomed back."

"I'm not going back," Peter announces to the ceiling.

"Excuse me?" my mother says, as if she couldn't possibly have heard what she knows she heard.

"You didn't ask," he says. "You just assumed."

"You're right. I assumed. Do you know why? Because you are lucky to be at that school in the first place."

Peter takes his keys out of his pocket and fiddles with a bottle opener on his keychain. "I'm not learning anything."

Because you don't go to class, I think.

"Peter, I think what your mother is saying is that attending Tufts is an incredible opportunity, and you're lucky to have a second chance there."

My mother shakes her head too fast. "That's part of what I'm saying." She's ramping up for battle now—she must have spent days preparing for this. "This family has invested in your education. If you're not going to pursue it, pay the money back."

Peter starts tossing his keys up in the air and catching them. "Everything is about money to you," he says, taking a shot at my mother's Achilles' heel.

If it hits the mark, my mother doesn't show it. "Oh, this is definitely about money," she says. "It's about the money I've given you to support yourself—while you're supposedly getting educated—going to drugs and alcohol. That is disrespectful, self-destructive behavior, and I don't need to be around that, nor does your sister. So follow the plan or leave my house."

Peter catches his keys, his hand frozen in the air as he tries to determine if she's serious. His eyes slide from my mother to me. I look at her.

"Don't include me in this," I say. "He doesn't affect me one way or the other."

"Oh, is that so? None of this affects you? Then why did I get a message from Principal Chen, asking us to come to a meeting when school starts next week because she's 'concerned'?"

My brain immediately whirls into overdrive.

The swim-thug party?

What Conrad did to Matt's car?

Matt beating the crap out of Conrad? As far as I know, Matt hasn't done a thing to Conrad yet.

I don't know what the meeting is about, but I do know this: I sure don't feel like going to the principal's office with my mother. It's bad enough when I have to go there on my own.

She sips from the glass of mint tea she made while we were in the waiting area. The look on her face tells me that she's been waiting to ambush me with this information.

"Unfair," I announce.

"What's unfair?" she asks, pretending she did nothing wrong. I feel like I'm fighting with Tracy, not my mother.

"You know."

"Rose," Caron asks, "is this the first you're hearing of this meeting?"

I nod. Caron looks at my mother, who suddenly decides to refresh her tea with hot water from Caron's super-high-tech water cooler across the room.

"Kathleen, weren't you going to talk to Rose about the meeting before you came today?" she says.

My mother watches the hot water filling her cup. "It must have slipped my mind."

Caron raises her eyebrows. "You realize that isn't what we agreed on in our conversation."

"It sucks that you two have your own sessions. It gives her an advantage," I say to Caron.

"You're more than welcome to come with me every week instead of every other week," my mother says as she makes her way back to the couch.

"Kathleen, these sessions are not meant to be a battlefield."

My brother smirks, enjoying watching our mother get verbally spanked by her shrink.

"Noted," my mother says.

Caron waits.

"I apologize, Rose," she says grudgingly. I can tell she's irritated by having to apologize to me when she feels I've totally wronged her in every way lately.

The feeling is mutual, Kathleen.

"Let's get back on track," Caron suggests.

"Peter, you have until tomorrow to decide what to do," my mother says.

Peter goes back to playing catch with his keys as if he doesn't have a care in the world.

"Is there something else you wanted to talk about?" Caron prompts.

When my mother's expression changes from confident to terrified, I know we're about to get to the real reason we're here today.

"I'd like to talk about Dirk. Taylor," she adds, as if there's any doubt who Dirk is.

My heart thuds to a halt. Peter misses his keys and they glance off his hand and clatter on the coffee table.

"Go on," Caron encourages.

My mother clears her throat. "Dirk and I have become friends—"

"You're not friends," I interrupt.

"Let her finish," Caron says with a gentleness that tells me my mother is about to announce something I'm going to really hate.

"He asked me to dinner. I said yes—"

"No, you didn't," comes out of my mouth.

"—and we're going out next week."

My mother holds her breath, looking at me with fear, like she's waiting for me to say something awful.

When did my mother start expecting me to hurt her?

Probably after I started hurting her.

"On a date?" I ask.

"Yes."

"But…what about Dad?" I whisper, my throat burning from the pain of holding back tears.

"Honey, I love your father. I always will." She rubs her forehead like she's getting a headache. "Going to dinner with someone isn't going to change that."

"But Dirk is… He's…" I can't find the words to explain my confusion.

Shouldn't my mother want to date someone like Dad? If she goes out with someone who's totally different, does that mean she never really loved him?

"He's nothing like Dad," I finally say.

Peter snorts. "So?"

"Well, doesn't that mean…"

"Oh, grow up, Rose," Peter says.

"Peter," my mother warns.

"So what if you go out with Dirk? It's no big deal. Dad's dead."

I start crying again. My mother whips around, grabbing Peter by the arm. Peter sits up fast, like he thinks he might have to physically defend himself.

"Do you know what concerns me most about you this year?" she says in a fierce tone I've never heard her use before. "You've become unkind."

Peter yanks out of her grasp and sits back with his arms crossed, trying to mask the fact that he needs a minute to recover.

If I didn't hate Dirk before, I sure hate him now. It's *his* fault we're here, doing this.

"What's going on for you, Rose?" Caron asks softly.

"He *just* died," I say, using the back of my hand for a tissue.

"He died two years ago," Peter says.

"A year and a half ago," my mother corrects.

"Why are you doing this?" I ask her. "Is it because Dirk is a movie star and Dad was just an engineer?"

My mother looks dumbfounded, like she prepared for everything I could possibly say except that.

"I am very proud of your father—of how smart he was, and of how he was trying to help people in Iraq rebuild. The fact that your Dad was an engineer and Dirk is an actor has nothing to do with anything."

"It's not right!" I argue.

"Rose, people grieve differently at different ages," Caron says, when it's clear that my mother can't respond to what I said. "Grief can cause adults to reflect on the fact that they are half-way through their lives—it makes them want to live as richly as they can. For younger people, grief can bring up feelings of abandonment. Are you worried that Dirk is going to take your mom away?"

My brain says that with the way I feel about my mother right now, I'd be just fine with Dirk taking her away—and my dad probably would, too. But the tears spilling down my cheeks say something different.

"If she gets to live *richly* by going out with someone who's not my dad, then I should get to have the website."

I hear my mother sniffle—she leans forward to take a tissue from the box in front of me.

"I feel like interacting with people on the website keeps you in a constant state of grief over your father, and you can't let go of it," she says.

"I don't want to let go of it." I can hear panic in my voice but I don't try to hide it. The idea of letting go freaks me out. I know Dad now through grief. If I'm not feeling sad about him, he'll just drift away and fade into the background of my life, which will go on without him. Like he never existed. "I don't want to let go of *him*."

"Dad and the grief are two different things," my mother says.

My brain goes into can't-compute mode. How can I keep him here if I'm not grieving for him?

My mother blows her nose. "I want you to remember him but I don't want his death to become your whole life. And when you're constantly checking that website to see if someone has posted something, I feel like that's what's happening. What if someone posts something that upsets you and you don't come out of your room for three days again?"

Out of the corner of my eye, I see Peter look at me.

"That was different," I say. "The posts haven't really been about Dad for a few months. Now they're about support groups and stuff like that."

As I say it, I realize that despite all my arguing to keep the website going, the purpose of the site changed while I wasn't paying attention. Time passed, and it became something else without my permission.

Maybe that's what happens with grief, too, whether you want it to or not.

"I'll make you a deal," my mother says. "I'll turn the posting function back on if you take down the photo."

"Which photo?" Peter asks, sitting up all the way, not trying to hide his interest anymore.

I didn't know, when I put up a photo of my parents saying goodbye the day my father left, that I was causing trouble. I truly didn't. But when I think about the photo now, I realize why it drives my mother nearly insane. My dad is standing by a black car that's waiting to take him to the airport with his bags on the ground next to him. My mother is moving toward him to hug him, and you can't see her face but if you look closely at her arms as they reach forward, it looks like she wants to grab him, to stop him from going. And the expression on his face is pure sadness. He obviously does not want to leave.

"The photo of us saying goodbye," she says.

I can tell Peter knows which photo she's talking about. "Why do you want her to take it down?" he asks.

My mother takes her time answering. "Because I can see in it so clearly that we're making a mistake," she finally says. "He doesn't want to go. And I don't want him to go. But he's going, anyway, because that's what we decided and we're sticking with the plan."

She's talking as if it's all happening right now in our driveway, outside our house. She shakes her head and refolds her hands in her lap.

"You sound angry," Caron says.

"He never should have been there."

Peter and I look at each other, surprised to hear her say this so bluntly.

"Is that what the photo represents to you?" Caron asks.

She nods. "It was our last chance to change our minds."

"We should have said something," Peter says to me.

My mother closes her eyes. "Kids don't participate in those kinds of decisions for a reason."

"But we knew it was crazy," he says, clearing his throat when his voice cracks. "We talked about it."

"Honey, it wasn't your job to say anything."

"But what if—" I start.

Her eyes open. "What-ifs don't matter," she says, cutting me off.

"Finish your thought," Caron says to me. My mother bows her head and waits.

"What if Peter and I had told you and Dad that we knew he shouldn't go?" I ask.

My mother shakes her head but I can see the question in her eyes.

After some silence, Caron says, "Several months ago, Rose, you would have said it was your mother's fault that Alfonso went to Iraq. Now it sounds like you and Peter think it's your fault, that you could have prevented it."

"If your father and I couldn't stop what we set in motion, you sure as hell couldn't have," my mother says before I can form a response.

It's not every day that we hear our mom use the word *hell*. She sounds like she's convinced herself she's right, and that she believes there's no way we could have made a difference.

But during the silence that follows, I'm pretty sure all three of us are imagining the alternate universe where Peter and I made our parents see the light, where we sat them down in the living room one night before going to bed and said, *We'd rather never go to college than have Dad go to Iraq just to pay tuition.*

It's the universe in which Dad is still alive, and right now, we're all there together.

The Panofka book that belonged to Jamie's mom has way more dates and notes in it than I first thought.

I've been using my keyboard app to figure out the melodies of each exercise, and every time I turn the page, I can picture her a little more clearly. At first, the handwritten notes just remind her to do certain things as she practices, but halfway through the book they get more and more personal. On one page, she writes, *Sometimes singing makes me so tired I could weep.* On another page, it says, *Everything is so loud. It's almost impossible to hear.* A note toward the end says, *He's crying again. Again. Again. It never ends. Nothing ever ends.*

I wonder if Jamie read these, and if he did, how they made him feel.

I flip back to the beginning of the book and start singing the first exercise, which is the one I know the best at this point. I sing it an octave below where it's written, and it's hard for me—I can feel that I don't have the training or the vocal discipline to do it right. But it feels good, anyway, like I'm working out, exercising my muscles.

The knock on my door startles me. I close the book and put it in my desk drawer for some reason. I open the door, and Peter is standing there. "What were you just singing?"

"A vocal exercise," I answer, feeling weirdly embarrassed, like he caught me doing something I'm not supposed to be doing.

"It sounded sort of classical."

"I guess it is."

When he doesn't say anything else, I step back and sit on my bed. He hovers in my doorway, looking around. He hasn't set foot in my room in months. When his eyes land on my battered, torn school copy of *Julius Caesar,* which I haven't read yet for Camber's class, he asks, "You know the definition of a tragic flaw?"

I look at him and say with as much pointed irony as I can possibly manage, "A trait that causes a person's downfall."

Peter laughs a little. He's still pretty skinny with bags under his eyes and he hasn't shaved in a while, but he doesn't look as bad as he did over the summer.

"Did Camber give you that assignment where you have to identify your own tragic flaw?"

"Yeah."

"What's yours?"

I've actually been giving this a lot of thought today. As soon as we got home from therapy, I took down the photo on the website because my mother's explanation of what it means to her made me feel terrible for putting it up in the first place. I didn't know how she felt about that photo, but if I'd thought about it for half a second, I probably would have figured it out.

I think my tragic flaw might be insensitivity.

The web design program is still open on my laptop on my desk, and I can see the blank space where the new photo will go. The borders sort of pulse a little, reminding me that there's nothing there yet, and that I have a decision to make. Again.

"I haven't chosen my tragic flaw yet," I lie. "What was yours?"

"I can't remember," he says, probably also lying. "Can I come in?"

I'm surprised he wants to. "Okay," I say, sliding back so I'm leaning against my headboard.

It's weird to have Peter in here. He sits at my desk chair, looking at my laptop screen. Without asking, he starts scrolling down the page, checking out the site. I let it go because I've never seen Peter look at the site before. I don't know if he ever has. At first, when I told him I was going to build it, he wanted nothing to do with it. I was pretty surprised when he agreed to let me use his credit card to pay for it.

"Do you want to help me pick a new photo?"

When he doesn't answer, I get off my bed and reach over his shoulder to click on my photos folder. When a screen full of Dad pictures comes up, Peter sort of moves my hand out of the way and clicks back on the website page.

Dad disappears.

I'd be annoyed if I hadn't realized that Peter can't look at photos of our father.

He scrolls down to the bottom of the homepage and sees all the links to the people who died alongside Dad. The first one is for Vicky's son. Peter clicks on it and Travis's website pops up.

"This is that woman's son? The woman Mom doesn't like you to be friends with?"

"Yeah, Vicky."

I reach past Peter again and go back to my photos folder. He looks away from the screen when Dad reappears. I find my Vicky folder and open the Christmas Eve picture of her.

"She's from Texas," I say, as if that explains the antlers on her head.

Peter makes the picture bigger like he wants to see her face more closely. As he's looking at her, he says, "What was Mom talking about when she said you didn't come out of your room for three days after the anniversary?"

There's a hint of concern in Peter's voice. Something inside me gives way just a little.

"It was nothing. I was just reading people's posts and trying to write back to everyone. It took a lot of time."

"What were the posts like?"

I close the photo of Vicky and go back to the website. Peter starts reading the posts that are still up there from June.

When I think back to the anniversary, it feels like a blur, but not a bad blur. It took a lot of time to figure out what to write back to people—I wanted to say the right things—so I was up super late and then at it again after an hour or two of sleep.

It was like an avalanche, those three days. I'd answer a few people, and then sleep for a while, and there'd be fifteen new messages from other people when I woke up. I'd never thought of Dad as having lots of friends before, and then suddenly, there were fifty of them, telling me stuff I never knew.

"What's the post she's talking about, that she says upset you?"

I scroll around and find the one from the guy who said it made him happy when Dad said he was going to stay in Iraq another six months. I point to the screen and Peter reads it in silence.

"He was going to stay?"

"She says he made the decision right before he died, so he didn't have time to tell us."

Peter doesn't address that one way or the other. He just scrolls some more, reading more posts.

"You haven't ever looked at the site? I mean, you paid for it," I say. "Which made you as guilty as me, in Mom's mind."

"I didn't know she was going to freak out about the credit card," he says. "Did you?"

I shake my head. "I sort of thought she'd like the website."

"Why is she so worked up about those few days?"

I lean over and rest my elbows on the desk next to him. "She couldn't get me to do anything. Like, I wouldn't leave the computer to shower or go outside."

"Did you eat?" he asks.

"A little."

"She hates it when we don't eat."

I reach over and tug on the side of his waistband. There's about two inches of space between the fabric of his jeans and his skin.

"Yeah, I know, I know," he says.

I take my laptop off the desk and bring it with me as I crawl back onto my bed.

"So what are you going to tell Mom tomorrow?" I ask.

Peter leans back in my chair and spins himself in circles. "I have no idea."

"What does Amanda think?"

He drops his feet to the floor and stops spinning. "Amanda? We broke up when she left school."

"You did?"

Peter scratches at the stubble on his face, looking a little embarrassed. "Her asshole father came to campus, dragged her out of her room and forced her into his car without even letting her pack. And then I got a text. Somehow I went from being the love of her life to 'totally toxic' in under an hour."

I can hear Amanda talking in her fake sweet voice, telling Peter I'm "cute" and asking him what it's like to have a little sister while she looks up at him with her big, bloodshot eyes. "She called *you* toxic? What a loser."

The left side of Peter's mouth lifts in a tiny smile as he stares down at the floor.

"Did you text her back?"

"Her cell phone was disconnected, probably two seconds after she sent that text."

"Do you miss her?"

"Sometimes."

I want to slam Amanda some more, but I don't. If I've learned one thing from Caron since Peter's been back it's that no one is to blame for Peter's addictions but Peter. Period.

I don't know if Peter agrees with that, though.

"You're going to rehab, right?"

"You think that's what I should do?" he says. He doesn't sound pissed when he asks—he sounds like he really wants to know.

"It's better than getting kicked out of the house."

Peter raises his eyebrows like he's not entirely sure, and he starts spinning around in the chair again.

I look down at my laptop and bring up the screen with Dad's photos. I turn the computer around and click play on the slide-show so that Peter can see it. I don't need to see it—I've got it memorized.

He doesn't want to watch—I can tell. But he can't look away. I know which photo he's seeing by the expression on his face—which changes every few seconds—because I'm pretty sure it's the same series of expressions that cross my face when I'm watching the slideshow.

When it's over, he gets up out of the chair and sits on the edge of my bed. Then he points to the photo that's still up on the screen, the last photo of the slideshow. It's the first photo Dad sent back to us when he got to Iraq. He's smiling at the camera, with all his laminated IDs hanging around his neck. "That one."

It wouldn't have occurred to me to use this one, because it's barely Dad to me. But it is who he was—an engineer in Iraq. I drag it into the box and it appears on the homepage. It's a good choice. A much better choice than the photo of the day he left.

Peter looks at the screen and nods.

"You have to go to rehab, Peter. He'd want you to."

"I'll go," he says quietly, still looking at the laptop screen. Then he says, "You sound good, Rose."

I'm confused by the change of subject. "What do you mean?"

"Your singing. You sound good. You can't tell?"

"Um…I don't really…"

"Well, you do," he says. "You should keep doing it." Peter stands up. As he walks out the door, he smiles at me. And I recognize my brother for what feels like the first time in a year.

torrid *(adjective):* hot and steamy
(see also: Principal Chen's office...the Valentine's Day dance...*)*

12

PRINCIPAL CHEN'S OFFICE WOULD BE A SAUNA EVEN
without all the extra people packed into it. The school's vintage
radiators—which look like they were made during the industrial
revolution—clank and hiss like harbingers of the torture to come.
The principal's anticipatory Valentine's Day construction-paper
hearts literally droop off the walls, weighed down by condensa-
tion. Everyone is sweating, but no one as much as Matt Hallis.

I reach for my phone to text Tracy and tell her how fun it is
to see Matt so scared before I remember that texting her doesn't
really complement my plan to ignore her as punishment for lying
to me. She finally admitted last week that Peter had sent her a text
asking her to meet him at the house on Christmas Eve to help
him break the news about getting kicked out of school. I then told
Peter to go get his own friends. He told me I was being stupid.

So no texting Tracy about Matt. Which is fine. I can't fully delight in his suffering right now anyway—I'm too freaked myself.

Conrad and his mother sit on one side of the principal's desk.
I wonder if this is the first time Mrs. Deladdo has left her house

since the summer. My mother and I sit directly in front of the desk, Matt and his dad are on the other side, and Ms. Maso and Mr. Donnelly are behind me. I turn around and see that Ms. Maso has a bunch of fliers in her hand that say *Join Union High's GSA!*

Based on the grim faces in this room, I'm fairly certain that this meeting is about more than Ms. Maso starting a Gay-Straight Alliance at Union High.

Matt's dad can't sit still—he keeps jumping out of his chair and pulling out his BlackBerry, the top of his head grazing the red plastic hearts hanging from the principal's ceiling. He bats them away without even looking to see what they are.

I wonder if he's as big a homophobe as his son is, or if Matt picked that up all on his own.

Mr. Hallis finally settles down when the door opens and Union's own Officer Webster comes in. Officer Webster and I go way back to last year, when he saved me from being stoned to death by my classmates as his partner confiscated all the alcohol at the homecoming party, thanks to me.

Officer Webster says a general hello to everyone, and then—lucky me—gives me a special shout-out. "Rose, right? Good to see you again," he says, leaning against the door like he's blocking someone from escaping.

My mother turns to me with an expression that says, *You'll be explaining that to me later.*

I can't exactly blame my mother for hearing warning bells when a police officer addresses her daughter by name. My mother is still adjusting to the fact that her son—who should be in the middle of his sophomore year in college—gets up every morning at seven-thirty and signs himself into an outpatient rehab program at the local hospital.

"Thank you all for coming," Principal Chen says. "We have a situation here that could potentially involve criminal charges for both Matt Hallis and Conrad Deladdo. But I believe that we can avoid that, if we all work together tonight." The principal seems to direct this at Mr. Hallis.

"I'm mainly concerned with what you propose as punishment in place of the law," Mr. Hallis says, looking at Conrad.

Mrs. Deladdo looks from Mr. Hallis to her son and back. "Excuse me, but I don't understand. Punishment for what?" she asks, her tone offering an apology for not being up to speed on current events.

"You don't know?" Mr. Hallis says, incredulous, his shiny, black leather shoes creaking as he shifts his weight forward in his chair. Mrs. Deladdo leans back slightly.

Principal Chen offers Conrad's mom a reassuring smile. "Due to the fact that teenagers don't always tell their parents everything, I'll start from the beginning."

Mrs. Deladdo nods and pulls her dark blue jacket around her more tightly, as if she's cold despite the triple-digit temperatures in the principal's office. Conrad slouches down in his chair, glaring at me as if totally convinced that I'm the reason we're all sitting here, not the fact that he practically signed his name on Matt's car and our principal is smart enough to do the math.

"At a swim-team party at Mike Darren's house in August, before school started, Matt and other members of the team hazed Conrad as part of his 'initiation.' The hazing involved homophobic slurs and violence. When Conrad was thrown in the pool and didn't immediately surface, Rose became concerned. Matt then shoved her into the pool, too. Jamie Forta helped Conrad and Rose out."

My mother looks at me for confirmation, but I keep my eyes fixed on Principal Chen's candy dish, which is full of little pink hearts. From where I'm sitting, it looks like one of them actually has the words *Bite Me* on it. Is that possible?

"Several weeks into the school year, I got word that Conrad had quit the swim team. I was unable to ascertain why," she says to Mrs. Deladdo, who is now so pale I'm afraid she's going to slide out of her chair and onto the floor. "We held an assembly, organized by Ms. Maso and Mr. Donnelly, to educate students about tolerance."

"Shouldn't high school students already know what tolerance is?" Mr. Hallis asks, looking at his watch to convey his opinion that this meeting should be moving more quickly, oblivious to the irony of his asking this particular question.

I'm tempted to offer him the *Bite Me* candy heart.

"Everyone can use a reminder from time to time," the principal replies evenly before continuing. "In December, Officer Webster—whom I kept in the loop regarding all of this— informed me that Mr. Hallis had called 911 to say that someone had spray-painted Matt's car with the word *faggot,* and variations of that particular slur, and that his son was fairly certain Conrad had done it. Mr. Hallis, Officer Webster and I met the next day, during which I explained to Mr. Hallis what had transpired be- tween the two boys before school started in August." The prin- cipal looks pointedly at Conrad and adds, "Mr. Hallis kindly agreed to withdraw his complaint, provided a satisfactory agree- ment could be reached once the holidays were over and we were able to arrange this meeting."

By the way Mr. Hallis is glaring at Chen, I'm guessing she did a lot more than just tell him what had *transpired* between Conrad and Matt in order to get him to *kindly* withdraw his complaint. She probably told Mr. Hallis that if he didn't let her handle this exactly as she saw fit, Matt would find himself on the wrong end of the law, thanks to all the witnesses who had come forward after the party.

All the witnesses being me, of course.

My mother and Mrs. Deladdo seem to be astounded by all this information. Mr. Hallis is just annoyed by the process of getting everyone up to speed.

"In other words, Mrs. Deladdo," he huffs, "I won't press charges if your son pays me back for the paint job."

"You have evidence against this boy that I don't know about, Mr. Hallis?" Officer Webster asks.

"Principal Chen, please," Mr. Hallis says, ignoring Officer Webster. "I've been more than patient. Let's just get to the bottom of this so we can all move on."

"Conrad?" Principal Chen says.

For a second, I think that Conrad is going to deny what he did, despite the presence of a police officer in the room. He might have, too, if it weren't for his mother.

"Corrado," she says, barely audible over the hissing radiator next to her, "was it you?"

It turns out Conrad's Achilles' heel is his mother. Go figure.

Conrad nods.

"Okay, good," the principal says, pleased to be getting somewhere. "Conrad, would you explain to everybody here why you felt compelled to do what you did?"

"I'm not really up for rehashing it," he says.

"It would actually be in your best interest to do so," she replies firmly.

Conrad shifts in his seat. "The guys on the swim team decided I was gay. When I didn't tell them otherwise, they gave me shit—"

"Corrado!"

"—sorry, Ma—they harassed me at the swim-team party. Then practice became a nightmare. Matt threatened me just about every day, so I gave him what he wanted and I quit. Then I spray-painted his car," Conrad says. "And it was sort of the most fun I've ever had."

No one touches that with a ten-foot pole. Not even Mr. Hallis, who is closely observing his creaky shoes.

"I'm not gay," Matt says to Conrad.

"It's called irony. Look it up," Conrad replies.

Principal Chen turns to me. "Rose, will you tell us what happened at the party?"

No. No, no, no. I've already had enough trouble with *both* Matt and Conrad, and frankly, I would love it if our lives were a little less intertwined. Telling a roomful of adults what happened between them at the party is going to have precisely the opposite effect.

"Conrad pretty much covered it," I say.

My mother reaches out and touches my arm. "I'd like to hear your version," she says. I look at her, thinking about how she defended me against Peter in therapy even after all the crap I'd said to her.

I can give her this one.

"At the party, Matt and the other swim thugs—"

"The swim *what?*" Mr. Hallis says.

I feel my face get red. "Oh. Uh, the swim thugs. That's what the Union High swim team is called."

Mr. Hallis looks at his son in disbelief. Matt, already embarrassed to the point of muteness, merely shrugs. I continue on, keeping my voice as neutral as humanly possible.

"They called Conrad homophobic names, chucked cups of beer at his head, sprayed him in the mouth with a hose, choked him and threw him in the pool. Twice."

Mrs. Deladdo lets out a little sob. Conrad rolls his eyes but he takes her hand, anyway.

"Matt, is Rose's account true?" Principal Chen asks. I half-expect him to say that he wants to lawyer-up but he nods. "I happen to believe that both Matt and Conrad have the potential to be positive influences here at Union High, in their own ways. Rather than expelling or suspending them—although that would be well within the school's rights here—I'd like to ask them to make retribution for what they've done. So here's what I propose, if Mr. Hallis and Mrs. Deladdo agree. Conrad has a year to pay back the Hallis family for the damage done to the car with funds he earns by assisting the police department with graffiti removal. Mr. Hallis has already agreed that this can be done on a payment plan."

"And Matt's punishment?" Mrs. Deladdo asks as forcefully as she can.

"Matt is banned from sports for the rest of the year."

Matt leaps out of his chair, red-faced. "Wait! That's not—"

Mr. Hallis yanks him back down. "You did this to yourself," he says coldly. Matt drops his head into his hands and starts groaning like an injured animal, tears dropping through his fingers to the orange carpet below. Principal Chen patiently waits until the noise subsides to continue.

"Officer Webster and I feel it's important for the boys to do something together, and to that end, Mr. Donnelly, our drama teacher, has come up with a brilliant idea. Mr. Donnelly, would you share it with everyone, please?" Principal Chen asks.

Mr. Donnelly stands up. "This spring, the new Union High Gay-Straight Alliance and the drama department are doing a production of *The Laramie Project* in honor of the Matthew Shepard Act, and as part of the school's year-long tolerance project." He pauses for effect, and then seems to remember that this isn't the best venue for dramatic pauses. He hurries on. "Matt and Conrad will both have roles in the play."

Matt's head jerks up out of his hands.

"Who's Matthew Shepard?" I hear Mrs. Deladdo whisper to Conrad.

"Later, Ma," Conrad answers, his eyes locked on Matt.

"I'm not doing a play," Matt says.

"Would you prefer to be expelled?" Principal Chen asks brightly.

"No, he would not," Mr. Hallis answers for him.

"Fantastic. So, is this settled? Does anyone have any questions?" When no one answers, Principal Chen smiles and claps her hands once. "Then we've found our solution."

"Yo yo yo, Union High, whassup? Happy Valentine's Day! This is your very own Angelo Martinez—aka, DJ Motormouth—back in da house! You ready? This is your Dance for Tolerance, yo, and it is time to BRING IT! Oh, and a special shout-out to gorgeous girl Stephanie over there!"

A cheer goes up as Stephanie giggles and flips her perfect red hair, waving at Angelo. Angelo clutches at his chest like he's having some sort of heart attack, and then hits Play on Usher and Pitbull, "DJ Got Us Fallin' In Love."

I literally can't believe my ears. This is a guy who used to be a walking advertisement for Metallica and Nirvana—except for that day he showed up in that Neko Case T-shirt. But I guess he knows his audience because pretty much everyone in the gym cheers as they follow Stephanie onto the dance floor and start throwing themselves around. If Stephanie is this popular as a sophomore, I can't even imagine what things are going to be like by the time we graduate. Stephanie has half the guys at Union High begging to go out with her. The other half are waiting for Holly to wake up and dump Robert.

I look up at the five-foot-tall, black, plastic letters that spell out *Tolerance* hanging from the ceiling above our heads, next to a banner that says Sponsored by the Union High Student Council and The Sharp List.

I don't really know what makes this a "tolerance" dance, but no dates are allowed—you are supposed to come by yourself or with friends. Only single tickets were sold, no discounts for couples. And when the student council hired Angelo to DJ, they made him promise that he would play only one slow song the whole night.

The point was to make Valentine's Day fun for everybody,

not just couples. It was a nice try, but high school couples can stay away from each other for only so long. I already count three couples smushed against each other and swaying slowly, even though there's a fast song playing and insane dancing going on around them.

Also, shouldn't a dance that's about tolerance welcome couples of all kinds, not pretend that couples don't exist?

Weird political statements aside, the gym looks good. The student council converted it into a club as best they could by renting a lighting rig and a giant disco ball that spins around, sending pools of silver light flying across the walls and the floor. There are little red lamps on red cabaret tables surrounding the dance floor with red plastic chairs. But despite all the red, there are no hearts anywhere.

I wasn't planning on coming, but Stephanie's on the student council now and she begged me, saying it could be a great night for me and her and Tracy to hang out. Stephanie has been working overtime to make things better between Tracy and me. Though Tracy and I have been working together on The Sharp List, neither one of us has apologized for Christmas Eve. I know she thinks I owe her an apology for the way I talked to her, but I think she owes me an apology for…being the person Peter turned to. Instead of me.

I didn't say it was rational.

Stephanie and Tracy picked me up just as Peter was getting home from his job at the video store that's going out of business any second now. He looked like crap, but Tracy insisted that his sweater was fabulous and that she needed his picture for The Sharp List.

Total lie. She wants his picture for herself so she can look at it anytime.

It still bugs me that she's never once taken my picture for the list, even when she's dressed me herself. I swear, if Peter ends up on The Sharp List before I do, I'm never talking to Tracy again.

It's weird—Tracy has always had a crush on Peter. But something's different now. Now, it seems like she actually believes he could like her back.

I guess that's called confidence.

I should be happy for her that she has the confidence to think that a guy who's in college could like her. But it's a little hard when the college guy is my brother.

The flash from Tracy's new, super-fancy digital camera goes crazy as she takes photo after photo, practically blinding me and everyone else in the gym. Stephanie is busy checking in with the freshmen volunteers at the ticket table to make sure everything is going okay, so I decide to say hi to Angelo.

Angelo is wearing sunglasses, headphones and a headset microphone, kind of thrashing around in place as he stares at a glowing laptop that is so scratched up and dented and covered with band stickers, it looks like it should be resting comfortably somewhere, preparing to die. I've never seen him happier.

"Sweater!" he cries out, his nickname for me reverberating throughout the entire gym because he forgot that his mic was still on. People look over with puzzled expressions, and he gives everyone a thumbs-up, like he meant to do that. He switches off the mic, slides his headphones backward so they're resting around his neck and gives me a high five. "I got so much shit to play for you tonight," he says. "You look good, Sweater!"

Stephanie lent me her red wrap dress from last year. Her mother won't let her out of the house in it anymore—now that she's so tall, the dress is way too mini. Of course on me, it covers my knees.

Angelo slips his headphones back on and starts talking before he realizes he forgot to turn on his mic. He grins, and starts over.

"Union High, it's all about the love, yo. Live and let live, right? And believe. Just listen to Katy—she knows what's up."

He starts playing "Firework." I start laughing.

"Katy Perry? For real?"

I have no problem with pop music—in fact, pop music probably takes up more than half the space on my phone—but it shocks me to see Angelo playing it.

"Huh?" he says, lifting up one side of his headphones so he can hear me.

"Since when do you like Katy Perry?"

"Listen, Sweater, good music is good music. Genre ain't nothin' but a thang." He grins, looking at me over his sunglasses. "Plus, you gotta play the hits if you're gonna DJ. But don't worry—I got *good* stuff comin' up. It's gonna rock your world."

He goes back to studying his screen intently while he pounds his fist on the table in time to the music. I'm still amazed at his transformation. The only sign of the Angelo Martinez I used to know is the grease under his fingernails from working in his dad's garage.

I turn around to watch the mania. Stephanie is in the middle of everything with a circle of guys around her, watching her dance. Kristin and a few of the other cheerleaders walk through the crowd in their uniforms with armloads of carnations, making deliveries for the flower sale they're having to raise money for the squad. Kristin stops in front of Stephanie and basically hands over the entire bunch. Stephanie grins and holds the flowers in her arms like a giant bouquet as she tries to keep dancing.

The people who can't—or won't—dance hang out on the fringes in their usual groups, making fun of everyone. Mr. Camber and Ms. Maso sit under a banner that reads *Tolerance for All*, chaperoning from behind a table loaded with pamphlets that no one is going to touch in front of their friends—"Union High's

Gay-Straight Alliance," "The Dangers of Unprotected Sex," "Bullying Sucks," "Mixing Energy Drinks with Alcohol KILLS."

A cheer goes up as Kristin makes a big show of walking over to Camber with a bunch of flowers for the annual ritual. Angelo stops the music, playing a sound effect that sounds like a car screeching to a halt.

"Mr. Camber, it's Valentine's Day," Angelo says in a sing-songy voice, dragging each syllable out for maximum effect.

Everybody in the gym goes "Oooooh!" as Kristin tries to hand Camber the flowers and then ends up leaving them on the pamphlet table when he politely refuses to even touch them. Kristin starts to walk away, and then stops dramatically as she looks at the card on the last flower she's holding. She turns back around and hands it to Ms. Maso, and the crowd goes wild.

"Aw, Ms. Maso, you gonna read that card out loud for us?" Angelo says into the mic. She shakes her head and yells across the gym, "You'd best start playing music, Angelo Martinez. I can still change your grade and recall your diploma."

Angelo grins at her. "Okay, Union, check this, we're goin' back in time. This is for Rose Zarelli," he says. "Sweater, meet The Runaways. Cherie Currie *is* Cherry Bomb!"

I have no idea what he's talking about. I freeze as all heads turn my way—usually, when I'm singled out, it's not for a good reason, so my first instinct is to run or hide. But then Stephanie lets out a loud "Rosieeeee!" and Angelo starts the song.

At first, no one dances. The song sounds old and too simple—like someone recorded it in a garage or something. The singer's voice is low at first, and I can't even really tell if it's a girl or a guy. But then, she starts yelling, and by the time she gets to the first chorus, the dance floor is full of writhing, thrashing bodies.

Everybody shrieks when the singer moans over the guitar solo in the middle of the song. I look at Mr. Camber and Ms. Maso, expecting Angelo to get in trouble, but Ms. Maso is reading the cards on Mr. Camber's flowers out loud to him and he's actually laughing. Neither of them seems to care that the gym has exploded over a song called "Cherry Bomb."

Suddenly, Stephanie breaks free of the mosh pit that's formed around her and runs over to me. With a scream, she throws her entire bouquet of red carnations up in the air and they rain down on my head in a cascade of red petals and love notes she didn't even open, like some kind of coronation.

Stephanie grabs my arms and starts making me jump up and down with her while she throws her hair around. Angelo is staring at her like he's never seen anything so beautiful in all his life. I can't stop laughing. He points at me like I'm supposed to be learning something from all this.

Stephanie is singing along at the top of her lungs. She's got a great voice, but it doesn't sound right with this music. I realize that her voice is…pretty. Too pretty for this. I start singing, too, just to hear the difference between our voices. There's nothing pretty about my voice compared to Stephanie's—it's got something scratchy and harsh in it, and it's pissed off and rough.

Just like Cherry Bomb's.

When the song comes to an end, I spin around and scream, "Cherry Bomb!" at Angelo. He grins at me. "See what I mean?" he says into the mic as if he's having a private conversation with me, not DJing a high school dance. "And The Runaways are, like, only the beginning! There's Kim Gordon and Siouxie Sioux—"

"Dude, play stuff we know!" somebody calls out in the sudden quiet of the music-less gym.

"Yeah, like, from this century!" somebody else says.

Without missing a beat, Angelo hits Play on "Raise Your Glass" by P!nk, and the satisfied masses go back to jumping around. P!nk is cool, but I can barely even hear her—The Runaways are still vibrating in my head.

I'm not an opera singer. I'm not a musical theater singer.

I'm a lead singer.

I wasn't wrong after all.

Stephanie runs back into the fray, on to the next song. Somehow, even though she's been jumping up and down in heels for the past few minutes, she's not even sweating. I, on the other hand, am totally drenched. I decide I don't care, and I'm just about to go ask Angelo to play "Cherry Bomb" again when I see Jamie standing next to Angelo's table.

I'm so jacked up that my first impulse is to run at him full-force, grab his face and kiss him like the world is ending.

But the practical side of me wins out. I can't let him see me like this, not after what happened last time we were together. What if I gross him out and he doesn't want to touch me again?

I bolt to the bathroom, adrenaline blasting through my veins as "Cherry Bomb" plays on the iPod in my head. I push open the door and see Ms. Maso in a gold sparkly sweater dress, checking the stalls to make sure nobody's doing anything they're not supposed to be doing.

"Hi!" I yell, making her jump. I tear off a piece of industrial-grade paper towel that is for sure going to leave scratches on my face and stand in front of the mirror trying to mop myself up. I see someone who looks deliriously happy. It takes me a second to recognize myself.

"Rose!" Ms. Maso replies, looking at me with a mixture of delight and concern. She's never seen me like this—I'm sure she's wondering if I'm on something.

"Cherry Bomb!" I sing at her, unable to keep from spinning around in a circle.

Luckily for me, Ms. Maso laughs.

"That's what I should be singing!" I say to my reflection. "Forget 'la-la-la'! Forget 'Oohs' and 'Ohs'! Forget musicals!"

Ms. Maso just shakes her head as I start spinning again, my arms waving above my head.

"Hey, Ms. Maso, when are you going to go out with Mr. Camber?" I clap my hand over my mouth when my brain catches up with my ears. Adrenaline is wreaking havoc with my impulse control.

"I did not peg you for a rumor-mill kind of girl," she says, scolding me with a smile in her eyes. "Don't go jumping around in here by yourself for too long."

"I like your dress!" I yell as the door closes behind her.

I mop up as much sweat as I can, giving up when I realize that it's appearing on my face as fast I can make it disappear, probably because I'm still dancing.

So what? What do I care?

Destiny just found me in the gym at Union High.

I run back to the dance and see Jamie still standing next to Angelo's table watching everybody, his hands in the pockets of his green army jacket.

With "Cherry Bomb" still echoing in my head, I grab his hand, pulling him onto the dance floor. He's so surprised he doesn't even put up a fight. I can feel a drop of sweat sliding down my face—probably bringing what's left of my makeup with it—but I truly don't care. I just start dancing. He watches me for a few seconds with a smile as I sort of spaz around, and then he starts dancing, too.

And the thing is, Jamie can dance.

He doesn't do any of that weird lip-biting or fist-thrusting that most of the other guys are doing—he just dances. And it's…sexy. I almost stop moving just so I can watch without any distractions.

All around me, people are working so hard to be hot—the cheerleaders are doing weird sandwiches with the jocks, where the girl is in the middle, grinding her miniskirt against a guy in front of her and a guy behind her. And the couples who are determined to make this Valentine's Day about romance are still pretending there's a slow song playing, pressed up against each other like they're glued together.

But the sexiest thing in the room is happening right in front of me, and it's not big or flashy or obvious. It's just...Jamie.

I think about being with him in my kitchen on Christmas Eve and what happened between us that night—how he apologized because he would have done things differently if he'd known I'd never done that before. But as I watch the way he moves, I get that strange aching feeling that I get whenever he touches me— even though he's not touching me now—and I realize that what happened in the kitchen was probably all I could handle. If it had been any more than that—if it had been a Thing instead of just something that happened—I probably would have freaked out.

You want more—you want everything—and then you're afraid of it. It's all so weird.

Jamie reaches out for my hand and holds it for a few seconds as I get the message to slow down. When I get the hang of what he's doing, he pulls me just the tiniest bit closer. He waits until I slow a little more, and he pulls me closer again. I practically want to jump out of my skin as the distance between us closes and I feel him looking, watching what we're doing, seeing how we move together. It's like he can see through my red dress, like he can see my body.

Like he gets it in a way that I don't.

Just when he's going to pull me against him, I see Conrad. He's leaning against the wall near one of the exits. For a second, I think he's staring at me, but it's not me he's looking at, it's Jamie. He pushes off the wall and heads toward us.

I can see him coming—Jamie can't. But I'm just as surprised as Jamie when Conrad grabs his shoulder and pulls him backward. Jamie stumbles, catches himself and spins around, ready for a fight, confusion in his eyes when he sees who it is.

"What are you doing?" Jamie loosely grabs the front of Conrad's coat and gets in his face a little.

"What are *you* doing, Jamie?" is Conrad's brilliant reply.

That's when I know he's been drinking. If he were sober, there's no way that would be a good enough answer for Conrad, the master of insults.

Jamie looks around to see if anyone important has noticed that Conrad can't really stand up straight. I can tell that he's trying to figure out a way to get Conrad out of the gym.

"Let's go," he says, throwing an arm casually around Conrad's shoulders and trying to turn him around.

"Aw, you wanna leave already? But we haven't danced yet!" Conrad insists, grabbing for Jamie's hands.

Jamie steps back, both hands up in the air. "You can't be drunk here."

"I want to dance with you!" he yells in Jamie's face. I can smell the alcohol from where I'm standing. Ms. Maso and Mr. Camber look up to see what's going on.

"Conrad, be quiet or you're going to get Jamie in trouble," I say.

"Every fucking thing's about Jamie. Everyone wants Jamie. Must be hard to be Jamie," Conrad says, his eyes glittering brightly. "Not as hard as being you, though."

I've been waiting for this.

"What do you have against Deladdos, huh? Last year you go crying to the principal about Regina, and this year you go crying to the principal about me?"

"I didn't say anything about Matt Hallis!" I yell at him, knowing that what I'm saying is technically true—but only technically.

"Sure, that's why we all ended up in Chen's office," he replies, rolling his eyes. "You're dull and predictable, you know that?"

"Did you even think about Jamie when you asked him to go with you to Matt's? What if he'd gotten arrested again?" I spit the words out, forcing him to take a step backward. "You're selfish."

"Let's *go*," Jamie says again as Camber stands up and starts to make his way over to us.

"You don't understand the first thing about me," he slurs. "You don't understand a fucking thing about a fucking thing."

"You're not that hard to figure out, Conrad."

"Go on, tell me *one* thing you understand."

"I understand why you've always been a jerk to me."

"Jerk." He laughs, snorting. "Can you even say the word *dick?* Or does it scare you?"

"Rose," Jamie warns, his eye on Camber.

I keep going. I hate myself for it, given what I now know about Conrad's life, but I keep going.

"First I thought you hated me for taking Jamie away from Regina. But now..."

I hesitate—the words I intend to say are setting off air-raid sirens in my head. I try to listen—I really do—but I just can't.

"What? Say what you were going to say!"

"Now I know it's because you think I took Jamie away from *you.*"

I got him—I got him good. I wasn't even sure I was right, but I can see now that I am. And that Conrad totally thought no one knew his secret.

Jamie closes his eyes like he wishes he could go back in time just ten seconds and stop me from saying it.

He knew. Jamie already knew.

It's the first time I've ever seen Conrad speechless. He wobbles from side to side for a second, and then turns toward the exit. Camber tells him that if he leaves he can't come back in, but Conrad blows past him. Camber watches how he's walking and then follows him.

Jamie's eyes go dark as a wall comes down between us.

"I hate how he talks to me, and to you," I say, sounding angrier than I am because I'm embarrassed by the crappy thing I just did. But I'm sick of Conrad—I haven't been able to get away from him since I first saw him standing on that diving board.

Talk about destiny.

"His life sucks right now," Jamie says.

"Yeah, well, so does mine," I answer.

"No shit," Jamie says, making it completely clear that he doesn't understand my lack of compassion.

I don't, either, to be honest.

Jamie goes after Conrad. Should I follow him? Apologize to him?

Or should Jamie apologize to me?

I wonder as I watch him walk away from me again—after getting close to me, after touching me—to take care of a Deladdo.

I'm officially done with the tolerance dance.

Stephanie is dancing her heart out in front of Angelo's table, but I don't see Tracy anywhere. I grab my coat and put it on even though I'm still sweaty from dancing—I don't want to see even a glimpse of the Valentine's-Day-red dress I'm wearing.

I head to the hall where a photographer was set up, figuring Tracy might be there taking her own photos. But the photographer is packed up and gone.

The hall is quiet and slightly eerie, with only the emergency lights on, but I can see someone down there. I take a few steps to get a better look, and I can just make out Tracy leaning against the lockers with someone.

I hear her laugh her special flirty laugh that she's perfected over the past two years, and I turn around to head home on my own.

And then I hear Peter.

Now I understand why Tracy's been so confident lately about college guys.

I turn back around and stand very still, listening, trying to make sure I'm hearing what I think I'm hearing. Then I head down the hall. When I'm standing a few feet away in a pool of red light from the emergency exit sign and Tracy finally sees it's me, her flirty look slides off her face. For a second, even Peter looks freaked out to see me standing there.

"You guys are such liars."

"Rosie, we didn't—" Tracy starts.

"Hang on," Peter says to her. "What are you talking about, Rose?" He is suddenly super pissed off. "We didn't lie to you about anything."

"You're together, and you didn't tell me. That seems like a big fat lie to me."

"It's not any of your business," he shoots back.

"It's *not?*" I ask, astounded.

Tracy looks like a deer caught in the headlights. "Rosie, I swear, we haven't seen each other since Christmas Eve. This is the first time."

"I'm such an idiot. You both suck," I say.

"Anytime you'd like to grow up would be great, Rose," Peter says angrily.

As I stalk off down the hall, my phone vibrates and I furiously yank it out of my pocket, tearing the lining of my coat, and see a text from Vicky.

Wishing you romance the size of Texas on this Valentine's Day. Now go kiss someone already!

SPRING

veracity *(noun):* reality; truth
(see also: once you learn or say something,
you can't unlearn or unsay it)

———————

13

IT'S THE FIRST DAY OF SPRING, AND IT'S SNOWING.

My mother and Dirk Taylor have gone out three times. At least.

I lost my best friend to my brother. I also lost my brother to my best friend. I'm not sure which bothers me more.

Jamie hates me for what I said to Conrad. I still can't figure out why I said it, to be honest.

Normally, I'd be punching walls over all this.

But today...I'm fine.

I don't mind the snow. I'm not mad about Kathleen and Dirk. I don't care what Peter and Tracy do.

Because today, after school, I'm auditioning for Angelo's new band.

I am ready to meet my destiny.

It takes me three tries to open my gym locker. I'd like to say it's because my hands are shaking from a post-gym-class endorphin rush—we did sprints—but I can't remember the combination to my lock, even though I've probably used it a thousand times by now.

I'm nervous.

But it's a good nervous. I know "Cherry Bomb" backward and forward. I can sing it in my sleep. I probably *do* sing it in my sleep.

Angelo has been emailing me MP3s of old-school punk to "educate" me, as he calls it, since FTS broke up. Their lead singer got signed to a label, but the rest of the band didn't. Angelo says he doesn't care because the guy was a loser, but I know he's totally bummed. So now he's starting a new band, and he wants a "badass girl singer" because he's "done with dicks."

He thinks I could be the one.

I think maybe I could be the one, too.

First the MP3s he sent were just girl singers, but now they're guys, too. Bad Brains, Social Distortion, Black Flag, The Dead Kennedys, The Sex Pistols, The Clash. Until now, Peter was responsible for my taste in music—Amy Winehouse, Snoop Dog, Led Zeppelin—but Peter's got nothing on Angelo. He's probably never heard of half these bands.

The truth is, I don't always know what to do with the stuff Angelo sends me. I mean, I don't know how to study it, or make myself sound like it. I don't even like all of it. But it's furious, and furious singers blow my mind. I go down in the basement and sing myself hoarse for an hour before I go to bed, and it's like someone just opened up the top of my head and let all the rage out into the atmosphere. When I'm done, I'm so calm I can fall asleep in minutes if I want to, and I hardly ever see freaky things in my head anymore.

Bye-bye, Insomnia; later, Horror Show. Take that, suckas.

The bell rings for the end of the period and I barely have my clothes on. I was so sweaty from sprints that I had to take a shower and although I tried not to let the water touch my face, I still need time to fix my makeup. I am going to be seriously late for French. I hear the herd shuffling out of the locker room to go to the last period of the day. I grab my bag and run to the mirror.

The girl who's staring back at me has on cat-eye black liner and thick mascara; choppy, short bangs that she did herself last night with a pair of pinking shears; and a single blue streak in her hair.

Needless to say, the girl's mother flipped this morning.

I told Mom the blue would wash out and the bangs would grow in. She forced herself to calm down—I actually thought I saw her mouthing the numbers as she counted to ten—and then looked me up and down. I said I was going for an Excene Cervenka sort of thing.

I waited for her to ask who or what I was talking about, but after a second she nodded—is it possible that she could actually know who Excene Cervenka is?—and I saw her make the decision not to say anything about the black tights with holes in them, or the Doc Marten's and vintage dress I borrowed from Holly.

Holly said I could keep the dress because it never fit her right, which is just Holly's nice way of saying it's way too big for her.

I look different. I *am* different.

I'll bet Tracy would totally put me on The Sharp List today. Not that I'd let her.

Things actually aren't terrible between me and Trace. It just feels like we've been taking a break from each other since Valentine's Day. Peter and I haven't really been acknowledging each other, either, which isn't that different from how things have been since he came home anyway, except for that one night.

I have to admit that I miss Trace—more than him, probably because I'd already been missing him for a long time and I'd gotten used to it. It's just that I don't want to be around her. I don't know how things are supposed to work now. Like, if I tell Tracy something, does she automatically tell Peter? And does Peter tell her stuff about me, stuff that I might not even tell her?

I think she gets it, because she hasn't been sending me The Sharp List. To be honest, it's sort of a relief not to be working for her anymore.

When I think about it, I know I should be happy for them. She's liked Peter forever, and he's probably having the second worst year of his life. He needs someone right now, and she can help him in ways that my mom and I can't. Or won't.

I *want* to do the mature, grown-up thing and be happy for them. But I can't. Not yet.

I'm fixing my eyeliner and hoping that Monsieur Levert won't care if I'm a few minutes late—as long as I can explain why in French—when the next class starts to come in.

"It's black with a really low back—I'm totally going to need double-sided tape to keep my butt from showing," I hear Lena say. "What's yours look like?"

"I don't have mine yet. But Anthony likes me in red," Regina answers with the enthusiasm of someone talking about cat litter.

They come around the corner and stop short when they see me.

"You can pay professionals to cut your hair, you know," Lena says, looking at my ragged bangs. "They can color it for you, too."

When I don't say anything, she asks, without bothering to hide her disgust, "Why do you look like that?"

Regina stays silent, staring at me.

"I have an audition," I reply.

"For a freak show?" Lena says, pleased with herself, looking at Regina for approval.

"She's her own freak show," Regina says.

In the mirror, I watch her go down one of the rows of lockers to start getting ready. Lena follows her like a devoted pet. Other girls come in, see Regina and Lena together and decide to find a locker in another row.

"This is what it looks like," Lena says, showing Regina something on her phone. Regina barely glances at it. When Lena sees me watching them, she asks with totally fake innocence, "Going to the prom this year?"

Regina laughs flatly. I pretend I can't hear her, digging through my bag for my makeup remover so I can clean up the mascara smudges under my eyes. Lena tosses her phone into her locker and pulls her sweater over her head—she's wearing a push-up bra that makes her look huge—and she shakes out her hair like she's in a movie or something.

"You guys want to share a limo?" she asks Regina.

Without thinking, I spin around.

"Wait a minute," I say to Regina. "You and Anthony are going to prom with Lena and Matt?"

I think it's probably the first time I've ever spoken to Regina first.

Now it's her turn to pretend she can't hear me.

"After everything Matt did to your brother?" I continue.

She starts to pull off her boots.

I surprise myself by adding, "You remember him, right? Conrad?"

Lena rolls her eyes dramatically. "Everybody goes through initiation when they join a team. Conrad made way too big a deal out of it. So did you."

"All I did was help Conrad out of the pool," I say. "I didn't make a big deal out of anything."

She readjusts herself as if she's not satisfied with the way her push-up bra is working. "Everybody knows you told Chen it was Matt," she says. "You can't keep your mouth shut when it comes to Chen."

I look at Regina to see if she's going to get in on the action, but she's weirdly focused on getting ready for class. She's modest compared to Lena, who is now stripping off her leggings and prancing over to the mirror in her matching lace bra and panties, pretending she doesn't notice people noticing.

But Regina turns her back to us as she steps out of her jeans.

I look in the mirror again, finish erasing the mascara smudges and spend a little more time arranging my messy bangs just so it doesn't seem like I'm rushing to get away from Regina and Lena. I stick my eyeliner and remover back in my bag and I'm just about to leave when Regina pulls her shirt over her head.

The bruises on her back are fading. In fact, if it weren't for the hideous fluorescent lighting in the locker room—which is for sure designed to keep students from looking at themselves when they should be going to class—I probably never would have noticed them. But right now, in here, they're unmissable. And big. Fist-sized, you might say.

They make me wonder what she's hiding on her front.

Lena is now going on and on about the prom after-party, debating the merits of renting a cottage on the beach or just going to a hotel like last year. When she finally senses my stillness, she looks at me, and then turns to see what I'm staring at. She gets just a quick glimpse before Regina pulls her gym shirt on and yanks her blond hair free of her collar.

Lena's eyes get huge, and she can't help but turn back to me for confirmation that we're seeing the same thing. We look at each other for a long moment, trying to read each other, trying to figure out what to do.

Lena makes a decision before I do, spinning around and picking up right where she left off, babbling about how she might be able to scam her parents into renting the cottage on the beach. But I'm not that fast. When Regina sees my face, she knows instantly what I saw. Or what I think I saw.

"Anthony likes it rough," she says.

"Likes what rough?" I ask without stopping to think.

"Sex. Do you know what that is?" she asks in a fake little-girl voice. She's in bitch mode, and she's going to do everything she can to turn this around on me. I brace myself. "You better figure your shit out fast if you're still after Jamie. Because he needs certain things," she says, drawing the words out to make them sound as dirty as she can. "I lost it to Jamie when he was living with us. So I would know."

I want to put my hands over my ears—I can't have this conversation with her. I don't want to hear the details. I don't want to know how it was. I don't want to hear anything about it. I don't want to spend a second thinking about the fact that she knows way more about what to do with a guy—with Jamie—than I do, and that there's no way I can compete with that.

I find myself thinking about how I knocked her to the ground on the track last year.

Breathe, I tell myself.

Regina knows exactly how to get me—she always has. She and her brother are both so good at it. They must have gotten that particular talent from their father. Because I've been in a room with Mrs. Deladdo, and there's no way Conrad and Regina learned how to destroy people from her.

Regina waits for me to say something with that dead smile on her face.

How is it possible to hate someone so much and feel bad for her at the same time? My head is going to crack open with the pressure of those two conflicting things.

"Why do you want to keep Jamie and me apart so badly?" I ask her as calmly as I can, trying to keep my hands from balling into fists. I want to hear her say it—I just want her to admit to me that she's still in love with him.

She tosses her bag in her locker and slams it shut with a bang. "Because you're full of shit, Rose," she says.

That's not even close to what I was expecting her to say.

"What does *that* mean?" I ask.

She takes her sweet time spinning the dial on her combination lock, then she picks up her sweatshirt and faces me.

"You're never gonna be with Jamie. You might give it up to him, or go out with him to piss off your parents," she says, knowing full well that my father is dead. "But you'll leave—you don't think Union is good enough for you. And you don't think Jamie is, either."

Her words lodge under my skin like tiny shards of jagged glass.

It happens so quickly that I almost don't realize it.

Almost.

The bell rings for last period.

Lena goes into the gym with a quick glance at me that I can't read.

Regina starts to follow her. "No way are you better than us," she spits at me. Her voice is hard but there's sadness in her eyes— actual, genuine sorrow.

She doesn't believe what she just said.

When the door to the gym closes behind her, I stand still, trying to get myself together, to shake off the waves of confusion and fear and fury that always follow a conversation with Regina.

Those word shards pulse under my skin.

I bolt, later than I've ever been for a class, catching a glimpse of blue-streaked hair in the mirror as I run by.

For a second, I don't recognize myself.

The snow slides down my bare neck as I stand in the slushy parking lot waiting for Angelo, who is fifteen minutes late. I didn't wear a hat or a coat or a scarf—they didn't look right with my outfit.

I'm freezing.

My brain has been stuck in an ugly loop since French and I haven't been able to get out of it. I picture Regina's bruises. Then I think about Jamie seeing bruises on her once, up close and personal; Jamie living in her house; Regina losing her virginity to him. And then I'm trying to imagine doing that. With him. And thinking about how it must feel to share that with someone, and then see that someone with someone else. And then I understand why Regina tried to hurt Jamie by going out with Anthony.

Thinking about Anthony sends me back to the bruises. And it starts all over again.

Those bruises are from Anthony. They have to be.

I remember the way he grabbed her arm at the swim-team party, hard enough to change the color of her skin. I wanted to peel his fingers off her. I wanted to help her and I didn't know why.

I knew something wasn't right.

Does Jamie know? Is that why he's so protective of her?

He can't know. He would have gone after Anthony a long time ago if he knew.

So do I say something?

If I tell Jamie, Jamie will start something with Anthony, and they will probably kill each other—literally. And what if I'm wrong? What if Regina was telling the truth, and she and Anthony do certain things—and I have no clue what those things would be—and she ends up with bruises? Then I'll look like a total and complete loser.

Is that possible? Do people do stuff like that?

But if I'm not wrong, and I don't tell Jamie, Anthony will keep hitting Regina and Regina will just keep letting him…because she doesn't know any better? Because she thinks she deserves it? Because it's all she knows?

What if she needs help, and I don't do anything?

The thing is, I made a promise to myself at the beginning of this year that I was going to stay out of other people's business and not open my mouth. I've already gone back on that once, for Conrad.

Do I really owe Regina anything after the things she's done to me and the way she treats me?

I kick at a giant pile of gray slush and send dirty chunks of ice flying. Why do I keep ending up with information that other people are supposed to have, information that I can't give them without causing a train wreck?

I can't think about this right now. I need to think about my audition—about all the music I've been listening to for weeks, about the fact that this could be my shot to be the kind of singer I want to be.

I shove Regina from my mind.

I'm looking for inspiration in the most depressing, hopeless, gray March sky I've ever seen when Jamie's car pulls up next to me.

"Angelo asked me to get you," he says, leaning over to talk to me out the passenger-side window.

Someone told me once that guys couldn't be beautiful—girls were beautiful, guys were handsome. Jamie's definitely handsome and hot and all that. But he's also beautiful, even when he's mad at me.

If Jamie's surprised by my new look, he doesn't show it. In the back of my mind, behind all the other stuff that's going on between us, I'm disappointed that he doesn't say anything, that he doesn't notice I've changed.

"Where's Angelo?" I ask.

"Still working. You ready?"

I'm freezing—there's nothing I'd like more than to get in the car and feel the heat blasting—but no, I'm not ready. I'm mad and confused and freaked out. I wasn't expecting to see him; I have no explanation for what I said to Conrad at the Valentine's Day dance; I can't say anything about Regina because I'm not sure what I saw and I don't want to seem clueless or stupid.

My brain ties itself in knots.

Jamie leans over a little more and opens the passenger door from the inside. "We gotta talk," he says.

I've been feeling pretty great about my hair and my outfit all day, but the second the car door closes behind me, I feel like an imposter, like I'm wearing a costume. As we leave the parking lot, I pull down the visor to check myself in the small mirror, to remind myself what I look like today, who I am now.

It's not lost on me that I've looked at myself in the mirror more in the past twenty-four hours than I have in the past two years. But I don't mind my reflection anymore—in fact, I sort of can't stop looking. Maybe because I finally like what I see. Or maybe it's that I no longer don't like what I see.

Is that an example of a double negative that actually makes a point clearer? I'll have to ask Camber.

I can feel Jamie watching me as I look in the mirror. I ignore him and shove the visor back up, my fingers raw and red from being outside with no gloves or pockets. I can barely feel them when I start picking at the holes in my tights to make them bigger.

"What you did was fucked up," he says.

My face gets hot. I yank on my tights too hard and two medium-size holes become one giant one. I pull my dress down to cover it. "You're mad at me?"

"You could say that, yeah," he says.

I hate knowing that I did something that made him not like me. Something still stops me from apologizing, though.

"So what happened after you left?" I say, trying to sound like I don't care.

"I took him home."

"You brought him home like that?"

"Mrs. D's seen worse," Jamie says.

"How did you get past Camber?"

"Camber's all right," he answers, as if that explains everything. While we're stopped at a light, he uses his sleeve to wipe off the inside of the windshield, foggy with our breath. Then he leans back against his door and just looks at me until I can't stand it anymore.

"I said it because it's true. And you know it."

"So?" he says, sounding genuinely confused, like he doesn't understand why Conrad being in love with him is a big deal.

The light changes.

He starts driving again.

And I realize that it's not a big deal. Not in the slightest.

Somebody loves somebody who doesn't love them back. It's just something that happens—probably all the time, if you're Jamie Forta. No biggie.

So why did I think it was a big deal? Because Conrad is gay? Because Jamie isn't?

What's my problem?

Regardless of the answer to that question, one thing is clear: Jamie Forta is obviously a way better person than me.

Maybe that's what Regina was really trying to tell me.

I suddenly feel defensive. "Conrad was being a jerk. I wanted to shut him up."

"You did a good job. He hasn't talked to me since."

"Well, maybe you can have your own life now instead of taking care of the Deladdos," I grumble.

As soon as the words leave my mouth, I see Regina's back in the harsh fluorescent light of the locker room.

"Can I turn the radio on?" I ask.

"You don't wanna talk to me, either, huh?"

I turn away from him and start making dots in the fog on my window. The more dots I make, the more I can see. A weird, spotted version of Union goes by in a gray blur of clouds and slush and road and buildings. I've never really thought about Union, about whether it's a good place or a bad place. It just…is. I *am* going to leave someday—I've always had the feeling that life is happening somewhere else and it's up to me to find it.

But I'm not the only one. I bet there are more people who leave Union than who stay. What's the difference between them? What makes one person leave and another spend the rest of his life here? Is one choice better than the other?

Do I think I'm better than Union? Better than Jamie?

I know I'm going to college when I graduate. I don't know what Jamie's going to do—he probably doesn't know, either.

Does it matter?

"I've never seen you like that," he says.

The sudden rush of shame makes me feel sick to my stomach.

"Yeah, you have. Last year, when you stopped me from hitting Regina."

I really wanted to hurt her. But she wanted to hurt me, too, in any way she could think of. Does that justify what I did?

I study the pattern I'm creating on Jamie's window. "Did you lose your virginity to her?"

It takes Jamie so long to answer that I wonder if I actually asked the question out loud or not.

"Where'd that come from?" he asks.

"Today she told me she lost it to you when you were living with her." He looks stunned, like he can't believe she told me that. "Is that when you first found out? About her dad?" I ask.

I can tell by the way his jaw is sort of moving back and forth that he's angry, but I'm not sure if he's angry at me or her.

"Why the fuck is she telling you stuff like that?"

Now it's my turn to be angry—it pisses me off that he even has to ask that question.

"Because she hates me, Jamie, and she's in love with you, just like Conrad! For all I know, Mrs. Deladdo is, too."

Jamie makes a sudden right, and I grab on to my seat belt because I feel like I'm going to go flying into him. He pulls into a parking space behind a random building and slams the gearshift into Park. Then he takes a long, hard look at me.

"You don't know anything about Mrs. Deladdo, or what she did for me."

Great. Another Deladdo mystery. "Well maybe you'll tell me someday," I snap. "Otherwise, I can just find out from Regina next time she wants to use something she knows about you against me."

Jamie rubs his face with both hands like he's trying to erase this whole conversation, and then he crosses his arms. "You're sort of a pain in the ass, you know that?"

"Me?" I ask, totally floored. "*I'm* the pain in the ass? *You're* the one who kisses me and takes me out on a date to tell me we can't go out on any more dates and then comes to my house and puts his hands up my shirt and kisses me—again!"

In the silence, the snow turns to sleet, rattling on the outside of the car, bouncing off the hood. Jamie lets out a long exhalation and runs a hand through his hair.

"I haven't been a virgin since I was thirteen."

This information sends such an unexpected, crazy rush of heat through my body that I get dizzy. The car suddenly feels like a million degrees inside.

"You were thirteen?" It comes out a whisper.

"Uh-huh."

"With who?"

"Girl at a party. She was high. We all were."

"You were at a— When you were— But—"

I don't know which question to ask first. I can't conceive of a world in which a thirteen-year-old boy would be at a party getting high and having sex.

Shows you how much I know.

"How old was she?" I ask.

"Seventeen."

"Isn't that…illegal?"

"Probably."

"And you were high? When you were thirteen?"

"Yes," he says deliberately, like he'd like me to stop asking questions.

It works. I am silenced, confused by the jealousy and desire and awe competing for attention in my brain as I try to picture Jamie Forta at thirteen, high, having sex with a seventeen-year-old.

When I was thirteen, I was collecting horse stickers.

I'm silent for so long that he shifts forward a little to get a better look at my face.

"Did you like it?" is the only thing my addled brain can think to ask.

"There was nothing to like." The way he says this doesn't tell me how he feels about what happened, but the words themselves make me want to take his hand and feel the warmth of his skin against mine.

"How did you end up at that party?"

He shrugs like he's not quite sure. "I was on my own a lot then. I did shit I shouldn'ta done."

"You've been…having sex since then?" I ask quietly, both afraid of and excited by what I know he's going to say.

He gives me a half smile. "Yeah, nonstop," he teases.

I'm too intrigued by his crazy story to be embarrassed by his teasing. "Do you like it?"

It's at that moment that Jamie notices that I look different. His gaze goes from the top of my head down to my feet, taking in the bangs and the blue streak, and the dress, the tights, the boots. I can't tell if he likes what he sees—I can't read his expression at all. But when he meets my eyes again, he reaches up and traces his fingers down the blue.

"Sometimes."

He likes it. Sometimes.

My stomach does a weird little flip and I want to roll the window down for air and let the frozen sleet land on my face. My head is tingling from the feel of his fingers in my hair and my eyes want to close.

"Like when?" I manage to ask.

"When it's somebody who means something."

"Are there a lot of people who meant something?"

"No."

"Did Regina?"

He doesn't hesitate. "Yeah."

I suddenly realize that Jamie might be the only guy who has ever been good to Regina in her whole life.

Ever.

"Do I mean something to you?"

His warm hand slides around to the back of my neck and just rests there.

"What do you think, Rose?"

The sleet comes harder now, the rattling louder.

"You remember the kitchen on Christmas Eve, and outside Tracy's before school started, and last year—Valentine's Day and homecoming?"

He nods.

"Why do you always disappear after?"

He looks at me as if I should already know the answer to that question.

I suddenly wonder if Regina has ever told Jamie her theory about me, about how I think I'm too good for him and would never truly be with him.

"What if I told you...I love you" is what I say.

Jamie's beautiful hazel eyes lock on mine, and his whole body freezes—I don't even think he's breathing. Then his hand slowly disappears from the back of my neck and he turns his head away from me slightly but keeps his eyes on me, as if he's not sure he heard me correctly, but if I said what he thinks I said, then there's something very, very wrong with me.

"You're looking at me like I'm crazy," I whisper.

"Yeah, well…"

"You can't say you didn't know."

Jamie turns away, placing his hands on the steering wheel like he wants to drive away from our conversation before I can say anything else.

"Don't, Rose."

"Don't what?"

"Everything's gonna be different soon. It's not worth it."

"To you?"

"To *you*. You don't love me, Rose. Trust me."

All the air leaves my lungs in a rush.

His cell phone buzzes and he digs into his pocket. "Yeah," he says, answering it. "Yeah, we're coming." I can hear Angelo's voice, though I can't hear what he's saying. "All right." He jams the phone back into his pocket, twisting to look over his shoulder while he backs out, pulling onto the main road as if we hadn't just been talking about love.

As if I'd never said anything at all.

meddlesome *(adjective):* being nosy; interfering
(see also: my mother, and—yeah—me)

———————

14

MY MOTHER HAS A PLAN FOR MY BIRTHDAY.

On Saturday morning, she hands me her credit card and says, "Go to the mall and get yourself a dress. Something you love." And then she adds with a mischievous smile, "People like you in blue. It brings out your eyes."

I try to get more out of her but she won't give me anything. As I'm walking to the mall, I think about calling Tracy to invite her along for this unprecedented moment in my life when I have my mother's credit card and permission to buy whatever I want. But I don't call.

Now that I'm not editing The Sharp List anymore, I have to go online if I want to see who she's featuring. This morning I logged on, and there was "The Sharp List: College Edition!" Peter, of course, was her pick, which I find pretty ironic, given that he's currently not allowed to attend college. Plus, she totally cheated—she dressed him and took fake candid pictures. I can tell because he looks like a J. Crew model, and there's no universe in which my brother could—or would—look like a J. Crew model on his own.

When I get to the mall, I wander through all the usual stores, but everything they have is normal, basic, boring—Union. There's one more store I can check, way at the end of the mall, called Tried & True. It's half vintage, half stuff that's made to look vintage. I went in there once in eighth grade—I didn't see anything I liked, but I was also pretty much wearing only leggings and sweatshirts back then, so that's not saying much.

There's a mannequin in the window of Tried & True wearing a black sequin minidress and high, lace-up boots with spiderweb stockings. She has skull-and-crossbones tattoos drawn on her arms, hot pink nail polish on her fingernails and bright blue eye shadow. There's a microphone on a stand in front of her, and someone has positioned her arm so it looks like she's about to grab it and start singing.

I wonder if I could pull off that look as a lead singer with Angelo's band. Of course, I have to get the gig first.

My audition was not the greatest. In fact, it was terrible. I tried to sing "Cherry Bomb" a bunch of times, but I couldn't do it the way Angelo wanted. He kept stopping the band and coming over to coach me, but I couldn't get the style he was after. "She's, like, dangerous—totally wild," he kept saying. "She explodes! She's on fire!" he'd yell as the band would launch into the intro again, and again, and again.

I started to feel bad and sound worse. It wasn't until Angelo asked me if I was okay that I realized I wasn't.

I had just told Jamie I loved him. I didn't know I was going to say it to him, and I'm not really sure I said it to him for the right reasons, but I said it.

I'd never said it to anyone before.

And he told me that I didn't love him, that he wasn't worth it. I think I went into shock.

When the audition was over—or maybe it was just when Angelo and the band couldn't take it anymore—Angelo drove me home. "What the hell was that, Sweater?" he asked in my driveway, giving me one of his famous shoulder punches.

That was all it took. I started to cry.

I told Angelo everything—almost. Regina saying she'd lost her virginity to Jamie; me telling Jamie I loved him; Jamie telling me that I shouldn't.

I didn't say anything about Regina's bruises.

It's not the first time I've cried in front of Angelo, but it was the first time he knew what to do.

"Look, Sweater," he said to me, looking around like he was afraid of getting caught. "I can't really talk about this. But I'll tell ya one thing—if a girl says the L word to Forta? It don't matter whether he loves her back or not. Game over—he can't deal."

Then he practically shoved me out of the car, like he knew he'd said too much. On my way out the door, he told me to watch Cherie Currie singing "Cherry Bomb" on YouTube at least forty times, because he wanted me to audition again in a few weeks.

It took me a second to realize he was giving me another chance. As I was mopping up my mascara and blowing my runny nose, I told him I'd kill it next time for sure.

And I meant it. As bad as my audition was, it taught me exactly what I have to do next time. I could feel that knowledge inside me, clear and solid. It wiped away the embarrassment, the shame, the doubt—and what was left was a plan of action.

When I got inside, I called Vicky and told her what I'd said to Jamie, and what Angelo had told me. She asked me right away if Jamie and I were having sex, like she was asking if he and I talked on the phone regularly. I said no, and she said, "Take a little piece of advice from a gal who got herself knocked up at fifteen. Most girls lose it to someone who doesn't give an armadillo's ass about them. They do it just to get the guy and then it blows up in their faces when the guy moves right on to someone else. Before you do anything, you ask yourself if you can trust this boy with your body and your heart. And don't you go lyin' to yourself about either one."

Vicky kind of missed the point, but I kept thinking about what she said anyway. I totally trust Jamie with my body—I feel absolutely safe with him when he's touching me. But I probably can't trust my heart to someone who says I shouldn't love him, no matter how much I trust him with my body.

I don't know what to do with that, so I put it aside.

The door to Tried & True is propped open, and Sleigh Bells is blasting from the store speakers. I go in and start poking around the racks, which are full of awesome dresses. Everything in the store is arranged by color—there's a red section, a black section, a green section.

I head to the blue section—it's the least I can do for my mom, since she gave me her credit card. I'm going through the dresses, trying to figure out what this new me likes, when I hear, "Can I help you?"

I am as surprised to see Regina as she is to see me.

Her face goes white. "What are you doing here?" she hisses, like I'm going to get her in trouble or something.

"I— You work here?"

She points to her Tried & True name tag and folds her arms. She's glaring at me but she looks nervous—she wants me out of the store, like, now. I look at her bright red 1950s dress and matching cardigan with rhinestone buttons, and her hair in a French twist. I feel like I'm in a parallel universe.

"I'm looking for a dress. A blue dress."

She points to the rack I was already looking at and goes back to the counter without saying anything else.

I start with the first dress, sliding it to the right. Then I slide the second dress to the right, too. I go through about five before I realize I have no idea what I was just looking at.

I'm standing in front of Regina at the counter before I realize what I'm doing.

She's stamping plain brown paper bags with the store's logo. I don't say a word—I just look at her. It's not a tactic. I truly don't know what I should say or do, but here I am, standing here, looking at her.

For a second, as she looks back at me, it seems like she might actually say something important. But she just reaches below the counter and turns up the music. "You're so weird," she scowls.

I keep standing there, waiting for her to tell me to get lost. It feels like an hour goes by. I have no idea where I get the courage to keep standing there staring her down, but I find it somewhere.

Finally she stops, slamming the stamp facedown, getting ink on the counter.

"It isn't any of your fucking business."

Her words are angry but not her voice.

She won't look at me.

And that's when I know I'm right about Anthony.

She grabs an armful of clothes that she has to put back on the racks and leaves me standing there. I drift back to the blue dress corner and start going through them again. I find a simple, dark blue sleeveless chiffon dress with a pleated skirt that has a high-button neck at the front and a super dramatic open oval in the back. I take it off the rack and hold it up.

"Can I try this on?" I ask Regina, who's as far away from me as she can get while still being in the store.

"Knock yourself out," she answers without looking.

I go into the dressing room and pull off my clothes.

Whatever it is that I'm trying to do would be easier if I could tell Regina that I know about her father—she wouldn't be able to blow me off then. But it would probably just make her even angrier to find out that I know something else about her that's so private, something that Jamie wasn't supposed to tell anyone. Something that makes her seem less like the badass she wants everyone to think she is.

Well, she *is* a badass. Just not with all the people in her life, I guess.

I wonder if Regina is mad at her father. I don't know how that works with people who get abused—are they mad at the people who do it to them? Or does that happen later, long after they're gone?

Is it worse for her if she's mad at her father, or if she misses him?

And I thought it was confusing for me to be mad at *my* dad.

Caron was grilling me last week about being angry at Dad. I admitted I was mad at him for not being here, for not figuring out a better way to make money than going to Iraq, for not telling me that he'd decided to stay longer. I didn't bring up the other reasons because I didn't think I could explain how I get mad thinking about how he used to say that I was beautiful because now I know he was saying those things just to make me feel good.

When I think about Regina's life, I feel like an idiot for being mad at my dad for anything.

I pull the blue dress over my head, and it slips right on like it was made for me. It's totally different from anything I've owned before, and I know I'm getting it the second I see my reflection in the mirror.

I change back and step out of the dressing room. Regina is behind the counter again, staring out the window into the mall. Although the music in the store has gone quiet, I'm not sure she even hears me come out.

I put the dress on the counter, take out my mom's credit card and wait.

Without looking at me, she picks up the dress and scans the price tag.

"Tell Jamie," I say.

I watch as she carefully folds the dress in thirds and wraps it in a piece of tissue paper. She takes her time putting a sticker with the store's logo on the tissue paper, and then reaches out for the credit card.

"If you knew him at all, you'd know what would happen."

She swipes my card and together we wait for it to go through. The machine starts whirring and churning, printing out the credit-card slip.

"I bet you anything he'd rather you tell him the truth than protect him from getting in a fight."

She tears the slip off the machine and puts it on the counter for me to sign along with a pen. I lean over and sign it, and then separate the slips, taking my copy and holding out the store copy for her.

She doesn't take it.

I lay it on the counter.

"He's done enough already," she says. As we look at each other, I can tell she's trying to figure out how much I know. I don't give her anything.

"Please, you have to—"

Fire lights her eyes. "Don't you tell me what I have to do. Stay out of whatever you think this is, and don't say a fucking thing. I don't need anything from you."

She takes the wrapped dress off the counter and drops it into a freshly stamped brown bag, which she shoves across the counter at me.

"It's wrong, what he's doing," I say.

Tears fill her eyes and she looks even angrier.

"What do you care," she says, turning her back, pretending to be busy with the computer on the desk behind her as she furiously wipes the tears off her face. "Get out."

I pick up the bag and turn to leave, stopping in my tracks when I see Conrad standing at the entrance. I have no idea how long he's been there, but he's looking back and forth between Regina and me, confused, worried, maybe even scared. "What did you mean?" he asks me.

It's the first time Conrad has ever said anything to me without sounding angry.

Regina spins around at the sound of her brother's voice. Her eyes shift to me and she goes still, waiting to see what I'm going to do.

I wait to see what I'm going to do.

"Something's wrong?" Conrad says to me.

As I look at him, I see him on Valentine's Day, his love for Jamie laid bare by me, for better or worse.... I see Tracy using her slut list fame to create The Sharp List.... I see myself trying to blend and realizing that maybe I just don't, or can't, or won't.

And I have what I think could be a moment of clarity.

Sometimes people help each other, and get messed up in each other's business; sometimes we stay out of it and let people find the way themselves. It's always right to offer help, but not all help is right.

I will keep telling Regina that I know what Anthony's doing, and that it's wrong, and that there are people who can help her. But I won't disrespect her by telling her brother—or anybody else—about something she told me to stay out of. Regina has to be the one to tell people. If she doesn't, won't she just end up in the same position again with some other guy later?

I don't answer Conrad's question. Instead, I say, "I'm sorry, Conrad, for what I said at the dance."

Conrad looks stunned and even more confused than before. I walk out of the store with my beautiful dress, leaving the Deladdos alone.

* * *

I keep getting glimpses into the restaurant's gleaming kitchen as tuxedoed waiters glide in and out of the swinging doors. A chef uses a big pastry bag to put the last flower on a giant chocolate cake sitting on one of the stainless-steel tables while an assistant figures out the perfect spot for each one of my sixteen candles.

I could have skipped the first four courses of the meal Dirk arranged for us—duck consommé and foie gras aren't really my thing, although to be honest, I don't really know what they are—and just had birthday cake. But after seeing *The Laramie Project* tonight, I decided that I could be polite and grateful and just go with the flow for the night—even if it meant spending my birthday with Kathleen and Dirk, and Holly and Robert.

When my mother returns from her trip to the bathroom, Dirk gets up from the table to pull out her chair, ignoring the giddy hostess who rushes over to be of assistance the second he needs anything. She's been finding every excuse possible to come over to our table since we got here, and I can tell that Dirk is getting annoyed. My mother, however, barely notices the hovering woman. She's just thrilled that this evening is actually happening.

I'm guessing my mother wanted to do something special for my birthday, knowing that I'd spent my fourteenth at home watching TV with her and my fifteenth recovering from mono and crying in the kitchen, also with her. But I was pissed when I found out earlier tonight that my mother's secret plan—going with Dirk to see Robert and Holly in *The Laramie Project* and then out to dinner in New Haven—was actually Dirk's plan.

The thing is, Dirk's plan was kind of genius, because it's super hard to stay pissed off during a play like *The Laramie Project*.

The play was beautiful and heartbreaking. It was about people who knew Matthew Shepard in Laramie, including the people who killed him and the people who tried to save him. It's about how what happened to Matthew changed all of them, and changed what they believed about all sorts of things. Basically, it's the kind of play that makes people want to be nicer to each other. I guess it gives you perspective—I don't think anyone walks out of *The Laramie Project* and still thinks that their stupid fights with their friends and siblings are worth it. I bet Dirk figured he could capitalize on that for my mother's benefit.

Note to self: Dirk Taylor is not dumb.

Everyone in the show was good. Holly was as lovely as always, and Robert did a super-solid job. Even Matt was okay—he said his lines at the right time and didn't intentionally mess anything up, which was sort of a surprise. Clearly Mr. Donnelly is some kind of miracle worker.

But it was Conrad who turned out to be the star. All the actors in the ensemble play a bunch of different parts, and Conrad transformed himself for each character in a way that nobody else did. The most amazing moment was when he was playing an E.R. doctor, and he had this really hard monologue about what Matthew looked like when the ambulance brought him in. It was incredible, the way Conrad did that. I got chills, not just because of the play or Conrad's performance but because Conrad became an actor in front of our very eyes. He found the thing he can do, and he did it perfectly.

It's the first time I've ever been jealous of Conrad Deladdo.

By the time the play was over, I felt like I'd been to Laramie and talked to the people who knew Matthew Shepard myself. After the curtain call, there was a talkback where the cast answered questions, and Mr. Donnelly explained how he hoped that the show would help people to understand what it means to truly accept others for who they are.

I think half the audience was at least sniffling at that point, if not wiping tears off their faces.

When we were waiting for Robert and Holly, I watched Conrad being congratulated by people. He looked like a totally different person—he looked happy.

"The writing is just so interesting," Dirk says as he refills my mother's wineglass. "What did you think of the script, Rose?"

The kitchen door swings open again, and this time I see someone with a handful of real flowers, placing them in between the candles on the cake.

"It was really smart the way it was different people talking but not necessarily to each other. It was like the lines spoke to each other, even if the people weren't actually speaking to each other."

My mother smiles at me as if she's impressed with my comment.

"But did it move you?" Dirk asks. "Ultimately, did the structure work?"

"Dad," Holly scolds. "This isn't class. It's Rose's birthday."

"Sorry, Rose." He apologizes with his trademark smile that can get him pretty much anything in the world—I think the obsessed hostess swoons across the room.

"No, it's okay," I say. "The structure of the play did move me. And so did the production. Especially Conrad. I can't believe that was his first play."

"Conrad was really good," Holly says. "He worked harder than anyone else in rehearsal."

Robert is bristling before she can even finish the sentence. "He came a long way during the process. He needed a lot of help."

"Well, he'd never acted before," Holly explains. "I think he's a natural. Don't you, Dad?"

"He has great—"

"He's not a natural," Robert scoffs, cutting Dirk off.

Dirk looks at him in surprise, clearly not used to being interrupted.

"Stop," Holly says to Robert quietly.

Robert doesn't answer.

I look back and forth between them. All is not well in paradise.

"What do you mean by natural, Holly?" Dirk asks.

Holly doesn't get the chance to answer because ten guys in suits suddenly materialize and surround our table. They start singing an elaborate a cappella version of "Happy Birthday" in, like, six-part harmony. As they sing, the waiter brings over the giant cake lit with sparklers and covered in roses both real and made of icing. When they're done singing, I lean over and blow out the candles, and the whole restaurant applauds.

"Thanks, guys. Thanks for coming tonight," Dirk says to the singers, rising to shake their hands as a few flashes go off in the restaurant. "You've got quite a voice, Cal," he says to one of the younger guys in the group. "Cal is in my first-year class," he explains to us.

"Thank you, sir," Cal says, beaming, forgetting to let go of Dirk's hand as his eyes drift over to Holly.

"Rose?" my mother says, raising her eyebrows, reminding me to be polite.

"Oh! Thanks. That was really nice," I say to the group as I half stand and give them a weird little thank-you bow. Even though a cappella singing sort of makes me want to yank my hair out by the roots, I have to admit it's pretty cool to be serenaded by a bunch of college guys in suits. Cal smiles at me, and then his gaze shifts back to Holly.

"Hi, Holly," he says with a grin.

"Hey, Cal," Holly answers with a little wave. "That sounded so great. Thanks for singing for my friend."

Despite the fact that Cal is super cute, with messy blond hair and bright green eyes, Holly's greeting is totally innocent. But Robert doesn't see it that way.

While Dirk walks the singers to the door of the restaurant and my mother is engaged in strategic conversation with the head-waiter about how to serve the giant cake, Robert turns to Holly.

"How do you know *that* guy?" he asks.

"Like Dad said. He's in his first-year class."

"That still doesn't explain how you know him."

She gives him a long look, like he's trying her patience. "You are not in a position to accuse me of flirting with someone right now."

Robert takes a deep breath. "I'm sorry." When she doesn't acknowledge his apology, he says, "How long are you going to be mad at me?"

"I don't know. Maybe I should ask Rose how long I should stay mad at you."

"Tell her," he says, his crystal-blue eyes blazing. "Just tell her."

"Okay," Holly says sharply. She turns to me. "Robert told me that *he* liked *you* last year, not the other way around."

"He did?" I say, unable to hide my surprise that Robert finally told Holly the truth.

"Rose, why didn't you tell me?"

Holly looks hurt and it makes me feel terrible.

"I, uh...I felt like he should tell you. And I told him that. I did, Holly, I swear." I think about adding the fact that Robert asked me not to say anything, but I figure he's in enough hot water as it is. "It just didn't feel like my place to say anything."

My mother goes to the front door of the restaurant to say goodbye to the singers as the headwaiter starts cutting the cake and resetting the table for six.

Six?

"Well now I know why he's weird about you sometimes," she says to me. "You chose someone else over him."

Robert's not even listening at this point. He's staring at Dirk, who has his arm over Cal's shoulders and is telling my mom something obviously complimentary about him. Robert looks like he's contemplating the best way to murder Cal.

"No, Holly, it wasn't really like that—"

"Do you want to be with that college guy?" Robert interrupts. "Because if you do, you should just go."

Holly looks at Robert, and then looks over her shoulder to see Dirk chatting with Cal. Slowly—dangerously slowly—she turns back to Robert.

"Oh, should I?" Holly asks sarcastically. I've never seen her look angry before. For the record, she's just as pretty when she's angry as when she's happy.

Robert says, "Yeah, you should."

I want to grab the words and stuff them back into his mouth. He has no idea what he's doing.

Holly slowly picks up her sparkly silver clutch and stands just as the headwaiter puts a piece of cake down in front of her. She walks over to her father, says something to him and then continues right out the door.

Dirk and my mother aren't quite sure how to respond, but Cal is. He doesn't waste a second—he goes after her instantly.

Robert is out of his seat and halfway across the room before I can tell him he's being an idiot. Dirk stops him and hands him off to my mother, who is still talking to the singers, before going after Cal and Holly. My mother then sends Robert back to the table, presumably so he doesn't have to withstand the coldly appraising looks of the college guys who can't understand what a beauty like Holly is doing with a high school sophomore.

Robert sits down heavily in his seat and rests his forehead in his hand. "Sorry to mess up your birthday night."

The waiter puts a piece of the perfect cake down in front of me. "Robert."

"Yeah?"

"What are you doing here?"

He looks up at me. "What do you mean?"

I shake my head. "Why are you listening to Dirk and my mother?"

It takes him a second, but he stands up and starts to run. Then he comes back. "Rosie, I'm sorry I—"

"Yeah, I know, I know. Go."

He doesn't have to be told again.

I look down at my chocolate cake with a real red rose on it and I pick up my fork, wondering whether being the birthday girl means I can start even if no one else is at the table.

"That is some dress, Rose."

I look up and Jamie is standing next to me in a suit.

An actual suit.

It's black, and it fits him perfectly. He has on a tie. His hair is still wet from the shower, and he's holding a thin package neatly wrapped in brown paper with a bow made of twine and my name carefully printed in that meticulous block handwriting. I almost reach out to touch him, to make sure he's not some weird hallucination I'm having.

"Your mom invited me. I couldn't make the play or dinner, but she said come for dessert."

The headwaiter materializes out of nowhere with another chair and places it in front of the sixth table setting.

"My...mom?"

How did she even know to call him? I haven't said anything to her about Jamie in months.

Jamie pulls out the chair next to me and sits. "Sweet sixteen, huh?"

"I guess so."

"Everything okay?" he asks, looking at the host stand where my mom is deep in conversation with Dirk, who has just come back in from outside.

"Robert and Holly are having some drama," I say.

Jamie nods. "How was the play?"

I pause, not sure if I should bring Conrad up, but I know that

Jamie would want to know. Since Conrad isn't talking to him—thanks to me—it's really the least I can do.

"It was amazing," I say, "thanks to Conrad. He was great. Really, really great."

"Yeah?" Jamie says, sounding surprised. And also proud. I understand, in a way that I never did before, what Jamie has been trying to explain to me all year.

Conrad is family to him.

And so is Regina.

I have to tell him. If I don't tell him and something happens to her, he'll never talk to me again.

"So he can act, huh?" Jamie asks thoughtfully.

"Yeah," I say. "He did this whole monologue that made everybody cry."

Jamie's eyes roam over my face for a second. "I don't like to hear about you crying," he says, and I know we're not just talking about the play anymore.

"It just happens sometimes," I say, picturing Angelo telling Jamie about the snot-fest I had in his car after I totally blew "Cherry Bomb." I take a deep breath, and say, "I'm sorry about what I said to you that day. About how I feel."

"Don't be sorry, Rose."

"I am, though. I know we're not..."

"It's good that you told me," he says when I don't finish my sentence.

"I could tell it made you feel weird."

After a second of Jamie staring me down with those beautiful, gold-flecked hazel eyes, he hands me the package I forgot he was holding and leans forward to whisper in my ear. "You look gorgeous."

My heart stops in my chest. Jamie stands to greet my mother and Dirk, who are coming back to the table without Holly and Robert. I know, without opening any of my presents, that I've just received the best gift I ever could have dreamed of for my sixteenth birthday.

"Jamie." My mother smiles, grasping his hand in both of hers. "This is Dirk Taylor."

"Pleasure," Dirk says, shaking Jamie's hand. "Glad you could join us."

"Thanks for the invitation," Jamie answers. As he sits, Dirk gives me an approving wink. My mother catches my eye and I can't help smiling at her. I can't believe she did this for me.

Now I know why she sent me to buy a dress—a blue dress, to be exact.

"I think we should get started," she says, discreetly implying that whatever is going on with Holly and Robert could take a while.

If someone had told me two years ago that I'd be spending my sixteenth birthday at a fancy restaurant with my mother and a movie star, I would have called that person nuts. If they'd said that I'd have Jamie Forta next to me, looking perfect in his suit and making polite conversation with my mother and the movie star, I would have said that person was totally certifiable.

"Are you ready to open some presents?" my mother asks. There's a little pile of beautifully wrapped boxes in the center of the table, but I'm most interested in the one in my hands.

"I'll start with this one," I say as I pull the end of the twine bow. The package is very light, like there's nothing in it. As I slide my finger under the tape and pull the brown paper away, I see what looks like a piece of cardboard. When I notice the frayed edge on one side, and realize it's the back cover of a notebook, I know exactly what I'm looking at.

I turn the cardboard over and see the beautiful house that Jamie was drawing in study hall on the first day we ever talked to each other last year, the one I told him I really liked. He finished it—it's a much bigger house and the woods that surround it are denser—and he inscribed it.

Happy 16, Rose. Love, Jamie.

Love, Jamie.

"What is it?" my mother asks.

I hold up the drawing.

"Jamie, is that your work?" she asks, as if he were a professional artist. When he nods, my mother says, "You have real talent. It's beautiful."

"What a spectacular design, son. Have you thought about architecture school?"

I make my second mental note about Dirk for the evening: he's supportive. Genuinely.

"See?" I say to Jamie, grinning at him. "It's not just me."

Jamie thanks my mother and Dirk but can't quite look at me, choosing instead to focus on putting sugar in his coffee. I let him off the hook and pick up my fork, cutting a perfect piece of dark chocolate cake, working around a real red rose. I'm just about to taste it when Jamie takes my hand under the table.

carnage *(noun):* violence; brutality; bloodshed
(see also: the inevitable happens*)*

15

"ROSE."

I hear Tracy's heels clacking down the hall.

"Rose!" she calls again when I pretend I can't hear her over the sound of yanking my locker door open. I'm checking my hair when her face appears behind me in my mirror. "Can I talk to you for a minute?"

I take another few seconds to check out my new blue streaks before grabbing my stuff and slamming my locker closed. I turn around.

Tracy doesn't look like a high school student anymore. She dresses like she works at a fashion magazine, which, I guess you could argue, she sort of does. The Sharp List now has followers all over the place, not just in Union. I think some reporters in New York even follow her blog. Stephanie told me that her parents are so excited that they are hiring a professional web designer to build her site.

It's all happening for her. Already.

But she still looks nervous about talking to me.

"Your hair looks cool," she says as she automatically takes in my outfit.

Today is my callback for the band, and I'm wearing torn-up black jeans with safety pins in the seams and pretty much every bracelet I could find in the house. Holly lent me a super-cool off-the-shoulder camouflage shirt, and she helped me with my makeup in the bathroom this morning before first period, so my thick black eyeliner is way better than it was last time.

I'm lucky that Holly was willing to help me.

After the birthday dinner, I called her to apologize and because she's Holly, she said not to worry about it, and that Robert shouldn't have put me in the middle like that. I told her that it was obvious that Robert was completely and totally in love with her, and that he's an idiot sometimes but a really good guy.

That's when she told me that they're on a "break" now.

I'm sure Robert is in a dark room somewhere, pulling his hair out and rocking back and forth, trying to figure out how he messed up the best thing that ever happened to him.

I'm going to call him later to check on him.

"Are you busy today?" Tracy asks.

"I have my callback for Angelo's band."

"Oh, okay," she says, sounding a little disappointed. "Chen asked me to do a special prom post for The Sharp List, so I have to get a dress before tomorrow night."

I wait to see how this involves me.

"Um, Peter is meeting me in the lot and we're going shopping. I thought maybe you could come along, too. And then maybe the three of us could get a slice after?"

"Sorry. Can't," I say. My voice sounds cold even to my own ears.

"Maybe some other time," Tracy says, turning to go.

Give her something, says a voice in my head.

"I'm walking to the lot now," I say, and Tracy looks back at me. "Want to walk together?"

A smile lights up her face.

As we walk out into the perfect May afternoon, I try to sort out what I want to say to her.

"It just makes me feel weird" is how I start.

She knows me so well, it's not a problem that I started in what should probably be the middle of the conversation. "I know," she says.

"Why didn't you guys just tell me?"

"It really didn't happen the way you think it did."

"Okay, so how did it happen?"

"When he texted me in December, he just needed help. He was afraid to tell you and your mom, and he thought if I was there, it would be easier. He asked me not to tell you because he knew you'd be upset that he didn't call you first. But I figured you'd want me to help him. So I said okay."

"So, between Christmas and Valentine's Day…?"

"Nothing, Rosie. I swear. We just talked on the phone a bunch. He was miserable and he felt like he had no one to talk to, so he called me." For once, Tracy is the one who blushes. "You know I've been crushing on him forever. Talking so much just made it…worse. And then, when I kind of couldn't take it anymore, I told him to meet me at the end of the Valentine's Day dance. And I kissed him. I felt bad that you found us, Rose. Peter did, too."

"He did?"

She's surprised by my surprise. "He hasn't told you that?"

"He acts like he didn't do anything wrong."

Tracy seems baffled by this, but she doesn't offer any explanations.

"See? That's why this is weird. You have all this information in your head about what's going on, but you can't tell me anything because of him."

"I want to be your best friend, and I also want to be Peter's girlfriend," she says. "How do I do that?"

We fall silent as we walk toward the hill.

Union High girls are calling out to Tracy, telling her that she's going to want to take their picture tomorrow night because they're going to be wearing this or that designer to the prom. The girls who want to be models have actually started giving Tracy little gifts when she puts them on her site, thanking her for giving them something for their portfolios.

It still seems weird to me that Tracy gets this kind of attention, but she handles it like a pro.

I'm proud of her.

Maybe I should tell her that.

"I'm proud of you." Tracy does a little double take, like she doesn't understand what I'm talking about. "The site. Everything you did with it. All the followers you have. You're going to be able to work anywhere you want when you leave Union. It's cool."

Tracy smiles. "I think that's the nicest thing you've ever said to me."

"It's true. The Sharp List is awesome."

"Will you start working on it again? The writing is so bad without you."

"Only if you put me on the thing for once." I try to sound like I'm joking, but she sees right through that. She lifts the camera that now lives permanently around her neck and snaps my photo before I'm ready.

"Wait—"

"You know what, Rosie? You used to wear whatever I told you to wear, and don't get me wrong, you looked good, thanks to me. But I just never felt like you had your own style—until now. I love those blue streaks. And as much as I wish I could take credit for them, I can't."

She keeps snapping photos as we start up the path on the hill. "You can stop now. You're making me self-conscious."

Tracy laughs and lowers her camera. "So how'd you like my birthday present?" she asks.

I think back to my birthday, to the pile of presents on the table for me at the restaurant. I can't remember a gift from Tracy. "Did you give me a present?"

"You don't think your mother figured out to invite Jamie to your birthday dinner on her own, do you?"

I grab her hand to make her stop walking. "Wait. That was you? You made that happen?"

"Me and Peter. She invited us. We told her you'd rather have him there, and she knew we were right."

I feel warm as I remember looking up and seeing Jamie standing next to me in a suit, holding a birthday present. "Oh, my god, Trace" is all I can say.

"Holly said your dress was totally amazing. I have to see it."

"Jamie told me I looked gorgeous. It was the greatest birthday present ever."

Tracy smiles. "You're welcome, Rosie."

She gives me a hug. I know somehow, as we stand there, that we can never go back to the way we were before she was going out with my brother. But maybe that's not a bad thing.

We get to the top of the hill and hear a crazy commotion at the same time. There's a big group of people standing around in a circle, watching something. As we get closer, I see fists flying.

Suddenly Stephanie is running toward us as fast as she can in her high-heeled clogs, yelling something I can't hear. When she stops and starts waving for us to hurry, I break into a sweat before I even start to run.

I push my way through the circle. Jamie and Anthony are locked together on the ground. Anthony's nose is gushing blood and Jamie's eye is starting to swell but they're still swinging at each other like they don't intend to stop until someone dies.

I look up and see Angelo on the other side of the circle, his eyes glued to Jamie. He looks like he's dying to get in there but he's holding himself back.

Which means that Jamie told Angelo not to jump in.

Which means that Jamie started this.

Which means he knows.

Conrad and Regina are near Angelo, and Regina is crying. I'd only seen her cry once before the other day, and I was pretty sure I'd never see it again. But she's actually sobbing, and Conrad is practically holding her up. Conrad looks at me—I can't read his expression. Lena is on the other side of Regina, and she looks terrified. When our eyes connect across the circle, I know exactly what happened.

Lena told Jamie. Did she also tell him that I knew?

Do I even have to ask that?

Anthony gets the upper hand and rolls on top of Jamie, getting in a good shot at Jamie's stomach. Jamie manages to shove Anthony backward and stand up.

Suddenly, there are two West Union guys in the circle. They grab Jamie from behind.

The Union crowd thinks this is unfair. Angelo now has the reason he was looking for to jump in. He starts swinging at Anthony. One of Anthony's pals lets go of Jamie to go after Angelo. And then suddenly Peter is shoving his way through the circle.

He gets Anthony in a headlock and drags him backward. Jamie shoves Anthony's guy to the ground and comes toward Anthony, fists clenched, face bloodied, fury pouring off him in waves. Peter yanks Anthony around so that Jamie can't hit him.

"Enough, man, enough!" Peter says to Jamie, breathless with effort. Even though Peter's older, he's struggling to hold on to

Anthony, who's way bigger. And while Peter has been sitting in a room with other addicts talking about his feelings, Anthony has been weightlifting with his puckhead friends.

Jamie ignores Peter and easily frees Anthony from Peter's headlock. Peter stumbles a little but quickly turns around so he and Angelo can block Anthony's pals as Jamie and Anthony go at it again.

Jamie lands a fierce punch and Anthony crashes to the ground. Anthony's up a second later, charging at Jamie. Somehow, he manages to pin Jamie to a parked car and he starts landing punch after punch. Jamie doesn't seem to be defending himself anymore, and I realize he can't really see because one eye is now swollen completely shut, and the other one doesn't look so good.

I think Conrad must realize the same thing because he lets go of Regina and takes a flying leap at Anthony, trying to keep him from hitting Jamie again. Conrad pins Anthony's arms long enough for Jamie to slide down the side of the car and land on the ground.

"What the hell is going on here? Break it up!"

As Mr. Camber runs toward the group, everyone who was watching starts to melt away, vanishing into nearby cars or stores.

"You!" Camber says to Anthony, who's struggling to get Conrad off him. "Get over here by this car and don't move. Conrad, let go and stand over there. Zarelli!" he calls to my brother, pointing to Anthony. "Watch him!"

Camber crouches down in front of Jamie and looks at his busted-up face. "This is not going to end well for you, Forta," he says, his voice full of furious disappointment.

Jamie doesn't even seem to hear Camber. He's focused on Regina, who is still sobbing.

"Fuck you, Rose!" she shrieks at me. "Fuck you!"

I open my mouth to tell her it wasn't me but Camber starts yelling. "Somebody start talking—now!"

"Forta don't like me goin' out with his ex-girlfriend," Anthony says, his voice weird because of his broken nose. His entire shirt-front is covered in blood and snot.

"Is that true?" Camber asks Jamie.

Jamie's semi-good eye shifts to Lena, and then lands on me.

This can't be happening. This can't be the way this is going to go.

"You have to give me something here, Jamie, or I can't help you," Camber says.

Jamie spits blood on the ground and stays silent.

As Camber keeps grilling him, Lena tries to sneak away. I grab her arm. "You told him?" I whisper.

She pulls away. "Of course I did. What's wrong with you?" she says.

The irony of her response is too much for me to handle right now. I let go of her and she disappears.

The paramedics and the cops arrive at the same time, and things start to happen really fast. Bobby Passeo, who used to play hockey with Peter and Jamie—and who I got to meet not once but twice last year—jumps out of the ambulance, opens the back and grabs his red box.

"Hey, Zarelli!" he says to my brother, as if seeing two guys on the ground with bloody faces is way more normal to him than seeing my brother back in Union. "Just like old times, huh? Long live puckheads."

He checks Anthony's nose and shoves gauze up his nostrils to stop the bleeding, making Anthony wince in pain. Bobby gives Anthony's forehead a shove.

"If you want to stop bleeding, keep your head back," he says.

As he checks Anthony's pulse, he sees me.

"Rose! What do you know—two Zarellis for the price of one. Hey, do me a favor and bring this ice pack over to Forta. You gotta crunch it up to make it cold," he instructs as he hands it to me.

I take the pack and bend it back and forth a few times, feeling the cold start to seep through the plastic into my fingers. It continues into my veins and travels through my whole body. I work up the courage to take two steps toward Jamie but the fury in his gaze stops me in my tracks.

I never thought I'd know what it was like to be on the receiving end of that look.

"I told her to tell you," I begin, trying to speak normally. "I told her you'd want to know. She said it wasn't my place—"

Jamie doesn't even bother to answer—I see the wall come down and he's gone.

The radio in Officer Webster's car is crackling to life. Webster goes to the cruiser, reaches in the open window and picks it up. After a second, he gets in the car, closing the door so that we can't hear his conversation.

Jamie watches Webster. When Webster gets out of the squad car a minute later, he crosses to Jamie and squats down next to him. I'm still frozen in place just a few steps away with the ice pack in my outstretched hands.

"Your dad wants me to bring you in."

I can't believe this is happening because of Regina *again*. I just can't. Conrad is trying to get her to leave but she won't move. She just keeps saying, "I'm sorry, Jamie, I'm sorry," over and over again.

But I don't think he hears her, either.

Webster extends his hand and helps Jamie up. But when the officer crosses to the car and opens the back door for Jamie to get in, Jamie doesn't follow him.

"Jamie," I say, though I'm not sure what comes after that.

It doesn't matter that I'm not sure because the next thing that happens is he comes over to me and says, "I don't know you."

And then he starts walking out of the lot.

No one knows what to do. Officer Webster looks at Camber, who seems to be wrestling with a decision. Finally he calls after Jamie.

"Forta, if you walk away, there's not a chance in hell you'll graduate!"

But Jamie just keeps going. He walks away—from Officer Webster, from Camber, from Union High, from me.

I feel like I might fall down. And in fact, I start to.

Angelo grabs my arm. Someone has my other arm—it's Peter. They walk me over to a curb and sit me down.

"It's going to be okay, Rose," Peter says from very far away. "Jamie's fine. He's not hurt that badly."

"Yeah, don't worry about him. He can take care of himself, ya know?" Angelo says. "He never cared about no high school diploma, anyway."

They don't know. They don't know what I did.

Tracy is in front of me suddenly. She's digging around in her bag, pulling out tissues. It's only then, when Tracy brushes the hair out of my eyes and starts working on the eyeliner and mascara that are running down my face, that I realize I'm crying.

"One, two, three, four!"

The band launches into "Cherry Bomb."

I close my eyes. My hands are wrapped around the microphone stand so tightly that my fingers feel bloodless. The music vibrates up my arms, into my neck and straight into my brain where it takes over, obliterating everything else. There's nothing but the guitar, the bass, the drums—and then, there's me.

I am not thinking about the parking lot...

I am not thinking about Angelo and Stephanie half-carrying me to the car where I fell into the backseat…

I am not thinking about Jamie….

Because this—what's happening right here, right now—is mine. And I got this.

I start out almost quiet, like Cherie does, because the notes are low in my range, but by the fourth line of the verse, I'm up an octave, right in my sweet spot, and heading straight for the chorus with more power than I ever knew I had.

I grab the mic off the stand and start jumping—I can't stand still. I see Angelo out of the corner of my eye, watching me, throwing his head around in time with the rhythm section. His eyes practically roll back in his head during the solo. When I come back in on another chorus, I start crashing into him.

The song goes up half a step, and now I'm not even singing anymore—I'm yelling in key. I swing the mic in circles and snarl just like Cherie did, which makes Angelo grin. By the end of the song, I'm on my knees, pounding on the floor with my fist as hard as I can. The song ends and I fall backward, my head hitting the floor, my legs folded under me, my arms thrown out to the sides.

I can't catch my breath. My hands are throbbing and bruised. My throat feels raw. I'm completely wrecked.

It's awesome.

Nobody says anything.

And then Stephanie screams. She jumps up from where she was sitting on the floor and screams like she's being murdered.

"Rosie! That was amazing! You're totally incredible!"

She bounces over to me, pulls me up off the floor and wraps me in a hug. We practically fall over, and then she shrieks again and jumps on Angelo, grabbing his face and kissing him over and over and over again.

"You're a genius! She's perfect!"

I reach out for the mic stand to steady myself. I'm doubled over, still trying to catch my breath. Angelo takes his guitar off and sets it on top of his amp. He comes over and holds his hand up for a high five. I give him one.

"*That's* what I'm talkin' about, Rose." Now it's his turn to crush me in a hug—I guess he doesn't care that I'm dripping with sweat.

For once in my life, I don't, either.

"Wait here," he says to me as he waves the rest of his band into the other room. Stephanie is still hopping around with excitement.

"Oh, my god, you're totally going to get it, Rosie! None of the other girls who auditioned were anywhere near as cool as you." I must look unsteady on my feet because she suddenly says, "Oh, here! Come here, sit down."

She reaches for my hand. I put the microphone back on the stand and let her pull me over to the ratty futon in the corner of the rehearsal space. I collapse, half on the futon, half on the floor.

"Did that feel as incredible as it looked?" Steph asks.

"It was like…I don't even know. It's a rush."

"You thirsty? Want some water or something?"

"Yeah, thanks, Steph."

She dashes over to the crusty old refrigerator in the corner. While she's looking behind moldy pizza boxes to see what she can find, I pull my phone out of my bag.

I have a whole bunch of missed calls. But none of them is the one I'm hoping for.

I don't have the strength to listen to the messages. I close my eyes and curl up on the futon.

As I lie there, I can no longer push away the image of Jamie's battered face, and his words start ringing in my head.

I lost him for real this time. I did the wrong thing, and I lost him for real.

But did you do the wrong thing? Jamie thinks it was the wrong thing. But do you?

No. I don't.

I didn't do what Jamie would have wanted me to do, but that doesn't mean it was wrong.

My bag is next to me on the ground. I reach into it without looking and feel around for the piece of cardboard that I've been carrying with me since my birthday. I run my fingers over it, and I can feel the indentations made by Jamie's hand pressing down hard with a pen as he wrote, *Love, Jamie.* His hands are burned into my brain…the way they look, the way they feel, the way they touch me.

If he gives me a chance to explain that I believed I was doing the right thing, everything might be okay.

And if he doesn't give you that chance?

If he doesn't give me that chance…it'll be his loss.

Something inside me falls away, something hard and restrictive and fearful. It crumbles, disintegrates and vanishes.

It'll be his loss.

It takes me a second to realize Angelo is crouching in front of me trying to get my attention. I take in his face, and notice he's got a black bruise on his cheek—he must have caught a punch in the fight earlier. I sit up, with no clue how much time has gone by.

"Whaddya say, Rose, you wanna be a rock star?" he says, offering me his hand.

For once in my life, what I want is completely, entirely, totally clear.

I take Angelo's hand and let him pull me to my feet.

"Yeah, I do."

He smiles. "Awesome, Sweater, you're in. Welcome to the band. We start rehearsing tomorrow night."

It's not like all the bad stuff that happened earlier didn't happen. But there's something else, something that's far away from all of that. Something that is more than the desire, more than the confusion and the fear, more than the random and the not-so-random acts of violence, more than the love I feel for Jamie Forta.

It's me. This is what I want. This is who I am.

And I am finally here.

* * * * *

ACKNOWLEDGMENTS

THANKS TO MY AMAZING EDITOR, NATASHYA WILSON, and the MIRA Ink editorial team, T. S. Ferguson and Annie Stone. Thanks for the awesome karaoke, you guys! (Oh, yeah, and all the support, too!)

Thanks also to my wonderful agent, Emmanuelle Morgen, without whom I would not sleep at night.

And a very special thanks to my parents, my brother and Lester, who keeps me honest.

ROSE'S RANDOM PLAYLIST

TAKE IT OFF
Ke$ha

WHATEVER LOLA WANTS
from Damn Yankees

MY MOON MY MAN
Feist

KARMA POLICE
Radiohead

MINE
Taylor Swift

MOSES
Patty Griffin

BE ITALIAN
from Nine

HOMETOWN GLORY
Adele

I WISH I WAS THE MOON
Neko Case

LOVE THE WAY YOU LIE
Eminem (feat. Rihanna)

REHAB
Amy Winehouse

DJ GOT US FALLIN' IN LOVE
Usher (feat. Pitbull)

FIREWORK
Katy Perry

CHERRY BOMB
The Runaways

KISS THEM FOR ME
Siouxsie and the Banshees

RAISE YOUR GLASS
P!nk

YOUR PHONE'S OFF THE HOOK, BUT YOU'RE NOT
X

KIDS
Sleigh Bells

Q&A WITH LOUISE ROZETT

Q. Tell us about yourself and your writing.

A. I was one of those kids who wrote lots of stories and plays. As I got older and started studying acting, I focused more on plays. I loved the collaborative nature of playwriting, but at a certain point, I really wanted to create something entirely on my own, that didn't require a director and actors. And that's when I went back to fiction. For me, writing is the best way to disappear into myself, to take a break from the real world. It calms me and absorbs me in a way that nothing else does.

Q. What inspired the Confessions series?

A. I have very vivid memories of being a teenager and trying to understand and cope with desire and other big, new issues. Desire is very tricky—people can really lose themselves in it and make bad decisions as a result of it—and I was interested in investigating what it's like to be a smart girl navigating that territory. Because it doesn't matter how smart you are—when you feel desire for the first time, it can really scramble your brain.

Q. Rose has been through so much over two books. How did you create such a realistic portrayal of grief?

A. Thanks for saying it's a realistic portrayal! I think the thing that's tough about portraying grief is the time frame. It takes a long, long time to process grief—it's not the kind of thing that can be dealt with quickly and cleanly. Based on my own experience with grief and trauma, the healing process is messy, and it's not linear—it starts and stops, and it's two steps forward, three steps back sometimes. Once I recognized that, Rose's journey became clear to me.

Q. In book 1, *Confessions of an Angry Girl,* Rose is bullied by Regina. In book 2, she sees Conrad being harassed by the swim team. What do you hope readers learn from Rose's experience, and what would you say to someone who is being bullied or harassed?

A. I think it's important for people experiencing bullying or harassment to speak up, in whatever form that takes, whether it's talking to an adult, or addressing the bully directly, or getting the police involved. Everyone has to make their own decision about how to manage the situation, and choose what feels right to them, as Rose does. But personally, I feel that staying silent is not the answer.

Q. What resources are there for someone who is being bullied or harassed?

A. There are a ton of different resources online, from websites like StopBullying.gov to sections on bullying on the Gay, Lesbian and Straight Education Network site, www.glsen.org. There's also a fantastic documentary called *Bully* that I think is a must-see for everyone, with a website called TheBullyProject.com that has great resources.

Q. Rose and Jamie have a rather complex relationship. How do you view their romance, and is there hope for them in the future?

A. I love Rose and Jamie together. I think they are very different people who broaden each other's minds and give each other new experiences of all kinds. I honestly don't know what's going to happen in their future—they haven't told me yet, if that makes any sense. But I will say this: the hardest thing to do in a relationship is stay together through change. And teenagers change quickly, and very often. It'll be interesting to see if Rose and Jamie can figure out how to handle that.

Q. Rose and Tracy's friendship has its ups and downs, but in the end they seem to make it work. What do you think is important in a friendship?

A. I think Rose and Tracy keep finding their way back to each other because they understand that they are different people, yet they respect their differences. They don't try to like the same things or the same people—they try to respect each other's opinions and decisions, even if they don't understand them. If you can master that in your friendships, you'll have a lifetime of great friends.

Q. Do you have a favorite among Rose's circle of family and friends? Who is it?

A. I love Angelo. I really do. He's a diamond in the rough. Angelo sees potential in Rose from the moment he meets her, and as he figures out who he is, he starts to help Rose reach that potential. He's also just fun, and funny, and kind, and uncomplicated in a way. I think Rose appreciates that in the middle of her very complicated life.

Q. Any words of advice for aspiring authors?

A. I have two pieces of advice for aspiring authors. The first one is just sit down and do it. Make a schedule for yourself, write it in your calendar like it's a doctor's appointment and commit to it. If you don't know what to say, then write about that. But get some words on the page.

The second piece of advice is, be nice to yourself while you're writing. I think this is really important. A lot of people stop writing after a few tries because they read what they wrote and decide it's terrible. But they're being completely unfair—they're judging something that isn't ready to be judged. Writing is a process of creation and revision, and more creation and more revision—it takes time. You have to be critical eventually, but if you do it while your ideas are still young and taking shape, you'll give up before you've even started.

Thank you, Louise!